# AUTHOR'S NOTE

As with other titles in this series, the story here is set in real villages in Cumbria. But all the homes and businesses have been invented. The points of interest on the slopes of the Old Man of Coniston are also more imaginary than real.

# The Coniston Case

## REBECCA TOPE

Allison & Busby Limited
12 Fitzroy Mews
London W1T 6DW
*allisonandbusby.com*

First published in Great Britain by Allison & Busby in 2014.
This paperback edition published by Allison & Busby in 2015.

A CIP catalogue record for this book is available from
the British Library.

10 9 8 7 6 5 4 3 2 1

ISBN 978-0-7490-1625-8

Typeset in 10/14.2 pt Sabon by
Allison & Busby Ltd.

The paper used for this Allison & Busby publication has been
produced from trees that have been legally sourced
from well-managed and credibly certified forests.

Printed and bound by
CPI Group (UK) Ltd, Croydon, CR0 4YY

*For Leonie Annette Keogh*

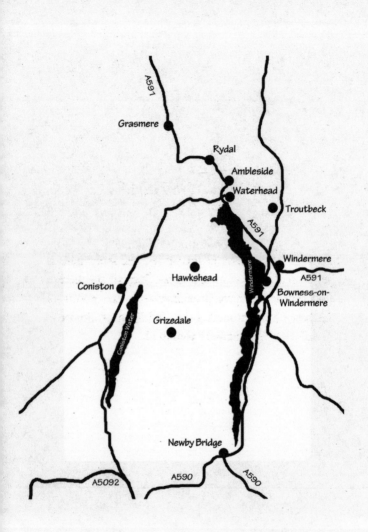

# CHAPTER ONE

'I won't care if I never see another red rose,' Simmy muttered to herself, while carefully arranging a bouquet comprising ten of the things. It was her eleventh Valentine's tribute of the day, and the sense of being swamped was becoming unbearable. 'And still another day and a half to go,' she sighed.

'Talking to yourself?' Melanie asked, coming through from the back room, holding another armful of blooms.

'Why are people so *unimaginative?*' Simmy wailed. 'Why not send a bunch of freesias for a change?'

'Symbolism,' said Melanie briefly, making it plain she knew full well that her boss already understood the way her romantic customers were thinking. 'At least they've placed their orders in good time. Imagine trying to do all this on the actual day!'

'It would kill me. As it is, I'll be out for hours delivering them all.'

'I'll do you a map,' said Melanie helpfully. 'You've got to go to Newby, Coniston, Troutbeck and Bowness. Coniston's going to be the snag. You might think of getting the ferry. Otherwise I suggest starting at Troutbeck and working south.'

'I don't like the ferry. I can go down to Newby and then up to Coniston after that. I expect the road'll be nice and icy. It's a long way, Mel.' She shivered exaggeratedly and looked out at the streets of Windermere where a scattering of shoppers were passing, bundled inside woolly scarves and hats. 'At this time of year, it feels like going halfway to the North Pole.'

'By rights you ought not to be doing Coniston deliveries, anyway, especially when you've only just started driving again.'

'I was there on Monday, remember. But the weather was better then and I wasn't in a hurry,' she conceded.

'Yes,' said Melanie patiently. 'But the fact remains that Coniston isn't really on our patch. There's a perfectly good florist there already. Watch out if she sees you!'

'If she's as busy as I am, she won't mind at all. I'd have cheerfully passed the order on to her, but the customer never gave us their name so there wasn't much choice.' It had been a peculiar business

10

transaction that might have led to more discussion if it hadn't been for the hectic Valentine's workload. 'I expect there's the same thing happening the other way around. I see her van hereabouts from time to time.'

'It's not the same,' Melanie argued. 'She can do some shopping when she comes here. Nobody wants to shop in Coniston, do they? Making a delivery over there really is a waste of time and petrol. And you're not supposed to do too much driving, remember.' Melanie's protectiveness had become a habit since Simmy had suffered an injury, shortly before Christmas, and been forbidden to drive until early in February. She had used crutches throughout most of January. Damage to her head had necessitated a shaven area, which prompted her to have a very short all-over haircut that still felt strange.

'Well it's too late now. I just hope it doesn't go mad tomorrow or I'll be turning orders away. You know you'll be doing all the local ones, don't you?'

'Yeah, yeah. My feet'll be worn away to nothing by the time I've done them all.' There had been a degree of discord about how Melanie might best make the deliveries of flowers in the streets of Windermere and Bowness. Her battered car was deemed by Simmy to be bad for the image of the business, but she had compromised slightly, and agreed that it could be left full of flowers in the

11

Bowness car park, and again at the northern end of Windermere, for increased efficiency. She had also, as a major concession, permitted Melanie to use the van while she herself had been unable to drive. As a resident of an area renowned for walking, the girl was almost a freak in her reluctance to use her own legs as a means of transport.

'If you work it out as cleverly as you've done my route, you should be fine,' Simmy said, not for the first time.

'It's crazy, all the same. Everyone's going to be out at work, for a start. At least with Mother's Day, it'll be at a weekend.'

'Don't!' begged Simmy. Mother's Day was only a month off and she was already worrying about the logistics. 'Let me get on with these first.' And she went to create more bouquets of red roses.

The middle of February in Cumbria was still a long way from springlike. There had been two nights of sub-zero temperatures and icy patches persisted all day where the ground was in shade. The roads were narrow and steep and Simmy had a morbid fear of skidding. She was secretly glad that driving had been impossible so far that winter, and had been in no hurry to get back behind the steering wheel.

February 14th was a Friday, which meant a relentless succession of orders had been flooding in all week. Wholesale delivery vans had arrived regularly with boxfuls of red roses. The back room of the shop contained almost nothing else. Brisk business, Simmy kept reminding herself, was a good thing – an essential thing. There had been entire weeks during January when barely one customer a day came in. There were hardly any passing shoppers and there had not been a wedding for a month. Funerals had been the mainstay, with a flurry of them at the end of January.

'The post's not been opened yet,' Melanie observed, flicking through a handful of envelopes and sheets of paper. 'Flyers, water bill, a couple of real things. D'you want me to open them?' Without waiting for an answer, she did so. 'Hey – this is an order, Sim,' she called. 'Come and look.'

Simmy came impatiently out of the back room. 'What?'

'See – they want a mixed bunch of spring flowers to go to a Mrs Crabtree in Hawkshead. Twenty-five pounds in cash, and no name or address. The message on the card is wishing her good luck in her new home. What's going on? That's the third one like this we've had in a week. Have we missed something about banks going bust, that nobody's using cheques or cards any more?'

'Third?'

'Yeah. The one for the bloke in Coniston on Monday and there's a Valentine one for Friday in Newby Bridge. That was hand delivered. Some man dashed in yesterday and just thrust the letter at me and rushed off again. I hardly even saw him. Said something about catching a train and hoping there was enough money to cover it.'

'I saw him, I think. The one in the long brown coat? I just caught a glimpse of him, the same as you. So they're not all from one person.'

'Course they're not. If they were, they'd all be in the same letter, wouldn't they?'

'But they're all anonymous? That's a bit odd, don't you think?'

'It's Valentine's, Sim. The whole point is to keep the person guessing. That part's not odd at all. It's the way they pay that I'm talking about. I wonder if Mrs Crabtree's going to know who sent her flowers.'

'Hmm,' said Simmy, vaguely, not entirely following what Melanie was trying to say. 'What's that leaflet about?'

'Solar panels. "Go green with Goff" it says. They're going mad for them at the moment, for some reason. My dad says they're just a flash in the pan and everybody with them's going to feel a right fool in ten years' time.'

'I don't know about that. My cottage might suit them rather well. It doesn't have to be sunny all the time for them to work, apparently.'

'Too many big boys getting in on the act, according to Dad. The whole thing's got very messy, with all those government subsidies up for grabs. Never works, he says.'

'He might be right,' Simmy nodded, not really caring either way.

'So I'll chuck it away, then? With the one about the pizzas and the one about the sale at the garden centre?'

'So much wasted paper,' Simmy sighed, and went back to her work.

As she fashioned yet another bouquet, very nearly on autopilot, the bell above the door signalled a customer and she peered through the shop to see who it was. Melanie was carrying a large box of oasis, leaving Simmy to greet the newcomer. A woman in her forties stood looking around, as people routinely did. Not someone likely to be sending red roses, Simmy thought hopefully. Something different would be such a relief. She produced a beaming smile of welcome. 'Morning,' she said, cocking her head enquiringly.

'Have you got any tulips?' the woman asked. 'Is it too early for them?'

Simmy pointed to a well-packed stoneware vase on the floor, boasting two dozen tulips of different colours.

'Oh!' The customer stared. 'What a gorgeous vase!'

'A local potter makes them. They are nice, aren't they?'

'Is it for sale?'

'Well – yes, I suppose so. He takes orders usually,

but I can let you have it if you really want it.'

'How much?'

Simmy paused. Her agreement with Ninian had been vague from the start; little more than a system where she displayed his wares and told people where they could find him. Prices had not been established. 'I really have no idea. We've never got around to discussing that – which sounds daft, I know.' She had no intention of explaining how hesitant and complicated things had been between her and Ninian since Christmas. 'I ought to call him and ask, I guess.'

'It's worth quite a lot,' said the woman. 'Hand thrown, probably a one-off. And it's *big*.'

'Everything he makes is lovely,' said Simmy, absently fingering the tulips. 'How many flowers did you want?'

'A dozen, please. Assorted colours. If I leave my number, could you get back to me about the vase? I haven't got much time just now.'

*Nor me*, thought Simmy, with a quick smile. 'That's fine,' she said. She sold the tulips and went back to the roses. She would phone Ninian after the end of the working day, if she remembered. The woman's number was on the back of a business card Simmy had found on her untidy little table next to the till. *Persimmon Petals*, it read on the front. *Proprietor: Persimmon Brown. Flowers for all occasions*. One of the few times she had been almost glad of her unusual first name was when it came to choosing a title for her new business.

The little room at the back was crammed with finished bouquets, as well as the wherewithal for additional ones. Melanie was trying to create order, laying out flowers, ribbons, cellophane and small cards in a sequence that would speed Simmy's nimble fingers for the rest of that day and into the next.

'Remind me to call Ninian and ask about prices for his pots,' said Simmy. 'I could have sold that big brown one just now if I'd known what to charge.'

Melanie blinked at her. 'Why didn't you make something up? He'd be happy just to sell it. You'll never get the person back.'

'Well – how much? Twenty-five? Fifty? He never gave me a clue.'

'You're both hopeless,' said Melanie. 'It should have been the first thing you agreed. Do you get a commission?'

'Probably. We were about to get the whole thing settled when I ended up in hospital, remember? Then it was Christmas, and it all got forgotten.'

'Six or seven weeks ago, Sim. You've been back at work for most of that time.'

'At least I managed to get him to bring some to display. Even that was a hassle.'

'Hopeless,' said Melanie again.

Ninian was a self-employed potter with a poor

head for business. He lived in a fellside cottage with no landline and a little-used mobile telephone, did not possess a car, and often went missing for days at a time. He and Simmy had established a fragile friendship, to the extent of her agreeing to do what she could to sell some of his vases. After a distressing series of events in late December, he had joined her and her parents for Christmas lunch – and then disappeared for two weeks, causing Simmy to worry that he was lost in a snowdrift.

'I'll try and phone him anyway,' Simmy resolved. 'Or maybe a text would work better. I think he quite likes texts.'

Melanie, at the ripe old age of twenty, was above responding to such a crass remark.

The morning flew by, immersed in the scentless foreign flowers ordered by self-satisfied swains for their expectant girlfriends. Husbands too were congratulating themselves for remembering the great day in good time to ensure a fitting tribute. Other customers had mutated from being welcome variations on the theme to irritating distractions at this point, wanting a pot plant for their new conservatory or something unusual as a birthday present for someone unwise enough to get born on or near February 14th. When the doorbell pinged at midday, Simmy heaved an impatient sigh and pulled off her rubber gloves. Modern roses might not have thorns any longer, but the stems were tough and bare fingers quickly became sore.

Standing in the shop, only a few inches inside the door, was a man she had first met five months before. Detective Inspector Moxon was dark-haired, broad-shouldered and rumpled. He knew more about Simmy than she found comfortable, especially as his knowledge apparently led to an affection and concern that made her feel young and vulnerable.

'Busy?' he asked.

'That isn't the word for it. Don't tell me you've come for red roses, or I might have to hit you.'

His smile was just sad enough to make her feel remorseful. She had come to the conclusion that he lived on his own. Within minutes of meeting him she had disclosed her own history – the dead baby daughter and subsequent separation from its father – and got nothing from him in return. He had met her parents, too. Angie and Russell Straw ran a well-known B&B in Windermere, and did their very best to avoid any encounters with the police. Angie could rant for several minutes about the idiocy of people pretending to want bobbies on the beat. 'The further away from us they are, the better,' she maintained.

Simmy agreed with her, but for different reasons. Her dealings with DI Moxon had been connected with a number of highly disagreeable crimes which had been upsetting at best and personally dangerous at worst. Floristry, she had discovered, put a person in the way of seriously heightened emotions, including rage, revenge and hatred. Despite the general goodwill associated with the sending of flowers, the major life stages that were marked in that way could easily be connected to darker feelings.

'I would have thought fresh business would be welcome,' he said.

'There's such a thing as too much business. There are only two of us, after all. I had no idea the world could be so romantic.'

'Just wait till Mother's Day,' he said. 'As far as I can see, that now extends to grandmothers, great-grandmothers and almost any female relative.'

'Not my mother,' said Simmy. 'She won't have it so much as mentioned. Says it's commercial claptrap.'

'We all know about your mother,' he said with a small shiver.

'So what brings you here?' she prompted, thinking it really wasn't her job to get him back on track.

'Ah. Yes. Coniston, Monday afternoon. Remember? You delivered flowers to a Mr Hayter, in a house called Rosebay Echoes.'

'Ye-e-es,' she agreed warily. She would have liked to explain that it had been her first week

20

back driving and that the lengthy trip to Coniston had been a somewhat stressful experiment. Instead she confined herself to simply answering his question.

'You saw him, I assume?'

'Briefly. Why?'

He ignored her question and produced another of his own. 'Can you remember the inscription on the card?'

'Not exactly. Something about a new job.'

'Was it signed?'

Simmy racked her memory. 'I don't think so.' She went to her computer. 'I might have logged it, even though it wasn't an online order. Oh, yes – here it is. "Good luck in your new job." No name or anything. The order came in the post, with cash. I assumed he would know who they were from without being told.'

Moxon waited a few seconds. 'Did you gain any particular impressions of him? His frame of mind, for instance?'

'Preoccupied. He hardly looked at me. But I thought he quite liked the flowers. He grabbed them off me and gave them a sniff before he shut the door in my face.'

'He's been reported missing, you see. And his landlord appears to be away, too. His daughter let us into the house earlier today and we had a quick look round. We found the flowers still in their wrapping

21

and your tape round them, but no card.' Simmy's tape had been an inspired innovation a few weeks before. *Persimmon Petals* was endlessly repeated along its length.

'What a waste.' It pained her to think of the blooms left to die unloved after her careful work in assembling them, not to mention the time-consuming drive to deliver them. 'They weren't cheap.'

Melanie came out of the back room, clearly having heard the conversation, and interrupted. 'Wonder what happened to the card.' Simmy and the detective both looked at her blankly. 'Why do you say that?' asked Moxon.

'No reason, really,' she shrugged. 'You'd think it would still be with the flowers, that's all. Probably he liked the thought after all and kept it for sentimental reasons. It might be under his pillow.'

'I doubt that,' frowned Moxon. Simmy became aware that the detective inspector was watching her closely, waiting for a more relevant reaction. 'It looks a bit worrying,' he prompted.

She put up her hands defensively and took a step back. 'Oh no,' she said loudly. 'No, no, *no*. Don't you go involving me in another of your beastly murders. Don't even *think* about it. I'm exempt. Immune. I've done more than my bit for society in the past few months.'

Movement on the pavement outside the shop

drew the attention of all three. They watched as Ben Harkness tried to push the shop door open, finding DI Moxon to be an obstruction.

Moxon himself sighed, shook his head and muttered an apology, before getting out of Ben's way.

# CHAPTER TWO

'Nobody said anything about murder,' Moxon objected. 'There's no sign of violence in his house.'

'Murder?' echoed Ben, with seventeen-year-old enthusiasm. 'Where? When? Who?'

'Aye-aye,' said Melanie with a grin.

'Go away, all of you,' ordered Simmy. 'I've got work to do. If the Hayter man isn't dead, then why are we wasting time like this?'

Moxon summoned every scrap of available dignity. 'He has been reported *missing*,' he emphasised. 'And after a brief search of his home, we found recently delivered flowers from this establishment, and as part of normal investigations, I came to ask if you knew anything that might help us.'

'Establishment,' muttered Ben, with a quick roll of his eyes. 'Is that what this is? I thought it was just a shop.'

Melanie poked him and hissed, 'Shut up, you fool.' She looked at Moxon. 'So who's his daughter? When did she last see him?'

'She's a Miss Daisy Hayter. She's getting married next week and arranged a dinner party last night for her parents and her prospective in-laws to have a pre-wedding get-together. Her dad never showed up, which she finds extremely worrying. Apparently it's totally out of character.'

'So much so that a detective inspector gets put on the case?' Ben queried.

Before Moxon could reply, Simmy said loudly, 'Well, I don't know anything. I hardly saw him. He hardly even *looked* at me.'

'This is a grown man we're talking about,' Ben persisted. 'I didn't think the cops were interested in people like that going missing. If he's not suspected of a crime, then he's free to go where he likes, surely?'

Moxon did not reply, which gave Ben all the information he needed. 'He *is* a suspect!' he crowed. 'You've lost someone who's on bail or tagged or something. Wow! Whoever said life in Cumbria was dull? It's a thrill a moment aboot these here fells.' His accent was recognisably local, albeit exaggerated for effect. In general he used standard English as insisted upon by his mother. Simmy, as an incomer, spoke with none of the Lake District tones, while Moxon and Melanie were detectable as Cumbrians as soon as they opened their mouths.

'No, he is not a suspect,' said Moxon firmly.

'What then?'

'If you must know, he's a friend of a friend of mine. I believe his family when they say this is a real cause for concern.' He turned to Simmy. 'You definitely can't say who ordered the flowers?'

'No. Sorry. I really have no idea, and we've thrown the letter away. Melanie makes me log everything on the computer and not keep any paper.'

Moxon rubbed his face and made a resigned grimace. 'I'd better let you get back to work, then. Although it would appear that I'm not the only interruption.' He gave Ben a severe look.

Simmy waited for him to go, but he made no move. She felt an odd mixture of resignation and apprehension. 'I do hope he's all right,' she offered.

'So do I. Does this happen often – orders with no indication of who they're from?'

'Hardly ever, usually, but we're getting a few this week, which Melanie thinks is probably quite normal for Valentine's. Anyway, it was fully paid up, so I wasn't worried. Lots of people don't use banks. I thought maybe it was a child, actually – although the message didn't sound like that, I suppose.' She spoke jerkily, trying to justify herself at the same time as seeing the whole business through Moxon's eyes.

'Whoever it was got the wrong florist,' said Melanie.

Everyone looked at her. 'Pardon?' said Moxon.

'There's a florist in Coniston. People sending flowers to someone living there should use the nearest shop. It stands to reason.'

'Establishment,' said Ben softly.

'It doesn't, though,' Simmy realised. 'The letter was delivered by hand. I found it on the floor when I opened up on Monday. It's a bit like booking a taxi, isn't it? I mean – you're never sure whether to call one from near where you live, or near where you're going. Either way, they have to do the trip twice. It's the same when you choose a florist, unless you do it online or by phone.'

'Which almost everyone does,' Melanie pointed out with dwindling patience.

'All of which demonstrates that there was something very unusual about that order,' said Ben.

Simmy sighed. 'I just thought it came from someone who isn't in the system. Someone old-fashioned but quite ordinary. And because it's Valentine's, everybody wants to keep their identity a secret. The usual rules don't entirely apply.'

'Dream on, Sim,' scorned Ben. 'This wasn't a Valentine, was it? It's obviously someone who didn't want to be identified for totally unromantic reasons. And you can't pretend it's ordinary at all. Ordinary things are not investigated by detective inspectors, for one thing. And even if he is a friend of a friend, grown men going missing don't warrant any police involvement at all without something really suspicious to attract their interest.'

Simmy saw Moxon's hands twitch, as if he would very much like to put them around the boy's neck and squeeze.

'Hush, Ben,' Simmy warned him. 'You don't know anything about it. And why are you here, anyway?' she asked him. 'It's Wednesday.'

He gave her a withering look. 'Free period, then some bod giving us more climate propaganda. I should stay and ask awkward questions by rights, but I didn't fancy it.'

'Propaganda?' Simmy blinked.

'Oh, he doesn't believe in man-made climate change. Surely you knew that,' Melanie explained. 'Haven't you heard the story about his mum and the solar panels?'

Simmy shook her head, thinking a theme was developing that was at least a distraction from Valentine's Day. 'What happened?'

Ben took over. 'She was on the verge of being persuaded by some salesman bloke to spend ten thousand on sticking panels all over the roof, until I showed her some of the facts and figures. This far north, she'd have been mad to do it, even if the basis for them made any sense – which it doesn't.' He leant forward, his voice rising. 'They *still* haven't managed to produce batteries that store the energy properly. So you have to go back to the old system once the sun goes down. All this guff about the national grid buying back your unused reserves is just a cynical bit of market manipulation. There is no way in the world it can ever make economic sense. But much worse than that, there was never any need to reduce carbon emissions anyhow. They're not doing a scrap of harm.'

'I don't believe you,' said Simmy.

'Suit yourself. Not believing is good. I woke up one day and thought – can all this man-made global warming stuff really be true?' He grinned. 'So I read all the counter science, mostly just to be perverse at the start. And now I'm absolutely certain the whole idea is rubbish. Mind you, some of those sceptic people are pretty bonkers as well. You've got to be selective. But it looks as if the computer models the scientists used in the 1990s are hopelessly wrong. It would be funny if it hadn't caused such economic havoc.'

Moxon was listening impatiently. 'You're wrong, boy. By the time you're thirty, you'll realise just how wrong you are. I just hope you change your mind before then.'

Ben scowled at him. 'I'm not wrong,' he insisted.

'But . . .' Simmy felt as if she'd just been solemnly assured that two and two made five. 'Surely the counter science, as you call it, is wacky off-the-wall stuff? The real scientists all agree – don't they?'

'Stop,' Melanie begged, before Ben could draw breath. 'I've heard him on all this, and believe me, it's not fun. And we haven't got time.' She gave Ben one of her unique glares, which carried added force thanks to an artificial eye. 'I suppose you thought we'd give you some lunch.'

'Brought my own,' he corrected, digging in his school bag for a plastic box containing sandwiches. 'And I guarantee you that I'll be proved right any day now.'

'You've got incredible timing,' Simmy said, anxious to follow Melanie's advice and dodge the climate lecture. 'Just as the inspector's here.'

'Yeah.' He smiled smugly and Simmy guessed the boy had witnessed the arrival of the detective and decided to investigate. He was quite likely to have been heading somewhere else and been diverted.

She had been watching all three faces, which were turned towards her in a pattern she was beginning to find familiar; as if everyone looked to her for a lead. DI Moxon himself was holding her in a steady gaze, with something of an appeal in his eyes. Ben was right, she concluded. There *was* some additional reason for his visit, which he was struggling to reveal.

'Tell us more about Mr Hayter,' she invited. 'If his daughter's so worried about him, there might have been an accident or something.'

The detective smiled unhappily. 'Well, for one

thing, she didn't believe he had ever been sent flowers before, not for any reason at all. For another thing, he has no plans to start another job, as far as anyone is aware. That implies at the very least that someone has been playing a rather nasty joke on him. Daisy suspects it was a coded message implying he was unlikely to remain long in the job he already has, and that would be very upsetting for him.'

Simmy cast her mind back, and volunteered as complete an account as she could of the events of the previous Monday. 'It was sunny, and I parked in the town car park without paying, because I was only going to be a few minutes. You know how expensive all the car parks are around here. It would wipe out practically all my profit if I'd paid, and you're not allowed to leave the car in the street. I walked up to his house, which is on the road that goes to the edge of Lake Coniston. It's pretty along there, with those big houses. Anyway, he answered the door quite quickly and then just stared blankly at me for about a minute—'

'Not possible,' Ben interrupted. 'A minute is *ages*. More like fifteen seconds.'

'Okay. It was much longer than normal, anyway. I said "Mr Hayter?" and he nodded, so I tried to give him the flowers. At first he didn't take them, but then he reached out and grabbed them and gave them a little sniff. Then he smiled a bit, thanked me and shut the door.' She shook her head. 'I'm not absolutely sure of every detail, or the sequence they came in. Do you think it matters?'

'Did he look at the card?' Moxon asked.

'Um – I'm not sure. He said, "Thank you, dear," and closed the door.'

'You said before that he seemed preoccupied.'

'Yes, that's right. He never seemed to pay full attention – as if he was listening out for the phone maybe, or in the middle of writing an important letter and wanted to keep the words in his head. I felt as if I'd distracted him from important business and he thought flowers were just frivolous and irrelevant.'

'And yet he opened the door quickly. If he'd been in the middle of something, wouldn't he have taken a long time to get up and go to the door?' It was Melanie, thinking aloud.

Nobody answered her. Simmy scanned her memory for any more details. 'I hope he's all right,' she said. 'He seemed quite a nice man, even if he didn't want me bothering him.'

'He called you "dear",' said Melanie. 'Is that why you liked him? Was he good-looking?'

'Fairly,' said Simmy with a repressive look.

Moxon closed his notebook, having written down the meagre facts so far elicited. 'Thank you,' he said. 'I think that's all.'

Simmy heard the silent *for now*, and sighed.

Unlike her two young friends she had no curiosity as to what might have happened to Mr Hayter from Coniston. It was blatantly obvious that it had nothing whatever to do with her, and she had eight more Valentine bouquets to construct, with more orders very likely to come through before she was done.

'I'm sure you'll find him,' she said.

'I'm sure we will. Enjoy your lunch.' He nodded at Ben, his expression part reproach and part admiration. The boy was, after all, highly intelligent and basically on the side of the angels when it came to matters of law enforcement. 'And don't you get above yourself, my lad,' he said.

Before Ben could speak, the detective had gone, leaving the youngster red-faced and wide-eyed. Simmy could see he was upset and thought he probably deserved it.

'Silly old bugger,' said Melanie, patting Ben lightly on the shoulder.

'Yeah,' said the boy thickly.

Seventeen, Simmy dimly remembered, was an awkward age. Emotions ran wild and careless words cut deep. Ben might be genius-level intellectually, but he could still be brought down and humiliated all too easily. Even so, it was time he learnt to respect authority and not flaunt his brains. 'I've got work to do,' she said, with little hope of being allowed to get on with it.

'I'm going to google him,' said Ben. 'That Mr Hayter.'

'You can't. I need to keep the computer free for any new orders. Melanie – tell him he can't. He might listen to you.'

They both looked at her pityingly, and Ben proffered a gadget she realised was the latest in communications technology and was sure to be able to manage some googling. Somewhere in her conscience was a sense that it was intrusive to search for people's backgrounds without their permission. Rationally, she knew they willingly displayed all sorts of personal information for the world to see, but that didn't help. Everybody could be an investigative journalist now, which meant everyone was also vulnerable and exposed.

'Look,' said Ben, 'you go and smell your roses, and I'll just keep out of your way.'

'They don't smell,' said Melanie. 'It's a bit of a swindle, really.'

Simmy gave her a dirty look and marched off into the back room. She switched on the radio she kept in there, but only used when Melanie was in the shop. Radio Two played undemanding tunes while her nimble fingers assembled yet another bouquet of red roses. Within five minutes she had banished all thoughts of Ben and the missing man and DI Moxon.

Instead she found herself thinking of Ninian

Tripp and hoping she wouldn't forget to contact him about the vase. Or preferably, go to see him, if she could find his cottage. Melanie would know exactly where it was, being in possession of encyclopaedic local knowledge. Somewhere to the east, she thought, in the unexplored uplands of Brant Fell. It was within walking distance, but after nearly a year, she still hadn't once gone that way. No chance of doing so before the weekend, she concluded. The evenings were still very dark and uninviting and walking still led to aching bones where she'd been hurt before Christmas. Once back in her Troutbeck home, there was very little incentive to go out again.

Ben put his head round the door, ten minutes later. 'Didn't find much,' he said. 'Incredible the way some people have no Internet presence worth mentioning. What are they thinking?'

'That they like their privacy, I expect. Didn't you find *anything*?'

'Oh, yes. Mr Jack Hayter won first prize for his runner beans at the Coniston Summer Show in 2011. Looks as if it was his only moment of glory. Somebody else won every year since.'

Simmy laughed. 'Nothing sinister, then?'

'It was sinister that Moxo has an interest in him. Of course, there wasn't time to check everything. We'd need to sign up for ancestry.co.uk to get the real stuff, as well as the newspaper archive. They both cost megabucks.'

Simmy waved a hand. 'Not interested,' she said firmly. 'I still think it's rude to go googling people.'

But the damage was done. She could not rid herself of the brief picture of Mr J. Hayter that remained in her memory. He had been thin, pale, middle-aged – the last person you'd expect to have flowers sent to him. He had not visibly reacted either positively or negatively to them – an impression confirmed by DI Moxon's information that they had never even been put in water. She was slowly discovering, to her astonishment, that flowers could be sent aggressively as well as lovingly. There could be any of a thousand messages contained in an innocent bouquet. Reminders, reproaches, accusations and warnings might all work their way into the blooms and the message card attached. This darker side of her business had tainted it for her once or twice already, and now she feared it might do so again.

So who had sent the unwanted tribute? A message that had seemed benign, sent by a person going to considerable trouble to ensure the flowers arrived despite not being competent to manage electronic communications, had now mutated into something ominous. Was it even possible that the receipt of the bouquet had driven the man to disappear, rushing out of the house that very day, leaving a bewildered daughter to raise the alarm? She was forced to concede, as Ben had said, that it all implied that something more serious was going on.

Ben had withdrawn his head and she could hear him and Melanie chatting together in the shop. She left it another fifteen minutes before going out to join them. She was just in time to see Mel picking up an envelope from the floor inside the door. As Simmy watched, the girl opened it.

'Who was that?' Simmy asked.

'Someone in a rush, with a new order,' Melanie told her. 'Never gave us a chance to say whether we could do it or not. You probably won't like it,' she warned.

'Why not?'

Melanie cocked her head teasingly, saying nothing. She simply passed the sheet of paper to her boss.

'Good grief!' Simmy exclaimed, when she read it. 'Yet another trip to Coniston, or very nearly. What's going on?'

'What?' Ben charged forward, almost elbowing her aside. 'Let me see.'

Simmy stood her ground and pushed him back. 'Get away,' she ordered. She peered again at the paper. 'It's supposed to go tomorrow. Don't they know how busy I'm going to be?'

'Are you saying you'd have refused the job if you'd had a chance to speak to the person who brought this?'

'Of course not. At least, not in normal times. This isn't a normal week, though, is it.' She read further down the page. 'Irises and anything in light colours. Hmm. Addressee – Mrs Maggie Aston, Goodacre Farm near Coniston. "With my deepest apologies." Something to the value of thirty pounds. Paid in cash.' She looked at Ben, who had made a small sound. 'What's the matter?'

'Looks a bit like the one to the Hayter man,' he said. 'Don't you think?'

'You both saw this person. Was it a man or a woman?'

'Didn't see, sorry. I wasn't taking much notice,' Ben admitted. 'I was trying to fix the bits that have fallen off the tower.' Two or three months earlier, Ben and Simmy had designed and constructed a model of a local landmark, which had formed a permanent centrepiece in the shop window display ever since. It was made from natural materials, such as dried seedpods and sticks, which were turning brittle and dusty with the passage of time.

'Mel?'

'A woman, I think. It was all so quick. Whoever it was just pushed the door open and chucked the letter in. They were gone again in about four seconds.'

'I must admit I'm starting to think this is all a bit funny – don't you? Another cash order for someone out towards Coniston way?'

'You know what I think. I bet it's always like this at Valentine's. Neither of us really knew what to expect, did we? We've never done it before.'

'That's true. I'll have to do it, I suppose, even if it feels rather weird. I can combine it with the Hawkshead one. Should I go round the lake to the north or the south?'

'North,' Melanie told her. 'The road from here to Ambleside is quicker, then you just pop down through Barngates. It's only three or four miles.'

'It's going to be about twenty miles altogether, then.' Simmy sighed. 'More, probably.'

'Do it after we've closed. Then you can go straight home, and it won't be so much driving.'

'Good thinking,' said Simmy gratefully. Melanie really did have a talent for logistics. Then she had another thought. 'No, I can't do that. It'll be dark. I'm not hunting for a strange farm in the middle of nowhere at night. I'll go at lunchtime.'

'Hey, hey!' Ben protested. 'First things first. We've got to tell old Moxo about this before anything else. Never mind how or when you get there – this is obviously the next victim of a serial killer. If I rush, I might even catch him out in the street. We need to act fast.'

Simmy's jaw clenched. 'You're much too late for that. And don't say such stupid things. It's not funny.'

For the second time in half an hour, Ben flushed

red. 'Don't call me stupid,' he said. 'Whatever I am, it isn't that.'

'Sorry. But you are being silly, all the same.'

'I am not. Think about it for a minute. Okay – the serial killer part was over the top, but you do have to report this. The person sending these flowers can't know there's been police interest in the Hayter man, can he? Or she. It could just as easily be a woman.'

'It's not all the same person, Ben. That's really ridiculous. They came in different ways. Posted and hand delivered. There's nothing going on. Just a massive amount of work that I need to crack on with.'

'Well . . . um . . . that's okay, except for the Hayter man. Let's just unpick everything we know about him. First – there's no proven connection between him going missing and you taking him the flowers, but it's obviously possible that there is one. He wasn't expecting to get flowers and he didn't treat them nicely. And then he disappeared, probably right after getting them. His daughter missed him, and told the police something important enough to arouse Moxo's interest. You took the flowers on Monday, and the dinner party was last night – Tuesday. So he vanished either Monday or Tuesday.' His voice was rising. 'Come on, Simmy – something's happening here. You must see that.'

Simmy experienced a familiar floundering in

the face of Ben's youthful logic and energy. His assumptions could equally well be right or utterly wrong. But there was some sort of coincidence at work, involving anonymous orders for flowers, and that meant she had no alternative but to give the matter some attention. 'I can't *bear* another murder investigation,' she burst out. 'I *so* wish these damned orders had gone to a different florist.'

'Well, they didn't. And you needn't worry. Moxon knows how you feel about it. He'll probably get some female detective to deliver this order for Maggie Aston, so they can see for themselves what's going on.'

Melanie whistled. 'That'd be clever. Go on, Simmy, call him and say you've had another cash order with no name. You've got his number, haven't you? Didn't he give you a card just now?'

'No, but I've got the one he left here months ago.' A small wooden box with a fancy inlaid lid, occupying a corner of the table that served as the shop counter, was used for business cards. Simmy turned it upside down onto her palm and inspected the dozen or so cards. 'Yes, here it is.'

'Efficient,' Ben approved.

Using the shop telephone, Simmy called the mobile number that Moxon had told her to use. 'He'll be in the car,' she said to her listening friends. 'It's not long since he left here.'

'It's forty minutes,' Ben corrected. 'He could

have walked to the cop shop and back four times by now. He walks as much as he drives.'

'How on earth do you know that?' Melanie demanded. Simmy flapped at them, as the call was finally answered.

'I probably ought to tell you there's been another order that might be connected to the flowers for Mr Hayter. Somebody just dropped in a letter and scooted off before we could even see if it was a man or a woman. Melanie thinks probably a woman. Oh, and I forgot to tell you there was an order in today's post, for a woman in Hawkshead and that's anonymous as well.' She blurted it all out quickly, hoping to dump the whole matter into his lap.

'Oh?' Moxon sounded cautiously excited. 'Who's the new one for?'

'A Mrs Aston on a farm near Coniston.'

'Address?'

Simmy read it from the note. 'A mixed bouquet of spring flowers. Same as the one for Mr Hayter.'

'What message?'

'"With my deepest apologies." Not the same as before. That was "Wishing you well in your new job." And the Hawkshead one is about a new home.'

Moxon made a wordless sniff.

'Should I just carry on as normal, then? They're both meant to be delivered sometime tomorrow. I thought I'd go about midday.'

'Why wouldn't you?'

'Well – Ben thought . . .' It sounded ridiculous now, as she began to say it. Nobody but Ben had read anything particularly sinister into the fact of a new anonymous order.

'Miss Brown – I'm grateful to you for this information. But there's no need at all for you to alter your usual practices.'

'Yes, but . . .' She realised she was actually nervous about delivering the order as requested, even if she did it in daylight. She had brushed too close to premeditated violence already – with the physical injuries to show for it – to blithely put herself in harm's way again. 'Are you sure it's safe?' she finished in a rush.

The faint clicking sound he made was impossible to interpret. Did he think her a fool, or was he reproaching himself for his own lack of understanding? 'I'll have a word with young Ben Harkness next time I see him,' he said. 'Let me assure you, there's no need whatsoever for you to worry. I have no doubt this is all perfectly innocent – and perfectly irrelevant to the case.'

'Yes, but . . .' Simmy repeated. 'You don't actually *know* that, do you?'

'When are you meant to take the flowers?'

'Any time tomorrow. I told you.'

'Okay. That gives us plenty of time to be sure, then, doesn't it? If there is the slightest reason for you to be worried, I'll let you know by first thing in the morning. Is that okay?'

'Yes,' she said. 'Thank you.'

'You're scared,' Ben accused her, when she'd finished. 'And Moxo told you there was no need to be. Right?'

'Exactly. And he blames you. He says it's all perfectly innocent.'

'But something is going on,' the boy insisted. 'That's obvious.'

'It is, you know, Simmy,' said Melanie, marginally more gently. 'And how does he know it's innocent?'

Simmy felt weak. 'Well, just leave it for now. We ought to be working, not gossiping like this. Ben, you'll have to go. You're too distracting.'

'Unless you want to order Valentine flowers for someone,' said Melanie mischievously.

'Huh!' snorted the boy. 'No girl of mine would want anything so obvious.'

'Thank you very much,' said Simmy. 'That's my livelihood you're belittling.'

'Luckily for you, most people are obvious, then.' As was generally the case, Ben Harkness got the last word.

# CHAPTER THREE

Russell Straw was cleaning shoes; his own, those of his wife and a pair belonging to a B&B guest who had stepped into a mud puddle the day before and soiled his brogues. Simmy found him in the kitchen, with a sheet of newspaper spread over the central table. 'You'll catch it,' she said. 'That has to be against any number of regulations. What if somebody trod in dog poo with those shoes?'

'It'll stay on the paper, which I'll screw up and throw away.'

'That's all right, then.'

Her father waved a round tin in her face. 'Have you seen what's happened to shoe polish?' he demanded. 'I bought this last week, without looking at it closely. They're not giving you that little catch to get the lid off, as they used to. Remember those catches? Brilliant idea. Why in the world would they scrap them?'

Simmy looked at him with utter blankness. 'I've never bought shoe polish,' she confessed. 'I mostly just wear trainers.'

'Scandalous,' said Russell. She wasn't sure whether he meant her sloppy lifestyle or the defective tin.

'Do you offer shoe cleaning as part of the service, then? That seems rather beyond the usual call of duty.'

'Not as a rule, no. This is a special favour, because he's a nice old buffer.'

'Sshh. He'll hear you. Wasn't that him in the family room just now?'

'Doubtful. That'll be the Spencers. They've embarked on a full-scale game of Monopoly that's sure to last till bedtime. And nobody can hear us in here anyway. I've told you that before.'

'And I don't believe you. You don't realise how much your voice carries when you're excited. You should have been in the theatre.'

'To what do we owe this pleasure, may I ask? You're not normally here on a Wednesday.'

'Exhaustion. I need tea and cake before I can face the final mile. And to tell you I don't think I'll be seeing you at the weekend. I'm going to sleep late on Sunday, and then just slob about. I might not even get dressed.'

'Scandalous,' he said again with a tolerant smile.

'What is?' asked Angie, in the doorway. 'What's so resoundingly scandalous that I can hear you all along the corridor?'

Simmy caught his eye and mimed *Told you so*. Russell made a rueful face. 'Our daughter is deliberately planning the most outrageously idle day on Sunday, to the extent of not paying us her usual visit.'

'Valentine's,' said Angie knowingly. 'I bet it's a dreadful rush.'

'You could say that. I never want to see another red rose.'

'It's a nice problem to have,' shrugged her mother. 'We're the same – fully booked all over the Easter holidays. If the weather's bad, we might easily go insane. At least we're only half full this weekend.'

'Ben Harkness doesn't believe in man-made climate change,' Simmy said to her father, only then realising she had carried this niggling discovery with her all day.

'And I don't believe in the Easter bunny,' he flashed back. 'Is it a matter of faith, then? Is global warming some kind of religion?'

Simmy paused. 'Sort of, yes,' she concluded.

'It has always been a grave mistake to put too much trust in science. I think I might have mentioned that to you once or twice, in the past?'

'You have. But isn't this one of those times when they're obviously right?'

'Quite probably, and yet I find the rage engendered by simplistic reporting and illogical conclusions can be harmful to one's health, and thus best avoided. I feel intensely concerned for the hearts of those anti-wind farm people.'

'Not to mention their sanity, poor things,' said Angie. 'Living near a turbine drives you mad, apparently. But most people I know still say they like the elegance and majesty of them. I think they look like invaders from outer space. But I decided to devote my energies to more immediate matters, some time ago. If your Ben's right, all the turbines will be taken down again in a few years' time anyway. I can't get myself too aerated about it.'

Russell tutted softly at her use of a word he had proved to her beyond dispute did not exist. 'You know what I mean,' she insisted. 'And nothing else quite says it.'

Simmy sighed, aware of a slight sense of shame at failing even to consider the matter of climate change up to then. 'DI Moxon came in today,' she told them. 'One of my customers has gone missing.' And she gave them the bones of the story in a couple of sentences.

Angie groaned. 'He ought to know better than to bother you again, so soon after the last time. Couldn't he have followed some other clue than a bunch of flowers?'

'That boy Ben was there, you say?' Russell had met Ben a few times, and had yet to pronounce judgement on him. Simmy had the impression that her father wanted to disapprove of the youngster but could find no real grounds for doing so.

'He was, as it happens. He got very excited.'

'It's not natural. Boys his age don't do excitement.'

Simmy laughed. 'He's not like other boys.'

'I had a call from a man today, wanting to know whether we did special Valentine weekends,' said Angie.

'What did you tell him?'

'I told him we were a B&B, not some pretentious boutique hotel. I wasn't very polite.'

'I don't expect you were. At least I signed up for romance when I went into floristry. I keep telling myself it's a lot better than Mother's Day is going to be.'

'It's a job, pet,' said Russell gently. Since Simmy had failed so disastrously at motherhood, the subject of Mother's Day was a sensitive one. The cards and flowers her stillborn daughter might one day have sent her were impossible to ignore, as were all the other might-have-beens that still crept up on them every little while.

'I know. It's all right, Dad. I just wish . . .'

'Yes,' he nodded. 'But Valentine's is upon us and you'll be too busy to brood over the business in Coniston, rushing round delivering all the red roses.

Lucky it's not set to freeze tonight. The roads should be easy enough.'

Weather (as opposed to climate) was an abiding obsession with Russell. He collected old country maxims with which to predict what would come next, and would often read out historical accounts of what the weather had done in the past, especially in the Lake District. One of his favourite stories came from Dorothy Wordsworth's account of two farmers perishing in a snowdrift and remaining undiscovered for weeks. Apart from the briefly sunny interlude two days earlier, it had been a wintry week, with a northerly wind blowing, bringing frequent vicious showers for good measure. Not a hint of a daffodil could yet be seen and the crocuses looked battered and pinched. Drifts of snowdrops had begun to appear here and there, but even they were hesitant in the teeth of such a bitter wind. The wooded slopes running alongside the lake were uniformly grey and lifeless, except for the odd clump of dark-green conifers on the lower levels.

'Tomorrow's going to be a nightmare,' Simmy said, feeling melodramatic. 'If I didn't have Melanie, I'd be desperate. It's a disaster that she's leaving in another three months or so. I'll never find anyone half as good.'

'It took you a while to appreciate her,' observed Russell.

'To my shame.'

She ate a modest evening meal with her parents and left for Troutbeck and home soon after eight. The night was deeply dark, traffic very sparse. The road up to her village was steep and winding, as were nearly all the roads in the area. But her white-painted cottage welcomed her, the heating already on and the scent from two large bowls of hyacinths wafting generously throughout the ground floor.

Automatically she picked up the phone to check for the broken signal that indicated a message. Messages from real people were rare, but not unknown. She kept her mobile off much of the time, disliking the distraction it created. The house phone was for friends and family and carried a benign aura accordingly.

There was a message, which when accessed turned out to be a very pleasant surprise. 'Simmy? It's Kathy – you know, from Worcester. Listen – I'm coming up to the Lakes this weekend – well, tomorrow, actually, and I wondered whether we could meet up. I'd love to see your shop and everything. I really don't want to lose touch, and it's already a year since I saw you. Thanks for the Christmas card, by the way. So call me back, okay. Any time up to midnight is fine.' And she recited her number.

Simmy remembered the number. Kathy had been her friend for years. The fact that she'd added 'from Worcester' was strangely sad, as if she feared Simmy might have made new friends with the same name and forgotten her. Over the past ten years they had been constant companions, with or without their menfolk. Leaving Kathy to move to Cumbria had been a wrench. Neglecting to invite Kathy to come and stay had been an omission she could hardly explain to herself, other than a need to sever all links with the painful events leading up to her separation from Tony.

She phoned back quickly, the sound of Kathy's voice proving to be a treat out of all proportion. 'I have missed you,' she realised. 'It'll be marvellous to see you again.' Then it hit her. 'But I am insanely busy this week. We're overflowing with orders.'

'Not in the evening, surely? I thought we could go somewhere for a meal tomorrow night.'

'Yes, we could,' Simmy decided. 'Of course.'

'I could even come and help you in the afternoon,' her friend offered. 'I don't have to be anywhere.'

'So why are you coming? Will you be on your own? What about Simon?'

'All will be explained. I need to do something on Friday and Saturday, so I thought I'd add an extra day at the beginning, to spend with you. Sorry it's such idiotically short notice. I only decided today.'

'Where are you staying?'

'That's another thing. Do you think your parents might have a room for me? Are they still running the B&B?'

'They are, but why stay with them when I've got a perfectly good spare room? You're welcome to it for the whole weekend, if you like.'

'Oh – thanks. I wasn't sure you'd have the space. And I didn't know . . . well, whether I'd be in the way.'

'Don't worry, there's no new man in the picture, if that's what you mean. Are you completely occupied for all of Saturday, or can we snatch some time together?'

'I'm not sure at the moment. It's a family thing. All a bit delicate. I promise I will explain when I see you.'

'What time will you arrive?'

'I'm leaving at first light, so should be there by lunchtime. I'll come to the shop first, shall I? Are you easy to find?'

Simmy gave brief directions, and tried not to think about the interruption her friend's arrival would create on the busiest day for many months. 'You might not get much sense out of me until the end of the day,' she warned. 'I'll be knee-deep in red roses.'

Only after the conversation ended did she remember she was supposed to go to Hawkshead and Coniston at lunchtime next day. Better, then, to do those deliveries earlier. Get into the shop by eight, make up the bouquets and take them to Mrs Crabtree and Maggie Aston right away. Melanie was primed to arrive promptly at nine. Everything would work out fine, she assured herself.

When she opened the shop next day and checked the post, she was relieved to find no further suspicious orders. All she had to do was prepare the bouquets for Mrs Crabtree in Hawkshead, with her new home, and Mrs Aston on a fell-side farm, who had earned abject apologies from somebody nameless.

She selected blooms from the cool back room, deftly arranging and securing them, writing the cards and wrapping them in cellophane, all in under half an hour. The florist van was parked at the back, taking two minutes to load. A scribbled message for Melanie was propped up beside the computer and the street door locked.

The day was grey and drizzly, and nobody was about when she set out at half past eight, taking a route that Melanie had suggested months ago. It avoided the centre of Windermere and Simmy liked to think she would have eventually worked it out for herself. It was, she realised, a sort of rehearsal for the much more demanding set of deliveries the following day, winding her way through the small lanes and finding obscure addresses. Except that Melanie had ordained that she go southwards for the Valentine flowers, and here she was today heading north.

Passing Rayrigg Woods, which rose steeply on

her right, she was quickly on the road to Ambleside. The lake to her left was calm and very low cloud banded the fells beyond. A monochrome world, with the bare trees and shrouded hills, as if all thought of blue or yellow or red had been firmly forbidden for at least another month.

Out past Ambleside, and through Rydal, she turned left for Hawkshead. Here it was impossible to hurry. The road was wet, with persistent lumps of dirty snow in places, heaped up on narrow verges. It curved and dived, forcing her to concentrate on every yard. Great trees, with their heads in the mist, watched her from behind stone walls. Sheep flickered like ghosts and she knew there was every chance of one appearing in the road, inviting her to run into it. A white-faced Herdwick stood like a sentry on top of a wall, staring up at the fells, ignoring Simmy as if she were the ghost. Herdwicks had caught her imagination over the winter, with their coloured fleece worn like a coat, the pale head creating the illusion that under the grey or brown body wool was a normal white sheep.

She was in Hawkshead at five to nine, the house she sought easily located on the right, before the town itself. A newish array of white-painted houses with grey stone porches, all alike, was scattered on a gentle slope. Still no colour, and still no people.

Holding the bouquet against her left shoulder, as

she always did, she rang the doorbell. How many times had she done this in the past ten months? It was almost always a happy moment, but there had been exceptions. Mr Hayter in Coniston had been one of them. He had not expected or wanted flowers. He had almost shut the door in her face, before snatching the bouquet and bidding her goodbye. Charitably she had assumed he was busy, or embarrassed or overcome with emotion. Now that someone had reported him missing the whole episode gained an aura of darkness and mystery which coloured her expectations of this new delivery, four days later.

A woman apparently in her sixties opened the door wide after a lengthy delay and stared at Simmy. 'Yes?' she asked.

'Mrs Crabtree? Flowers for you.'

'I *beg* your pardon?'

Simmy silently proffered the bouquet. Slowly, the woman took them.

'Who're they from, then?'

'There's a card.' Simmy took a step back. 'You've just moved in, then, have you?'

'"Good luck in your new home",' read Mrs Crabtree. 'But this isn't a new home. I've been here for twenty years. You must have made a mistake.'

'I don't think so. When were these houses built?' The question was irrelevant, she knew, but she felt she ought to say something neutral.

'Sixty years ago. Why do you ask?'

Simmy shrugged. 'They look more recent that that. Are you planning to move, perhaps?'

To her alarm, the woman's eyes filled with tears. 'My children tell me I should but I don't want to. This must be a horrible way of telling me to sell up.' She shook herself. 'But I won't. Why should I?' She blinked at Simmy. 'Who sent them? You must know.'

Simmy shook her head. 'I'm afraid I don't know. Someone posted the order and payment, without giving any details. The letter came yesterday.' It was a small but genuine relief to be able to explain truthfully, without hiding behind such notions as 'customer confidentiality', which always felt mean-spirited and obstructive.

'My children live in Barrow and Kirkby Lonsdale, and I can't imagine either of them using something as old-fashioned as a letter. You take orders online, I presume?'

'Yes. Of course.'

'Well, that's the way they'd do it. Or by telephone as a last resort. This sounds like somebody deliberately wanting to upset me.'

'Although your children *do* think you ought to move,' Simmy insisted gently.

'They do, but neither one of them would ever use such a roundabout way of telling me. Besides, I already know what they think. No – I did them an injustice just now, thinking it was even possible.

There's malice at the heart of this, and that's obviously not my Helen or Brian. They're nothing like that. It's probably all a stupid mistake. These flowers aren't meant for me at all.'

It was tempting to simply admit that this was probably true. Simmy had very little pride as a rule. She could live with someone believing her to be capable of getting something wrong. But she remembered Mr Hayter and the police detective and the fact that somebody was surely up to something sinister, and shook her head. 'I'm afraid they are for you, but I think perhaps we ought to tell the police about it. You're not the only person this week, you see, to receive something like this. It's probably just someone's idea of fun, but we don't know that for sure.'

'Police?' She looked aghast, and Simmy was reminded of her mother's repeated assertions that nobody wanted to be drawn to the attention of the police, however innocent and blameless their lives might be.

'Please don't worry. It's only that they might come along to ask a question or two. After all, if this person is sending flowers to random people with upsetting messages, they should be stopped, don't you think?'

'Oh . . . I suppose so.'

'I must get on now. I'm sorry to have disturbed you.'

'I'm really not moving house,' Mrs Crabtree repeated firmly, and closed the door. Simmy had a vision of the flowers being thrust head down into a pedal bin, and felt sad again.

She drove over Hawkshead Hill to Coniston, her van making much of the steepness. The views were mainly hidden by the persistent mist, but suddenly Lake Coniston was a few feet away on her left, shortly after passing the turning down to Brantwood. Her father's growing passion for John Ruskin had ensured that she'd paid an early visit to the house soon after coming to live in the area. She still remembered the romantic drawing by George Richmond, showing a delicately handsome young man who might break a hundred hearts. Combined with the story of poor Rose La Touche, whose heart had evidently suffered terribly through her relationship with Ruskin, the picture had given Simmy a lot to dream about.

The farm she had to find was somewhere past the village on the road to Torver. She had learnt not to trust a satnav for the finer detail of Lakeland navigation, and instead relied on the large-scale Ordnance Survey map. Now it served her well, and she found a gateway proclaiming her destination and a blessedly short track up to the house.

This order, she told herself, probably had nothing to do with DI Moxon's investigation. Besides, it was convenient that it came so close to the Hawkshead address, enabling her to deliver both bouquets in one trip.

The farm was to all appearances entirely traditional, with several barns and other buildings surrounding the house. Sheep were scattered across fields on all sides. The yard was relatively clean when she stepped out of the van and went around to the back. There was a smell of warm animal emanating from a nearby barn, along with sporadic bleating. She felt like an alien intruder, entirely out of place.

There were no human voices to be heard. The house stood behind a stone wall, at an angle to the main yard. A black and white dog with a sharp nose came around a corner and began barking, while at the same time wagging its tail. *Mixed message*, thought Simmy, standing her ground.

She walked firmly up to the house door, through a small gate and up a short path. She rapped the heavy knocker, and the dog barked more loudly. 'What's the matter with you?' came a female voice. 'What's going on?'

'Hello!' called Simmy.

At last the door opened and a woman a few years younger than Simmy materialised, with a toddler at her side. 'What?' she demanded.

'Flowers for you.'

'Me? What name did they tell you?'

'Mrs Aston.'

'There are two Mrs Astons. Me and my mother-in-law. Which one are they for?'

'Mrs M. Aston,' Simmy read from the card.

'That's me, then. I'm Maggie. The other one's Susan.'

'Here, then.' The morning was running away with her and there was still an awful lot to do back at the shop. For a whole hour she had managed to forget about red-rose valentines, but she knew that couldn't last.

Maggie Aston read the message and went a nasty grey colour. She swallowed gulpingly, and Simmy braced herself for a second bout of tears that morning. People did cry on florists, more than might be expected, but this was becoming excessive.

'Are you okay?' she asked. The child had disappeared inside the house, and was making contented animal noises. Simmy hoped that Mrs Aston would make every effort to control herself before rejoining her little one.

'No, I'm not.' The woman raised her arms over her head like a champion netball player and threw the flowers across the small front garden with the sort of strength that could only have come from hurling large bales of hay around, or bringing young beef animals down. The bouquet made it all the way over the wall and into the yard beyond. 'I think I'm probably going to be sick,' she went on.

'Oh dear.' Simmy did her best not to take

this personally. Her flowers had not deserved such treatment; it was rude to reject them so wholeheartedly while their creator was still on the doorstep. 'I'd better go.'

There was no response to this, other than the door closing in her face. *Such drama*, Simmy thought crossly, as she went back to her van, trying not to look at the poor flowers on the cold concrete. The mist had cleared minimally, and the Old Man of Coniston was patchily visible, looming over the proceedings with utter indifference. He had seen millions of petty human exchanges in his time, like an exasperated god watching his subjects. Simmy ducked her chin at him, in a silent thanks for helping her to regain perspective.

Even so, there was little romance in her thoughts as she drove back to Windermere as quickly as she could. Hawkshead Hill was easier in this direction, but still it was impossible to hurry. However light the traffic might seem, there were always delivery vans and farm vehicles highly likely to be around the next bend. There had been no road widening efforts on this side of Windermere, the narrow lanes rightly deemed to be part of the attraction for tourists. There were people who deliberately came in winter, seeking out the eerie sensation that all was not entirely safe, even if you kept to the roads and never left your car. There was ice, and inadequate signposting and sudden blanketing mist to contend with, even in this softer southern section of the Lake District.

It was ten-forty when she got back to the shop and Melanie gave her a reproachful look. All Melanie's looks – and she had a wide range of them – were enhanced by the fact of her artificial eye. There was always a hint of challenge lurking somewhere. The prosthesis was a good one, but it could never move in complete unison with its partner. The girl had learnt to capitalise on it in a variety of ways, but she was never going to be considered demure or compliant. Since her goal was a career in the hotel business, Simmy sometimes worried that she would find it impossible to abase herself before unreasonable guests or tolerate the many idiots she was doomed to encounter.

'A whole lot of stuff's been happening,' she said. 'Two more valentines, and that woman came back wanting Ninian's vase. I sold it to her for thirty quid.'

Simmy bit back a protest. It was her own fault, she supposed, for not phoning Ninian and asking him for a price. The place where the vase had been standing was now occupied by a lily in a pot, its buds just starting to swell. 'Oh,' she said.

'We're keeping fifteen per cent commission,' Melanie went on. 'Peanuts, but it's easy money, I suppose.'

'Is that what we agreed?'

'We didn't agree *anything*, Sim. That's the problem.'

'I liked that pot,' she said wistfully, realising this had been a strong element in her failure to sell it. The shop felt bereft without it.

'How did it go in Hawkshead? What did the woman say?'

'She cried. It was something horrible – intended to frighten or upset her. I ought to tell Moxon about it. He'll have to take all these weird orders more seriously now. I'm sure it's the same sender as Mr Hayter's, and the person's a menace, whoever he or she might be. They need to be stopped.'

'Wow! You sound really stressed about it. You were gone a long time. Did you have to console her?'

'Not really. And it didn't get any better after that. Remember I had to go to a farm near Coniston? That was really awful. The woman threw the flowers across the yard.'

'What?'

Simmy explained.

'Can't be a coincidence,' Melanie mused. 'That's three unwanted bouquets this week. Something *must* be going on.'

'I'll call Moxon,' she decided. 'Then we can get on in peace, with any luck.'

'Don't rely on it.'

In spite of herself, Simmy couldn't stop thinking about the innocent-seeming messages embodied in her flowers. The flowers themselves had been entirely innocuous, of course. It was all in the cards that were attached to them. The words were the problem. 'Isn't it beastly,' she said, 'to associate something so nice with an upsetting or threatening message? What sort of mentality is it that can do such a thing?'

'The farm one wasn't nasty,' Melanie pointed out. 'It was an abject apology. Usually that works pretty well, in my experience.'

'Does it?'

Melanie flushed. Her various relationships supplied ongoing interest to Simmy and Ben, not least because Ben's brother Wilf had briefly gone out with Melanie and harboured hopes that he could do so again. Meanwhile she had taken up with a police constable who was plainly her inferior in matters of wit and general desirability. No one seemed entirely sure where things currently stood. Joe sent frequent texts and Wilf was said by Ben to be hovering eagerly on the sidelines, awaiting an opportunity to resume his place in her affection. To Simmy's knowledge, neither of her beaux had ever sent Melanie apologetic flowers. 'My Dad does it sometimes,' the girl mumbled.

Simmy phoned DI Moxon again, thinking wistfully that she could expect no reward for her public spirit. He answered quickly. 'Mrs Brown,' he said, to demonstrate that his phone once again knew who she was.

'Yes. I suppose I should tell you what happened in Hawkshead this morning when I delivered the flowers.'

'You've been already? You told me you were going at lunchtime.'

For the first time since getting up, Simmy remembered Kathy and the reason for her change of plan. 'I changed the plan,' she said.

'So what happened?'

'Remember the message was good wishes for a new home? Well, she's not moving house and she was very upset at the suggestion that she was. She thought at first it was one of her children making a point, but then she decided they would never be so malicious. Somebody really must have been trying to upset her, on purpose.'

'I'll have to go and see her,' he said with a sigh.

'Have you got any more news of Mr Hayter yet?'

He hesitated, leaving an annoying silence of the sort that was always so much worse down a telephone line. 'Yes and no,' he said, eventually.

'That's all right. You don't have to tell me. I'd rather you didn't, actually.'

'Don't be sniffy.'

'I'm not. I really don't want to know. I don't want to be involved.'

'You've said that before.'

'And meant it.'

'Well, I'm afraid you'll have to find a new line of business then. It's been plain for a while now that flowers and crime go together all too nicely.'

A truth that she had been struggling to avoid finally pinned her down. 'It's horribly like last time, isn't it?' she said bleakly, and rang off without letting him reply.

# CHAPTER FOUR

Melanie was enraged by the 'yes and no' response to Simmy's question. 'The least he could have done was explain,' she said furiously.

'I didn't really let him,' Simmy defended. 'And listen, I forgot to tell you an old friend of mine is dropping in at lunchtime. She's called Kathy. She might help make up some of the Valentine things. I told her how busy we are.'

'Right,' said Melanie absently. 'What does "yes and no" mean, then? Yes, they found him, but no, they haven't managed to speak to him? Or what?'

'Don't ask me.'

'I guess I can find out from Joe, eventually.'

'Don't you dare! You'll get him into real trouble one of these days. It's not fair on him.'

'He likes it. It makes him feel important.'

'Have you sent him a valentine?'

Melanie shrugged. 'Just a card. It's pointless, really, isn't it? I'm a bit sick of the whole thing, to be honest.'

'Join the club,' said Simmy.

The hour from eleven to twelve saw intensive activity, creating the fresh orders out of yet more red roses. Space in the back room became hopelessly scarce and Melanie was banished to the shop. All the bouquets were carefully labelled, with instructions pinned onto their wrapping, and a special trough of water used to keep them in good condition. The aim was for their recipients to believe the flowers had only just been picked and magically transported to their homes by fairies. It was a point of pride with Simmy that no two offerings were exactly the same. She added misty sprays of gypsophila to some and feathery greenery to others. The stalk lengths were varied to create different shapes to the overall bouquet. Despite her claim of the day before that she never wanted to see another red rose, she could not help admiring them. Singly, they were gorgeous. The exact moment between the first opening of the bud and the full-blown blossoming of the flower was a small piece of perfection, achieved by extreme manipulation at the point of cutting them and impressive technology employed during their transportation from Africa. It was all wrong, looked at one way, but amazingly effective in the results.

'Somebody for you,' sang out Melanie, at twelve o'clock. Assuming it was Kathy, Simmy paused to run her fingers through her hair and pull off the gloves she wore. She didn't want to look tired and scruffy, even if it was her one-time best friend.

It was not Kathy. DI Moxon stood just inside the door, as was his habit, waiting patiently for her to appear. His feet were well spread, and while he did not quite bounce on them, there was a subliminal suggestion that he would start doing so in another minute.

'That was quick!' said Simmy. 'Have you been to talk to Mrs Crabtree already?'

He shook his head. 'Never got the chance. Something else cropped up.'

'Oh?' She experienced a sinking feeling of resignation, spiced with a thread of apprehension. 'And how does it concern me this time?'

'We found Mr Hayter.'

'Good.'

'Not good, I'm afraid. Not good at all. He's dead.'

'Murdered?' yelped Melanie. 'Oh my God!'

Moxon turned on her with the speed of a cobra. 'Be quiet!' he snapped. 'There has never once been any suggestion of violence in this case. You and Ben Harkness are far too quick to assume things. You for one should know better.'

'Sorry,' drawled Melanie, mulishly. 'So what, then?'

'He took his own life.'

'And that's not violence?' Simmy interrupted. She was shaking, she discovered. The detective had also noticed and was laying a supportive hand on her arm, directing her towards a plastic chair she kept beside the till. 'I'm all right,' she insisted. 'I'm being silly.' But she and he both knew there was every good reason why she should go into shock at the news. The two of them had a history of confronting sudden death at close quarters, joined together as witness and investigator. Moxon had been privy to her points of vulnerability, proving to be much more understanding than could have been expected.

'Sit down,' he ordered. 'And listen. I came to tell you because you're sure to hear about it anyway and I fondly hoped to be able to soften the blow a bit. You can be assured that there really is no suggestion that he was killed by anybody. It was an unambiguously self-inflicted overdose. He went off into the fells at night to do it, so the cold will have hastened the process. We found him yesterday evening.'

'Poor man.'

'Yes.' Something in his voice caught her attention. A familiar catch that took her back to her former husband's tone when speaking of their lost child.

'You knew him,' she remembered. 'A friend of a friend. It's personal for you, isn't it?'

His eyes glittered with something like gratitude. 'He was a good man. Nobody dreamt he was liable to do anything like this.'

'And his daughter's getting married. What a mess.'

Moxon's eyes held hers, his glasses magnifying them slightly, which made her feel strangely sorry for him. In all her dealings with him he had been gentle, even sensitive at times. He had a few of the classic traits of a police detective in his unwashed hair and rumpled clothes. He gave little sign of understanding human nature in its complex variety, manifesting real surprise on a number of occasions. Simmy suspected he found her confusing, Melanie unpredictable and Ben entirely beyond comprehension. None of them behaved towards him as he had surely expected. But he did try to be flexible. He did his best to avoid platitudes about risk and right behaviour, faintly aware that there were people in the world who did not see danger behind every bush; people who seldom even considered the matter at all in their daily doings. People like Simmy's mother, who broke fresh rules every day and never considered the consequences.

'But the flowers,' said Melanie. 'Was it something to do with the flowers?'

Moxon sighed and gave himself a little shake. 'I suppose it's best to get that part over with. The fact is, we don't know.'

'Why didn't you tell Simmy about Mr Hayter when she phoned you this morning?'

'She didn't give me a chance. I was telling her I'd be dropping in when I realised she'd hung up on me.' He gave Simmy a schoolmasterly look from under his brows. 'Not something I'm used to, actually.'

'So now we have three nasty messages and a suicide,' Melanie summed up. 'All in or near Coniston.'

Moxon ignored her, standing protectively over Simmy, who was doing her best to pull herself together. After all, she thought crossly, nothing that was happening presented any threat to her. She was just the invisible conveyor of sinister floral tributes. 'Mel's right,' she said. 'The farm delivery didn't go down well at all.'

'Farm?' said Moxon.

Simmy told the whole story, finishing with, 'But the message was different. I mean, it seemed really genuine. I suppose it's a two-timing boyfriend, and she's not yet ready to forgive him. I mean *husband*. She's *Mrs* Aston, with a mother-in-law and a small child.'

'A two-timing husband, sending flowers with a message of apology,' summarised Moxon. 'Quite possible, of course. And she threw them away.'

'It was quite a throw. They went halfway across the yard, poor things.'

Moxon wrote something down.

'But it can't be anything to do with the others,' Simmy said, with no real conviction. 'Can it?'

'Three orders for flowers, paid in cash, with no name or address for the sender. All causing upset to the people receiving them. How likely is it that they're from different people?'

'But it's not a *crime*, is it? Just mischief.' She grimaced. 'Malice, even. But it's not as if . . .' she tailed off, unable to voice the thought.

'Malice of such a degree that one person was driven to kill himself,' Moxon said severely.

Simmy went cold. 'You really think the flowers did it? That something in the message was so horrible he couldn't live with it? If I thought that, I'd never be able to deliver any flowers again.'

'Steady on, Sim,' said Melanie. 'That's going a bit far. Okay, you're being used, and that's sick. But none of it's your fault. You can't refuse to take an order just in case it might upset somebody.'

'I can insist on a name and address from the sender,' Simmy said tightly. 'I should have known better than to accept any of these three.'

Before the girl could answer, the doorbell pinged, and a familiar figure came into the shop. 'Kathy!' Simmy cried. 'I forgot about you.'

'Charming,' said the newcomer with a smile. She was tall, with a lot of frizzy brown hair. She looked from one face to another, eyebrows raised. 'Customers?' she asked.

'This is Melanie. She works here. And this is . . .' It was strangely difficult to admit to a visitation from a senior police detective. The prospect of Kathy asking endless questions, getting excited, shocked, intrigued, was unappealing.

'I'm nobody important,' said Moxon. 'And I'm just going. I'd better look into the farm woman,' he said, addressing Melanie more than Simmy. 'Thanks for letting me know.' And he went.

'Why are you being visited by a policeman?' Kathy asked, seconds later.

'What makes you think that's what he is?'

'Shoes. Hair. Notebook. What he said, and the way he said it. It was obvious.'

Simmy gave her friend a belated hug. 'It's so good to see you. You haven't changed a single hair. Did you drive up? Are you hungry? We usually pop out for a sandwich and work right through.'

'Carry on, then. Don't mind me. If you want me out of the way, I can walk down to the lake or something. It's very atmospheric out there.' They all looked out onto the damp street, and Simmy thought of her misty morning drive. It was true that the view across the lake from Bowness would be lovely, because it always was.

'It's up to you,' she said. 'We're over the worst now, so long as we don't get a lot of last-minute orders.'

Kathy's blank look quickly cleared. 'Valentine's!'

she realised. 'Of course! What a fool. I never made the connection.'

'Plus some other stuff,' Melanie said. 'We've had a few very unromantic messages this week.'

'Hence the policeman,' said Kathy astutely.

'Blimey!' said Simmy. 'Ben's going to have to watch out, with you here. He's been the unchallenged Top Brain up to now.'

'Ben?'

'Oh – just a boy we know,' said Melanie. 'You probably won't even meet him.'

Five minutes later, her words were proved wrong when Ben swung into the shop, with his usual air of coming to a place where he knew he'd be welcome. 'Uh-oh,' said Melanie.

Kathy was in the middle of a quick tour of inspection of the shop, during which she had greatly admired Ninian's remaining pots and expressed an intention of buying one. She looked up at the pinging doorbell, and glanced at Simmy.

'Ben,' said Simmy. 'He has a habit of turning up in the lunch hour. He's in the sixth form. This is my friend Kathy,' she told the boy.

'Greetings, Kathy,' he said carelessly.

'She's clever,' Melanie warned him. 'You'd better watch out.'

Ben gave the newcomer a closer look. 'I like clever people,' he said. 'You don't live round here, do you?'

'Worcester. I knew Simmy before she moved here.'

He nodded vaguely, as if Simmy's life before Windermere was entirely irrelevant. 'What news of the phantom flower-sender?' he asked.

'Mr Hayter topped himself,' Melanie burst out eagerly. 'Moxo was just here, to tell us.'

'Driven to it by a cruel joke,' he said, with a careful look at Simmy. 'Bummer.'

'We don't know that at all. It probably had nothing at all to do with the flowers. Don't put this onto me.'

'No, but – why else would Moxo keep coming here about it? And what happened with the Hawkshead person? Did you take those flowers?' He unslung the rucksack from his shoulder and extracted a plastic box containing his lunch. 'I'll eat while you tell me.' He eyed Kathy in a clear question as to whether she was staying.

'I was going to take myself down to the lake, but this sounds too fascinating to miss. You three are a real gang of amateur sleuths, aren't you? I did know there was something horrible at Christmas when Simmy got hurt, but she never told me any details.'

Simmy was still trying to adjust to the sudden appearance of her old friend in a new context. The Kathy she remembered had been a good listener, always ready with a witty joke, more or less contented with her life, despite a tendency to boss people about. She held similar views to those of Simmy's mother when it came to taking charge of events and refusing to accept foolish rules and regulations. 'We make our own destiny,' she would often say. When Simmy's baby died and her husband let her down, Kathy faltered slightly in this view, aware that it would come across as heartless. She had floundered uncomfortably, unable to offer anything beyond a helpless sympathy. 'What a *bloody* thing to happen,' she repeated every time they met.

Her own relationships apparently ran smoothly. A husband ten years her senior; parents who made minimal claims on her time; two ambitious daughters who had obviously chosen academic success over underage sex. 'They hardly seem to have noticed boys,' Kathy had said, a couple of years ago. 'Joanna's in love with the science lecturer and Claudia appears to be more interested in girls.' Neither passion had ever caused Kathy any lost sleep.

But now there was a mystery swirling somewhere close by. Why was Kathy in Cumbria all on her own? What did she have to do over the weekend? What was this new veneer of brittleness that had been plain from the moment she came into the shop? She could not keep still, her eyes darting from face to face, then to Ninian's vases and the street outside.

'So?' prompted Ben. 'Hawkshead.'

'Elderly lady, quite upset. The message wished

her well in her new home, but she's not moving. She thought at first one of her offspring was trying to persuade her, not very subtly. But it doesn't look as if it was either of them. More likely it's the same person as the one who ordered flowers for Mr Hayter.'

'But where's the crime?' Ben wondered. 'I still don't get why Moxo's so bothered about it. There must be a whole lot he hasn't told you.'

Kathy leant in, between Simmy and Melanie. 'Intimidation, possibly leading to suicide. False identity. Sounds fairly criminal to me.'

'True,' Ben conceded, plainly impressed at her quick grasp of the facts, 'but not the sort of thing DI Moxon would be involved in. He does murder and violent assault. The nasty stuff.'

'But nobody's been murdered,' said Simmy firmly. 'Not this time.'

# CHAPTER FIVE

Sandwiches, cakes and mugs of tea and coffee were distributed amongst the four of them, Ben and Melanie standing up, because only one chair would fit in the small central section of the shop and Kathy had been invited to use it. She sat sideways, jiggling one leg irritatingly up and down. Simmy perched on the small table holding the computer and a stack of paperwork.

A customer necessitated Melanie setting aside her lunch and leaning past Kathy to ring up the sale of a large bunch of blue irises. 'Not a Valentine,' laughed the man who bought them. 'They're for my mum, actually. Since Dad died, she's missed getting the card he always sent.'

'How thoughtful!' Melanie approved. 'She'll be made up, lucky lady.'

'"Made up"?' echoed Kathy, when the man had gone.

'Local idiom,' said Ben. 'It means pleased.'

'I've got to get on,' sighed Simmy. 'I need to order more supplies for next week, and get the books straight. Everything's stacking up.'

'Am I in the way?' Kathy asked. 'I can go for that walk, if it helps.'

'Well . . .'

'Say no more.' She jumped out of the chair. 'I'll disappear for a couple of hours to admire the scenery – I might even drive round to Coniston for a bit of a look.'

'You won't see anything,' said Ben. 'It's too murky. But I suggest you take the ferry, if you do want to go over there. It's more fun that way and a lot quicker.'

'So some people say,' muttered Simmy. She found the ferry unsettling, for reasons she couldn't properly explain.

Melanie's mobile phone beeped and she read a text message with a yelp. 'It's Joe. Listen to this. "Body found near Coniston Water. Your boss involved."' She looked warily at Simmy. 'I guess Moxon's going to be back before we know it.'

'Bloody hell,' said Simmy, not sure whether she was angry or scared, but suspecting it was probably both. 'Why does he say I'm involved?'

'Because you are, most likely,' said Ben. He gave Melanie a dark look. 'Still seeing Joe, then? Last I heard, Wilf thought you'd packed him in.'

'I'm not *not* seeing him,' said Melanie pedantically. 'We still go out once or twice a week, but I'm making sure he knows he's not to take anything for granted. He thinks if he feeds me inside information like this, I'll stick with him.'

'And is he wrong about that?'

'Mind your own business.'

'It *is* my business,' Ben flashed. 'I have to put up with Wilf going on about it all the time. And you can't pretend it's fair on Joe, either. Poor bloke probably thinks you'll marry him in a couple of years.'

Melanie dimpled complacently. 'Tough,' she said.

Kathy was hovering near the door, waiting for a chance to announce her departure. 'I'll be back by four at the latest,' she said. 'If you need me, call me. This is the number.' She produced a card from her bag on which were printed her name and mobile number and nothing else. 'I've got cards for every occasion,' she boasted. 'Like you with the flowers. Joanna does them for me.'

Catching up with the doings of Joanna and Claudia was going to be high on the agenda if she and Kathy ever managed to sit down quietly together, thought Simmy. 'Thanks,' she said, taking the card.

'You don't have to worry,' Ben reassured Simmy. 'Joe means Mr Hayter, obviously. It's nothing new.'

Melanie slapped herself lightly on the cheek. 'Of course that's it. What an idiot. I was thinking they'd found someone else.'

Simmy heaved a sigh of relief. 'I'm an idiot, as well. Tell Joe not to do that again. It's not helpful.'

Ben reluctantly went back to school, and Melanie conscientiously organised the assembled bouquets for delivery next day. She listed the addresses and amended the route she'd devised for Simmy to follow for maximum efficiency. 'You'll have to be closed for most of the morning,' she said regretfully. Melanie almost never managed to be in the shop on a Friday, due to the inflexible timetable at the college she attended part-time. Her diploma in hotel management was nearing completion and her results to date were so good that she was determined to get the highest possible mark overall. That meant diligent attendance and a lot of additional homework. In the six months that Simmy had known her, she had made astonishing progress on every level. She was even working on improving her accent, with special attention to the vowel sounds.

Work in the back room was almost finished, and no more orders had come through. 'We needn't have sent Kathy away,' said Melanie. 'You could have had a nice chat.'

'We can do that this evening.'

'She's nice. When did you last see her?'

'Not since I moved here. I thought she'd

forgotten all about me. And she's only here now because she's got some sort of business in the area over the weekend.'

'What does she do? Was she on the same course as you?'

'No, no. We met at a wine tasting, years ago. She's a civil servant. Never talks about her job. Our husbands were being all pretentious about wine, and we drifted off into a corner and got to know each other. We just clicked. You know how that goes.'

'Not really.' Melanie seemed a bit wistful. 'I haven't made a proper new friend since I was twelve.'

'Me. Ben.'

'S'pose so. But all my girlfriends are from school. I don't much like the ones at college. The best one packed in the course just as I was getting to know her better.'

'You'll meet loads of people when you start working in a hotel.'

'Yeah.'

The moment had almost arrived when Melanie would have to begin a serious job-finding effort. Her motive for working part-time in a local shop was primarily to improve her customer-service skills. Simmy had found it easy enough to knock some of the sharp corners from the girl, helping her to think twice before showing impatience towards customers. 'They might be newly bereaved, or wallowing in guilt, or having to adjust to a new situation. You need to go carefully with them.'

It had worked well, with increasingly few exceptions, although Melanie did have a persistent problem with ditherers that was hard to shift. 'You'll come across them all the time in a hotel,' Simmy warned her. 'Lots of people have no idea what they want.'

Melanie could scarcely imagine such a thing; her life decisions had been made years ago. With a mother who coped poorly with the challenges of life, the girl had quickly concluded that she was on her own and would have to concentrate hard if she wanted to better herself. The dramatic gulf between her and the rest of her disorganised family was one obvious explanation for her hesitancy over making friends.

'I need to start earning serious money this summer,' she said. 'I can't go on living at home much longer. It's driving me mad. There's nowhere to *put* anything.'

'You'll find something easily enough. There must be a hundred hotels within twenty miles of here.'

'A lot more, actually. I'm going to start at the top and work down. Can you practise interviews with me sometime, do you think?'

'Don't they do that at college?'

'Yeah, but they don't have much idea of what a real employer wants. You do, because you *are* one.'

Simmy laughed. 'That's true.'

The lull in activity was making her feel tired. All week she'd been in a controlled panic, afraid she could never manage to honour all the commitments she'd made. The unpleasantness in Coniston and the tears in Hawkshead had shaken her, making her realise that she was still not fully recovered from the tragic events in Ambleside just before Christmas. It took very little to frighten her now, and that made her angry. She had learnt how humiliating it was to become a victim and how steep a climb it was to emerge from that role without serious lasting damage. The expression on DI Moxon's face when he looked at her made her feel young and vulnerable, which was not the way she wanted to feel. There was a sneaking sense that he harboured other feelings towards her, as well. Without actually saying so, it was clear that Melanie believed him to be attracted to Simmy as a woman, rather than a witness. In short, he went soft when he was with her. He visited the shop in person when the matter in question could have been handled by a phone call or a visit from someone of much lower rank. He was concerned for her safety and eager to offer protection. There had even been one or two moments when Simmy suspected she had hurt his feelings.

Darn it, she thought. It's the same as Melanie with her Wilf – we've both got lovelorn swains who we're not at all sure we want. In fact, she could still not entirely shake off a mild sense of repulsion towards Moxon as a man. He was not good-looking. He did not have an easy manner. On the whole, taking everything into consideration, she would really quite like never to see him again.

But at least it was looking as if there would be no troublesome police investigation into the death of Mr Hayter. No repeated questions from the detective or eager delvings into people's motives from Ben. Spring was coming, business was flourishing and all was basically well with her world, she assured herself.

At half past three, she was amazed to find there was really nothing else to be done. It was all simply sitting in the back room awaiting delivery next day. 'I'm tempted to take the rest of the day off, if you can hang on here till five,' she told her assistant. 'I could take Kathy for a drive before it gets dark.'

'No problem,' shrugged Melanie. 'It's your shop.'

'I think I've earned it. And besides, I'd really prefer not to be here if DI Moxon shows up again.'

'Coward,' said Melanie affectionately.

Simmy phoned her friend, who answered instantly and was more than ready for a lakeside drive. 'We can go to Coniston,' said Simmy. 'Or Ambleside. Where are you? I'll come and find you.'

'Outside a big church in Bowness, trying to decide where to go next. I'll cross over and wait somewhere prominent, so you'll see me. Just below a smart hotel called the Belsfield – how's that?'

'Fine,' said Simmy, repressing a shudder that always came now when she visualised the central part of Bowness-on-Windermere. She had come close to dying there, as well as in Ambleside. And she had witnessed someone else's death a few yards from the spot where Kathy would be waiting.

Even on a damp February afternoon there were visitors wandering along the pavements, pausing to gaze at the fells, or to admire the swans which spent most of their time around the jetties. Bowness had more than enough shops, cafes, hotels and attractions to keep a family occupied for a few days, whatever the weather. By comparison, the little town of Windermere had almost nothing. The biggest shop, in prime position, sold ladies' underwear. There were few if any good views of the lake, either. And yet it had an atmosphere that was so serenely English, so unconcerned about what people thought of it, that it drew enthusiasts in plenty. Beyond the main street there were rows and rows of B&Bs offering sensible facilities as a base for fell walking or sailing or any other Lakeland activity. Simmy for one thought Windermere quite perfect, for the very reason that it hardly even occurred to it to try to please.

Kathy was standing very visibly at the edge of a pavement unobstructed by parked vehicles. She hopped athletically into the passenger seat, almost before Simmy had stopped. 'Hiya!' she said. 'You were quick.'

'It's not far. Where do you want to go?'

'It's up to you. I'm new here and it all sounds wonderfully romantic.'

'It's often a bit eerie out in the countryside, this time of year.' And Simmy told her friend about her early-morning drive to Hawkshead, that very day. 'The sheep are like ghosts, and the trees all seem to be watching you,' she concluded.

'What about Ambleside, then? I'd like to see all that.'

'I thought, actually, that we might do a loop around Windermere and go up the other side, maybe to Rusland or somewhere. Just driving. There are still plenty of places I've never seen. We might even do a circle, through Hawkshead or Ambleside. It'd be dark before we finished, though.'

'Let's not be too ambitious, then. It's just nice to sit in the car and talk and get some of the local atmosphere.'

'We must go *somewhere*,' said Simmy. 'Let's drive down towards Newby Bridge. You see Windermere from the road for much of the way.'

'Is it possible to drive up the other side of it?'

'Not close enough to see the water. You have to go westwards, along another little lake called Esthwaite.'

'Never heard of it.'

'Not many people have. It's got trout. They catch enormous ones, apparently.'

'Yum.'

'We could go for a quick look. There's a pub at Near Sawrey that might be open.'

'Just drive, Sim. I don't care where we go.'

Simmy was already driving, heading southwards out of Bowness. Something in Kathy's voice made her feel nervous. Her stomach was clenching ominously. 'Okay,' she said.

They passed Storrs, with its big hotel claiming to be a perfect wedding venue. Simmy briefly recounted the sorry story of a wedding there, for which she had done the flowers. 'It ended very badly,' she sighed.

'So I gather.'

'Oh? Did I already tell you about it?' She was sure she hadn't.

'You were in the papers, love. It was national news for a few days.'

'I suppose it was.' The idea that people who had once known her might have registered the name in the newspapers was an uncomfortable one that she had pushed away several times over the past months. 'You should have told me you'd seen it.'

'Should I? Why?'

Simmy was reminded of Ben's habit of googling anybody who came to his attention. She had never once considered that there might be people who would google her. 'It feels funny otherwise,' she said weakly.

Kathy didn't answer.

'We can go in here and admire the lake.' She turned into a car park which offered a good panorama across the lake, the fells beyond providing a dramatic backdrop. 'There's hardly anywhere else they let you park these days.'

'It's amazing,' said Kathy. 'I can't imagine living here all the time. Do you ever get used to it?'

'I'm afraid you do, rather, although I still feel I've wasted the day if I haven't stopped to look around me for at least a couple of minutes – but it does happen, more all the time. My father's very good at reminding me. He's been here for ages, and still thinks it's magical.'

'I never met your parents.'

'They didn't come down to Worcester much. When they're not working, they go off to a Greek island or a city break somewhere, like Berlin. They've always done that.'

'Listen, Sim – I suppose I'll have to tell you. I'm up here for a reason. It's going to sound ridiculous, so brace yourself.'

'Is it a man?' Kathy's husband, Simon, might well have proved too boring for sustained fidelity, once into their third decade together. He was a college lecturer in modern languages.

'A man? As in a *lover*? No, you idiot. Valentine's

Day must have addled your brains, if that's what you think.'

'I expect it has,' Simmy agreed. 'So what, then?'

'It's basically to do with Joanna. She's fallen in with some people—'

'A cult! You've come to rescue her from some bunch of lunatics who think the world will end next week!'

'*No!* Simmy, listen, will you. For God's sake!' The impatient, almost hectoring, tone reminded Simmy that Kathy could be bossy and impatient even with close friends. There had been times when this had made her wonder why she maintained the relationship. Perhaps, too, it explained why she had made inadequate efforts to maintain communication after she moved.

But she forgave Kathy completely on this occasion, saying, 'Gosh, I'm turning into Ben Harkness, aren't I. He makes stupid suggestions like that, all the time. Although quite often they turn out not to be stupid after all.'

'The idea isn't entirely stupid. I guess you might call it a sort of cult, but they're perfectly harmless. Their motives are actually very pure. Young and idealistic and all that.'

Simmy kept quiet with difficulty.

'The thing is, they're all studying physics at university, and there's a major module about climate. Meteorology and all that. And they've decided to do some experiments of their own, in a region that hasn't had much industry for ages. It's something about carbon dioxide, apparently, and some theory about water vapour. There's a tutor with them, who happens to be the one Jo fell for in her first term. She's badly smitten, and now they're up here with nobody watching them, I dread to think what could happen. She's had one or two health problems lately, on top of everything else.'

'I can see why you'd be worried,' Simmy sympathised. 'She's still pretty young.'

'Right. I really hate to come over as a mother hen, but I do have a bad feeling about it all. Plus, I think it's time I met this tutor. For all we know, he's married or something. I don't want him to break her heart.'

Hearts. Flowers. The symbols of romantic springtime matings seemed to be everywhere, Simmy thought. 'No,' she said weakly.

Kathy went on, spilling out all her worries, and the scrappy pieces of information she'd managed to glean. 'They've been here a week already – on the slopes of the Old Man of Coniston, setting up a whole lot of measuring equipment and so forth. But on Tuesday I had a call from Jo saying there's been some trouble. Simon says it won't be anything dangerous, but I'm not so sure. Obviously, I can't go marching in without warning, like a parent whose kid's being bullied at primary school. I've got to approach it carefully. But now there's all this bother with you and the police, which seems to be centred on Coniston as well. I can't believe there's any connection, but even so . . .'

'I see,' said Simmy, not sure that she did. 'It seems funny, though, the way you've just been drifting around Bowness this afternoon, instead of rushing off to find Joanna. Haven't you heard from her since Tuesday?'

'No – and I wouldn't expect to. She's quite convinced she knows what she's doing.'

'And yet . . . ?'

'If you must know, I was checking something out in Bowness first. One of the group is the daughter of a colleague of mine and she told me Mandy has an aunt living up here, and I found her address on the computer. I thought I'd call in for a chat, just to see if she knew anything.'

'And?'

'She wasn't in.'

'So what was the trouble Jo told you about?'

'The equipment was thrown about and some of it broken. They had to start all over again.'

'Is it out on the open fell? What if it snows? How are they going to keep guard over it?'

'Two of the boys have got all-weather camping gear. They were going to stand guard, around the clock.'

'It does sound a bit dramatic.'

'I wondered whether it might just have been some sheep trampling on the stuff. But Jo laughed at that idea.'

'Did they get permission from the landowner first?'

'I doubt it.'

'It'll be National Park up there. I'm not sure how ownership works, come to think of it. But people aren't likely to take kindly to a bunch of students playing at science in their precious landscape. They'll think it's a survey for a wind farm or a nuclear power station or something. Stuff like that is incredibly sensitive.'

'It all connects up, though. If they get readings about $CO_2$ that show – oh, I don't know – that the theories about greenhouse gases are all wrong, for example, then there'll be people wanting to stop them.'

'Surely a few students doing measurements for a week isn't going to prove anything? Even I know it's more complicated than that.'

'I'm not really up to speed with it, either. There is some mystery to it, if Joanna's anyone to go by. I got the feeling there'd been measurements made in the same place on and off for a long time. Centuries, even.'

'How could you "get the feeling" about something like that? Either she told you or she didn't.'

'Her exact words were, "We're not the first people to do this, you know. We're following in the footsteps of some very serious scientists. And their findings got them into some pretty bad trouble." Does that sound ominous to you?'

'When did she say that?'

'Tuesday. She was very excited about it.'

Simmy's instincts were powerfully against any sort of melodrama. If bad things were going to happen, she wanted to be a long way away at the time. But she had learnt that events could overtake you, however hard you tried to avoid them. And now if she was on Google, associated with murder and mystery, then events were going to follow her about all the more.

'Hmm,' was all she could think of to say to Kathy.

'The whole thing about climate change has got hopelessly out of control, you see. Projects and developments that looked absolutely sensible and benign have got corrupted by vested interests, until it's all a terrible mess. Jo met a scientist recently who doesn't dare publish his findings because they raise a few awkward questions. It's like a religious war, she says, with people scared of ending up on the wrong side.'

'Gosh! I had no idea.' Simmy remembered Ben's surprise announcement of the day before. 'But I know a boy who has. He should meet your Joanna.

I bet they'd find each other very interesting.'

It was a refreshing interlude in many ways. Driving a newcomer around the lake, she discovered how much local knowledge she had gleaned over the year. She pointed out various landmarks, reciting names her father had taught her on their sporadic days out. 'That's Finsthwaite over there,' she nodded to the right, across the lake. 'Isn't that a wonderful name! It's surrounded by lovely green woods in summer. People go there to see the bobbin mill, which is a museum. And it's got a very weird church.'

'You can't see much from the road,' Kathy complained. 'We ought to be rowing up and down in a boat.'

'Or walking. I don't much like boats.'

'I love them. How can you live here and not like boats?'

'Easily enough, especially at this time of year. It'd be freezing cold on the water.'

They reached Newby Bridge, and negotiated the confusing roads that took them northwards all the way to the Sawreys. 'We're going back to where we started – just on the other side of the lake,' Simmy explained inadequately. 'And if you insist, we might get the ferry across to Bowness afterwards. I hardly ever do that.'

'Because it's a boat?'

'I'm afraid so.'

'Has it ever sunk?'

'Oh, yes. An entire wedding party came to grief, sometime in the nineteenth century. It's operated by a cable now. Even that broke at one time and the boat drifted off for miles until it hit one of the little islands. For a while it was haunted by a horrible demon, so nobody would use it after dark. It does save a lot of driving, I have to admit.'

'We'll take it, then. It sounds totally enchanting. What time's the last one?'

'I'm not sure. Something like eight o'clock, I think.'

'That'll be nice and spooky – pitch-dark and freezing cold. I bet there are ghosts.'

'There are,' Simmy confirmed glumly. 'Old ones and new.' She was thinking of the poor young man drowned at Storrs not so long ago.

It was almost five o'clock when they reached Near Sawrey, and night was falling. The pub, which also offered accommodation, was open, but it would be a while before any food was available. 'Let's walk round the village for a bit,' urged Kathy. 'It looks gorgeous, from what I can see in this light.'

But the plan had to be aborted. Simmy's phone rang, jingling in her bag as if possessed by a special urgency. 'It must be Melanie,' she said. 'Got another last-minute order for red roses, I expect.'

But it was DI Moxon. 'I'm really sorry about

this,' he said, 'but I'm afraid I need you in Coniston as soon as possible.'

'*Where?* Why?'

'There's a sergeant who'll meet you in the Yewdale Hotel, in the middle of the village. You can't miss it.'

'But *why?* I've got someone with me.'

'You're going to hate this, and I'm very sorry. But I need you to look at a body for me. It's extremely important, otherwise I'd never ask you.' He sounded flattened, speaking in a soft tone full of pain. Not at all like a police inspector.

'A body?' she repeated, almost hysterically. 'Whose body?' The question was superfluous, or so she hoped. Obviously the body could only be that of Mr Jack Hayter, who died by his own hand on the slopes of the Old Man of Coniston. But Moxon's reply gave her reason to doubt her assumption, and shudder with apprehension.

'I'll tell you that when you get here,' he said. 'Where are you now?'

'Near Sawrey,' she admitted. 'Probably about fifteen minutes away.'

'Well, that's lucky, isn't it? Who is it with you?'

Simmy bristled, doubly irritated by both his remarks, her anxiety turning to anger. 'Nobody you know,' she retorted rudely.

'Sorry.'

His apology disarmed her and again the

comparison with Wilf Harkness occurred to her. Moxon should have been outraged at her lack of cooperation, her failure to show due deference to an officer of the law. Instead he spoke like a jealous lover and she felt sure he had heard himself and cringed when she spoke sharply.

'Yewdale Hotel,' she said with a sigh. 'All right, then.'

# CHAPTER SIX

From Near Sawrey to Coniston took them along
a zigzag route through Hawkshead and along the
same road Simmy had used rather a lot recently.
Kathy sat quiet and pale beside her, fully aware of
Simmy's fragile mood. The absence of questions
and guesses reminded Simmy of how well she and
Kathy had always got along. They had been known
to spend a contented hour together over a picnic
lunch or simply sitting in a park watching ducks,
barely speaking. Kathy had been a haven from
the irritations of married life, and she assumed it
had worked the same both ways. With Tony there
had always been a subtle sense of having to justify
herself at every turn. He would want to know why
she kept all the mugs upside down on their shelf;
why she favoured one particular teaspoon over
the others; why the cushions had to be plumped

up before going to bed. The answers were always utterly obvious to her; the questions therefore intended merely to remind her that he existed and might have other ways of doing things. Tony's sense of his own existence was oddly shaky, she'd learnt, and when their baby died it made this aspect of him very much worse.

'Yewdale Hotel,' Kathy read from the illuminated sign above the main entrance. 'Looks nice.'

'I've never been inside. Do you suppose they've got a dead body somewhere in there? He's been dead since Tuesday night, I think – why would he still be here? Why bring him to a hotel at all?'

'Don't ask me.'

They parked in the street and went into the hotel. A uniformed policeman jumped up, hands extended, as if fielding two difficult catches at once. 'Mrs Brown?' he said.

'That's me.' Her attempt at a sort of brisk levity was not very successful.

'Please follow me. It's a two-minute walk.'

He marched out of the hotel entrance and turned left. Then he turned left again and they were almost out of the village, heading towards the lake down a road that Simmy immediately recognised. Darkness was gathering, the sky blotched with pewter-grey clouds. Simmy and Kathy trotted after him like lambs. 'I know where we're going,' said Simmy. 'This is where I brought the flowers on Monday. But why, when Mr Hayter died out on the fells?' She did not expect a reply, but her questions continued to spill out, as her confusion deepened. 'Have they brought him back to his house? Would they do that? What would the neighbours think?'

Kathy snorted, but had no helpful suggestions to contribute. The policeman behaved as if nothing had been said.

When they reached the house, they were taken through a narrow gate into a paved area at the rear where someone had converted part of the garden into a patio surrounded by a stone wall. A white tent took up three-quarters of the paved area. A car door slammed close by and DI Moxon materialised. 'I really am sorry,' he said, looking as if he meant it. 'I couldn't find any way around it. Jim – take this lady away, will you, and put her in the back of my car.' Kathy was deftly removed and Simmy just stared at the tent.

'It's not as bad as you think it'll be,' Moxon said.

'Why is he *here*? It seems so callous, leaving him lying outside like that. Didn't you find him yesterday on the fells?' Already the time frame was eluding her, the week disintegrating into spurts of activity and a blizzard of contradictory information. 'Or even the day before,' she added with a frown.

'This isn't the man we told you about who we found on the fells. He's been in the mortuary since yesterday. This is another one. We don't know how long he's been here, because I'm sorry to say we didn't look outside when I was here with Daisy yesterday morning.'

She stared at him in horror. 'So he could have been here ever since I saw him on Monday. What on earth can have happened?' She shook her head to clear it. 'Did they die together? A suicide pact?' *Be quiet!* an inner voice ordered her, but she found herself unable to stop. 'And what on earth can I do to help?'

'I'm sorry,' he said again, in the same miserable voice he'd used on the phone. 'We know who he is – a mate of mine, as it happens. I'm godfather to his son. What we need from you is just to tell us officially that this was the man you delivered flowers to on Monday. I'm hoping you saw him clearly enough to know him again?'

'It's awfully dark,' she complained.

'Dave,' said Moxon, and a brilliant floodlight went on, turning the little garden into a vivid stage with every detail in stark illumination. A flap of the tent was pulled back so the interior was equally well lit.

Other than her own stillborn daughter, Simmy had managed not to look directly at a dead face before. Even in Bowness last year, she had turned aside and looked at something else after the first ghastly second. It was, as Moxon had predicted, much less awful than she'd feared and she let her eyes rest on the motionless flesh for a long minute.

'Yes,' she said. 'It's the same man. I remember his hair, and the way his eyes are set under his brows. Funny, isn't it – I had no reason to memorise him and yet I can remember the whole thing. He was tall and stooped a bit in the doorway. His head was bent and he looked at me from under those brows. His hair wasn't brushed very well, so there was a tuft over one ear. It's still there, see.'

'So this man was inside the house and opened the door when you knocked. Did you ask him his name?'

'Yes. I always do. I said, "Mr Hayter?" and he nodded. Then I said "Flowers for you" and he smiled in a funny way and took them from me.'

'What sort of a funny way?'

'As if it was a kind of joke. An ironic joke. I thought he might say "A bit late for that" or "Flowers won't change anything". That sort of idea. But he gave them a good look. He stood there holding them, the way people hold babies. But I told you all this before. He seemed preoccupied, as if I'd interrupted something.'

'Some details have changed in your account,' he observed without a hint of accusation. 'That's not unusual, and probably not too big an issue.'

'I'm remembering it better now I'm here,' she explained, feeling foolishly guilty.

'It's okay. Now tell me again – did he read the card?'

'Not while I was there. It was wishing him luck in his new job. I thought he looked a bit old to be starting afresh. But people do, don't they?' She returned her gaze to the dead face. 'Poor man.'

'So as far as you're concerned, this is Mr Jack Hayter. But it isn't, because Jack Hayter is lying in the mortuary in Barrow. His daughter identified him without hesitation. Besides, as I say, I know full well who this is. His name's Tim Braithwaite.'

Simmy almost put a hand on his shoulder in commiseration. The police officer had mutated into a sad middle-aged man grieving for his friend. 'Did he live here, then?' she asked.

'Oh yes. As did Jack Hayter. They lived here together.'

'A couple? So it *was* a suicide pact? Is that what you're saying?' She frowned. 'But if so, why does it matter which one I gave the flowers to?'

'Timing,' he muttered. Then he faced her full on. 'And this one wasn't suicide. What we have here is an unlawful killing by person or persons unknown. Murder, to use the normal term for it.'

Simmy thought of Ben and how thrilled he would be by the mystery. For a moment she envied him his youthful lack of empathy. 'So – Mr Hayter's partner told me a lie when he said he was Mr Hayter. I suppose he just did it for convenience, to get rid of me. I mean – if it was the right house, that's all that matters for a delivery, anyway. It doesn't have to mean anything menacing, does it?'

'They weren't partners. Jack was Tim's tenant. They had separate parts of the house. It's big enough, after all.' Simmy followed his gaze and agreed that the house obviously had at least four bedrooms, judging by the row of upstairs windows.

'It must be horrible seeing him like this – lying out in the cold. Can't you take him away now? Couldn't you have asked me to see him in a mortuary somewhere?'

'I could, but Melanie told me you were over this way with your friend, so I thought it would save you time and trouble this way.'

*He wanted to see me again*, Simmy realised. He was using this whole thing as an excuse to be with her. Was that possible? She felt exhausted by the thought, and mildly anxious. He was being inexcusably unprofessional, and yet at least two colleagues were standing within earshot, apparently unsurprised by what they heard. But deeper down, she felt sorry for him as well.

'What happened to him exactly?' she asked. 'Was it quick, do you think?'

'Looks like a knife between the ribs. He's been lying here for quite some time, so it's not easy to be sure precisely what happened or where he died. Not until . . .' He winced and Simmy understood that the thought of a post mortem on somebody you'd known a long time was horrible.

'He wasn't a policeman, was he?'

Moxon laughed without mirth. 'Far from it. Way too clever for that, was Tim. He's a scientist. *Was* a scientist. Some government department employed him to draw graphs and make predictions. I never really understood it. We didn't discuss it much.'

'What *did* you discuss?'

Simultaneously they noticed that the wrong person was asking the questions and both grimaced. 'Usual stuff,' he muttered. 'The news of the day. Rugby. Weather. His son and his problems. The son's problems, I mean. Cars. Money.' He stopped himself with a little shake of his head. 'All the usual stuff.'

'Should you be handling the investigation, then? If he was your friend? Won't it cloud your judgement or something?'

'Maybe.' He didn't appear to care very much. 'All I can think of for now is how nobody noticed he was lying here for God knows how long.'

'Might have been three days or more,' she calculated. 'In winter, with half these houses closed up, I suppose that's understandable. You can't see the patio from the road.' She should be eager to get back to Kathy and the security of her car. Instead she felt glued to the spot by DI Moxon's need of her. 'Who found him?'

'I did,' he said, the words echoing as if a great bell had just tolled. 'I came to ask him about Jack

Hayter, just as a routine, really. Even with a suicide, we like to get the whole picture straight.'

'Oh dear,' she said. Then she straightened up and added, 'Can I go now?'

'Of course.' He seemed disappointed in her.

'My friend will be wondering what's going on. And it's cold out here.'

He took a deep breath. 'She'll be fine. But it *is* cold, I admit. Turning icy tonight, shouldn't wonder.'

'All the more reason to get on, then. You won't leave him here all night, will you?'

'Don't worry. We've done all we can here. They'll be removing him any time now.'

*Removing* sounded callous, as if the dead man were a piece of furniture. As if there was no hurry to get him indoors and taken care of. If she hadn't known how distressed the inspector was, she would have mentally accused him of heartlessness. In another situation, with a total stranger dead at his feet, it might well have been different. He might have found it quite unremarkable, the way a human being could so quickly become a thing to be tidied away by men in a van.

Kathy got out of the police car bringing a cloud of warm air with her. The engine had been kept running to maintain the heat, with obvious efficiency. The two women walked back to Simmy's chilly vehicle, not speaking until they were inside it.

'Was it horrible?' Kathy asked.

'Not really. It's pretty silly being scared of a dead body when you think about it.'

'I didn't mean scary. If he was murdered, that means he died in pain and might have been terrified. There could have been blood or worse. I was imagining all sorts of things while I waited for you.'

'I didn't see any blood. They only showed me his face. It was definitely the man I saw on Monday. He said he was Mr Hayter, but the police say he's not. He and Mr Hayter both lived in that house and now they're both dead.'

'You're in shock,' Kathy diagnosed. 'Are you fit to drive?'

'Why do you say that? I'm not shaking.' She remembered a recent experience of real physical shock. 'I'm just a bit numb.'

'You're talking funny. Not making proper sense.'

'That's not me. That's how it really is. I delivered flowers to a man who said he was the one on the order, but he wasn't, because his daughter identified that man's body on Wednesday. Now the first man is murdered on the patio of the same house. He was the detective man's friend, which makes it all a lot more awful. He's upset. They'll probably take him off the case. The two men weren't a couple. This one – he's called Tim – was a scientist.' She was babbling, rehearsing what she knew she would have to explain to Ben and Melanie the next day. She thought glumly of Ben's inevitable excitement.

'Oh, well. Everything will become perfectly clear once the police start a proper investigation. They'll already have questioned neighbours.' Kathy looked back down the little road. 'Although it is a bit quiet around here. Not many lights on.'

'Holiday homes,' said Simmy. 'Or else people earning their living from tourism. They go to the Canaries in winter.'

'You say the first man committed suicide?'

'Right – although I gather we're not meant to call it that any more. I had a lecture the other week about it from a customer.'

'You're joking! Why?'

'Something about it no longer being illegal, so you don't commit it. I was going to tell my mum about it, but she'd have ranted so much I didn't dare.'

'Madness,' said Kathy. 'Not every act you commit is a crime – is it?'

'Some people think it is, apparently.'

'Anyway. We're getting off the point. He killed himself. Does anybody know why?'

Simmy groaned. 'I had an awful feeling at first that it was because of the flowers I delivered to him. There's been a run of unwelcome bouquets this week – all causing upset in various ways. But now I can rest easy about this one, at least, because it wasn't him they were intended for.' She paused. 'Except – I suppose Mr Hayter might have come

111

home on Monday and seen them, and something about them drove him to suicide.'

'I missed you, you know,' said Kathy, changing the subject in a soft, urgent tone. 'You just upped and moved and it felt as if you'd forgotten all about me. I never had such good talks with anybody else.'

'Really? I don't remember us talking much.'

'Oh, Simmy, we did! You kept me sane, a few years back when Simon and Claudia were fighting so much and Jo had that horrible glandular fever.'

Simmy was astonished. 'You always made that stuff sound funny, as if it was material for comedy, not something threatening your sanity.'

'Right. That's what I mean. You let me turn it into a laugh, so it all got put into a better perspective. Nobody else would do that.'

'I had no idea I was that useful.'

Kathy peered at her, but they could barely see each other inside the dark car. 'Why do I get the feeling you're still like that? I mean – that police chap seems to really need your help, for a start. And I imagine your parents are pretty pleased that you've come to be so close to them.'

'I really can't pretend that I'm of the slightest use to them. It's the other way round – they've had to rescue me a few times lately. My father's turned into a surprisingly good nurse.'

'But they'll be glad of the chance. That's how it works with parents.'

Simmy winced. 'I don't expect I'll ever get the chance to learn that for myself.'

'You might. Do you ever hear from Tony?'

Simmy had a feeling her friend was getting all the uncomfortable topics out of the way in a single sweep. 'Hardly ever. Only about the divorce business. It's all more or less finished now. I suppose he'll find a new wife.'

'Very likely. I saw him with a woman last week, actually.'

It was amazingly, irrationally painful. 'Ouch!' she said. 'I didn't see that coming.'

'Well, that's what happens, love. All part of the whole bloody experience.'

'And I'm supposed to pretend to be okay with it. I'd much rather you hadn't told me. I might never have known otherwise.'

'I don't hold with being an ostrich – you know that. Just get on with your own life, Sim. Aren't there any likely men around here?'

'Same as anywhere else. It's me that's not giving the right signals. It's driving Melanie crazy. She's desperate for me to find someone.'

Kathy laughed. 'Plenty of time,' she said, in a tone that clearly meant the opposite. 'Is that police detective available?'

'Moxon? Don't even suggest it.' She shivered. 'I have a feeling he'd be keen enough, if I gave him any encouragement. But there's something a bit . . . *greasy* about him. I am absolutely certain I could never fancy him physically.'

'Poor bloke.'

'I know. It doesn't seem very fair. But all he represents to me is death and violence and being frightened. It is a shame, but there it is.'

'Is he good at his job? Do we assume that he'll get to the bottom of all this confusion in Coniston?'

'I hope so, assuming he stays on the case. Preferably without me. I've got a ludicrously busy day tomorrow. What'll you be doing?'

'I'll have to find Jo, if I can. I need a cover story, which is where you come in.'

Simmy didn't answer. A large van was coming towards them on a narrow stretch of road, and she pulled as close to the wall as she could before stopping to let it by.

'He's going fast,' said Kathy, before a sharp report elicited a cry from Simmy. 'What was that?' Kathy wondered, turning to watch the other vehicle's rear lights disappearing around a bend. 'He never stopped.'

'My wing mirror,' groaned Simmy. 'Look. It's completely smashed.'

'I can't see. It's too dark.'

'I'd better try and find the pieces. It might fit back together, if I'm lucky.' She leant over in front of Kathy and took a torch from the glove compartment. 'Wait a minute.' Shining the light on the road, she collected up as many pieces as she could find, dumping them onto her friend's lap. 'My dad might get it together again, with some gaffer tape. He likes that sort of job.' She sighed. 'At least it's not the van. I'll be using that all day tomorrow.'

'Meanwhile, you're technically illegal, I believe.'

'Look at the poor thing.' The actual mirror was dangling by a few wires from a painfully exposed set of inner workings. 'It'll drop off if I leave it like that.' She got out of the car again and fiddled with the mechanism, managing to straighten the mirror and click it into place. 'That's better.' They drove carefully back to Ambleside, and then down beside the lake to Windermere, where Kathy had some difficulty in remembering where she had left her own car. 'It all looks different in the dark,' she complained. 'It was a side road with a name I associated with boats. I parked somewhere in Bowness, and then had to walk a good long way uphill to your shop.'

'Helm?' Simmy suggested.

'Right first time! That was it.'

'That's where Ben lives. It's just along here.'

They found the car and Kathy waited twenty minutes while Simmy went back to her shop to gather bouquets for the early morning deliveries, and switch to using her van. Then she followed Simmy back to Troutbeck and a promised meal. When they eventually drew up at the white-painted cottage, it was eight o'clock. 'What an adventure!' Simmy said. 'I'm sorry it all went wrong, though. It wasn't much of a guided tour.'

'I'm sorry I landed on you when you're so busy. I must say it's all amazingly efficient.'

'Don't say that. I've got a nasty feeling I've forgotten something vital. Melanie planned it all out for me, so it ought to work, but I should check with her that there wasn't anything new after I'd gone.'

'She'd have told you, wouldn't she?'

'I didn't stop to look for a message. I'll call her now.'

Melanie answered quickly, even breathlessly. 'Simmy! What happened to you? Moxo called here and said there *was* another dead man in Coniston, and he wanted you to ID him. I've been waiting for you to call and tell me about it.'

'That's it – the whole thing. We were on the way to the pub in Near Sawrey and Moxon phoned me, so we had to dash to Coniston. We never did get a drink, and now we're starving hungry. I've got those three orders with me for Troutbeck, so I can do them first thing tomorrow. Was there anything new?'

'But who *was* he? Was he murdered? Why are *you* involved?'

'I'll tell you tomorrow, Mel. I have to keep my mind on the job. So do you.'

'All right, then. And no, nothing new came in.

116

Only Ninian Tripp. He was sorry to miss you. And he said the price I charged for his vase was just right. He's bringing one or two more at the weekend.'

Simmy experienced a pang of regret at not seeing Ninian. Her mental image of his long fair hair and clay-stained clothes was a sweet one. 'Thanks, Mel,' she said with a sigh.

# CHAPTER SEVEN

Reminiscing with Kathy occupied the rest of the evening, assisted by a bottle of red wine, followed by a glass or two of brandy, which had been a habit of theirs in former times. Kathy's life had always been very different from Simmy's, but the divergence now was stark. She had earned promotion in her department, suffering resentful reactions from a close colleague, which had made her working days far from pleasant. 'I'm thinking of making a complete change,' she confided. 'Especially seeing what fun you're having, working for yourself. It's a completely different world. Nobody looking over your shoulder all the time, and always something new to do. I mean – that amazing model tower in your window, for a start. Such creativity! I feel only semi-human compared to you.'

'That was Ben,' Simmy said. 'His idea, and mostly his work. And it's really been there for too long now. It's getting stale, and bits are starting to fall off. I don't think we gave it enough varnish.'

'But what a lovely idea!'

'He borrowed it from some museum in New York. No – a botanical garden. The Christmas display or something.'

'He seems quite a special kid. And Melanie's impressive as well.'

'I know. We're a real little gang.' Simmy laughed. 'Even though I'm old enough to be their mother.'

'Well, I'm jealous.' Kathy drained the brandy glass and looked at her watch. 'Must be time for bed. I guess you'll want to start early tomorrow. Leave me here and I'll have a quick explore of Troutbeck before setting off to find my daughter.'

'Go and see the church. It's got very famous windows.'

Kathy pulled a face. 'I think I'll pass on that. I'd rather go and find a good waterfall or dry stone wall. It's all about the outdoors up here, after all.'

'Not in February.' Simmy shivered. 'It's dangerous on the fells in winter. People *die*.'

'So it would seem,' said Kathy in a hollow voice.

Simmy woke early on Friday, the words *Valentine's Day* the first to enter her head. The orders had

119

considerably exceeded her expectations to the point where she had seriously considered turning a few away. So many romantic souls in the world, she thought ruefully, and not one of them thinking of her. All those beautiful velvety roses, the colour itself a powerful suggestion of sensuality and warmth. Despite the absence of scent, they were still fabulous. Carefully packed in her van and the back room of the shop, they would remain in perfect condition for days, if necessary. Her disenchantment from earlier in the week evaporated completely as she indulged in a final five minutes under the covers, thinking about love and loss and the eternal hope that everyone carried with them, whether they knew it or not. As a florist, she was instrumental in fuelling those hopes, today of all days.

Except, she remembered, some of her contributions over recent days had done the very opposite. A man had killed himself, another had been murdered – Mrs Aston had flung the floral peace offering violently across her farmyard and Mrs Crabtree had cried. Had the same person arranged the flowers for Aston and Crabtree and also killed the man who was not Jack Hayter but an old friend of DI Moxon? She sighed, hoping that none of the undoubted police effort to answer these questions would involve any more demands on her. She had more than enough to do already.

Kathy came downstairs in a dressing gown, as Simmy was boiling the kettle for coffee. 'What time is it?' she asked blearily.

'Seven-fifteen. Sorry. Do you want a drink?'

'Tea, if that's okay. Surely you're not delivering flowers before it's even light?'

'I thought eight would be acceptable. A nice start to the day for the recipients, and I might catch them before they go to work. I've got everything planned out, starting locally and working southwards.'

'What do you do if they're not in?'

'Good question. It does rather take the shine off when that happens. I either find a willing neighbour or go back again later.'

Kathy thought about it for a minute. 'What if the willing neighbour is a sworn enemy and never hands them over? Or reads the message and tells everyone in town that Jenny has a lover called Frank?'

Simmy shuddered. 'Don't!'

'Well, I wish you luck. It looks a bit icy out there.'

'Does it? I haven't looked yet.' She pulled back the kitchen blind and was alarmed to see hoar frost covering the bare stalks of her garden as well as the grass and trees. 'Good God – the roads'll be lethal. It hasn't been like that since before Christmas. My father told me it was going to be fine. At least mild and ice-free.'

'When did it last rain?'

'It drizzles much of the time. The roads aren't dry, if that's what you're thinking.'

'But it's not *sheets* of ice. Your tyres should manage well enough if you go steady.'

'It scares me,' Simmy admitted. 'And the van's tyres are nothing special.'

'It doesn't matter. I can't let it stop me. I'm going out at nine, icy or not. I'm going to find Joanna and make sure she's all right. That's what I came for, after all.'

'Have you tried phoning her again?'

'Sent her a text, not saying anything much. I'll drive to her digs and take it from there. I can't imagine she'll be halfway up a mountain in this weather.'

'She might, if it's weather she's working on.'

'If I've got it right, there's plenty of research she can be doing. This Victorian weatherman left a whole archive of notebooks and stuff, which is kept in Carlisle. She can go up there and spend all day in the warm. It's the only way to read them, anyway. They won't let them leave the building, and they haven't got it online yet.'

'It sounds more like a PhD than an ordinary Bachelors.'

'I know. I have a feeling she and the others have got very carried away with it all. And it's term time, so they can't stay for long. She's got other studies to keep up with.'

'Funny that we're both focused on Coniston,' said Simmy. 'You with your maverick daughter and me with a murdered man.'

'Well, don't even *hint* that there might be a connection. I wouldn't say I'm an anxious sort of mother, but even I prefer not to think of my daughter confronting a killer.'

'I didn't mean that,' said Simmy, instantly realising that she *had* in fact meant something very much like it.

They sat together in the kitchen for fifteen minutes before Simmy went outside to inspect the road. Troutbeck was on high ground, with every route out involving a steep downhill drive. None was easy, but Simmy had come to prefer the most northerly option, past Townend and down to the busy lakeside road which was kept free of snow and ice. She stepped onto the road, testing it for slippiness. It seemed all right and while she stood there a car passed by at normal speed, heading downhill. A second one followed it and paused at the sight of Simmy. The driver opened his window and smiled at her. 'Doesn't look too bad,' he said.

'I hope not. I've got a busy day.' It was a man she vaguely knew, from the other end of the village. She had heard his name a few times, but could never recall it. 'I suppose the Townend way is best?'

'Probably. Not so twisty, at least. It's supposed to

turn milder during the day. I don't think there's any need to worry.'

'Thanks,' she said. 'That's encouraging.'

He looked at her kindly. 'Relax, okay? You'll get used to it eventually.'

'Will I?' She swung her foot over the road again. 'I just keep imagining the car sliding into a ditch. It seems all too likely to happen.'

'It won't. And even if it does, the ditches aren't deep enough to do much damage.'

She remembered her broken wing mirror. 'The walls are hard enough, though. I'd hate to skid into one. I think I'd steer towards another car, rather than hit a wall.'

He laughed. 'Think positive,' he advised and closed his window with another smile.

Simmy went back indoors and gathered up her coat and bag. All three of the Troutbeck deliveries were in the Town Head direction – uphill and away from the lake. Wishing Kathy a good day, she got into the van and turned its heater to full. It was so cold inside she worried that the flowers in the back might have become frosted and ruined, but when she checked, they seemed in perfect condition. The gentle upward slope presented no difficulties, and all of the Valentine recipients were present to show suitable joy and delight. Sighing with relief, Simmy felt ready for the day ahead, and the dozen or so further deliveries to be made around the area.

The relief increased when she saw no apologetic police detective lurking outside her house, as she passed it again on the way out of the village. Perhaps she would be allowed to forget all about murder and malice, at least for the rest of the day.

Fridays were generally complicated, because Melanie had lectures and could very seldom assist in the shop. There were a few people who could be called on in a crisis, including Ben Harkness, who welcomed any excuse to duck out of school for a few hours. Simmy's mother, however, was not on the list. 'I'm a useless shopkeeper,' she said and refused to take any responsibility of that sort. Russell had reluctantly lent a hand once or twice, rewarding himself for the service by seizing the chance to recount some of his local anecdotes to the customers, as a variation on the captive audience at breakfast time that the B&B guests comprised.

On this day, though, there was no option but to close for most of the morning. Thanks to Melanie's logistical skills, a delivery route had been worked out that would probably not take more than two hours. The temperature was rising and traffic appeared to be moving fairly normally, once she was down on the main road.

The necessity of going back to Coniston was regrettable. If she'd known DI Moxon was going to summon her there the previous evening, she might have cheated by delivering the flowers early. As it was, she would have to do very much the same journey as the previous evening's, down to Newby Bridge and several miles back up the western side of Lake Windermere to a house not far from the one she'd already visited twice. Then turn round and retrace her steps – or else carry on through Hawkshead and Ambleside as she had done with Kathy. That way was undoubtedly shorter, but the prospect of Hawkshead Hill was uninviting if there was any risk of ice.

The first two deliveries, in Bowness, were uneventful, but the one in Newby Bridge went badly. Nobody answered the door and there was no front porch or handy shed in which to leave the flowers. Kathy's theories about neighbours made it seem risky to try the next house. There was a phone number provided with the order, so she went back to the van and called it.

It was answered just as she was giving up hope, with a breathy 'Hello?'

'Miss Drury? This is Persimmon Petals. I have some flowers for you.'

'Oh! Gosh! Where are you?'

'Outside your house, in Newby Bridge.'

'But I live in Coniston. I sold my house a while

126

ago and I haven't got anywhere permanent yet. Who are they from?'

'The message says "From a secret Valentine," that's all. They gave your phone number when they placed the order.'

Miss Drury remained silent for half a minute, then stammered, 'Gosh! I have *no idea* who that might be. Surely you have the name of the person who ordered them?'

It was a question Simmy had begun to grow thoroughly tired of. 'It's confidential, I'm afraid.' Wasn't that obvious, she thought crossly. And come to think of it, this was yet another order that had been made in person, paid for in cash, and not logged on any computer apart from the daily tally of monies received. She had no recollection at all of the manner in which the order had been made, but she knew it hadn't been online. 'And – actually – I don't have a name anyway.'

'Why not?'

She explained.

'So what did he look like?'

'He had a long brown coat and a black scarf. That's really all I remember. We might get a bit more from my assistant, but I doubt it. I'm sure she didn't know him.'

Miss Drury tutted in frustration. 'Well, can you bring the flowers here, do you think? Why would this man give you the wrong address, anyway?

If he knows my mobile number, he must surely know where I live.' A thought audibly struck her. 'Um . . . where *exactly* are you?'

'It's a house called Primrose Paddock, just off the main road.'

'Oh, God! That's where my boyfriend lives. Someone's trying to make trouble for me. Listen – don't bring me the bloody things. Throw them away. And don't let Solly see them, whatever you do.'

'But—' Wasn't it possible that Solly had sent them, she wanted to ask, using his own address as a kind of proposal that she move in with him? 'Couldn't he be the one?' she stammered.

'Was your customer black?'

'Um . . . no, I don't think so.'

'Then it wasn't my boyfriend. He's a Somali. Six foot two and *very* black. You would probably notice.'

'Yes,' she agreed.

'And he'd be devastated if he thought I was cheating on him. Thank God he's not at home. Please – just get rid of those flowers, okay?'

'Okay,' said Simmy. 'But I'm coming to Coniston next, so I *could* just let you see them.'

'No. Don't. I'm at work out on the fells. It wouldn't be worth your while.'

This was the second rejected bouquet in two days, and Simmy felt sore about it. She also felt used

128

and exploited, part of some very nasty little game that she had hoped was all over and done with.

She also realised, with a sinking heart, that DI Moxon was going to want a description of the man in the coat and scarf.

# CHAPTER EIGHT

She would call the police when she got back to Windermere, she told herself. First she had to make five more deliveries, three to the same address in Newby Bridge and two in Coniston. The three turned out to be for a trio of young sisters from their doting father. They were at school, but their mother took the flowers in with a slightly rueful smile. 'He's away in Saudi, you see,' she explained.

Simmy bit back the question as to whether he had remembered his wife as well. It was definitely none of her business. At least it had been a very economical delivery. She went back to the van glad to have it almost emptied in so short a time.

The slow winding road up to Coniston gave her more than enough time to think about the latest puzzling bouquet for the disgruntled Miss Drury. She had not sounded particularly young, certainly over thirty. Why would anybody deliberately set out to cause trouble between her and her boyfriend? No former lover consumed by jealous rage had come to mind, it seemed; no racist parent furious at her choice of partner. She had sounded genuinely bewildered and not a little angry.

If it had not been for the fact of the murder of one of Simmy's customers, these bizarre orders for flowers would be quite easily dismissed as an annoying but essentially harmless set of pranks. As it was, there was a real underlying threat, and the fact that Simmy had innocently taken three, if not four, orders from a seriously malign individual made her very uneasy.

The police would presumably devote their efforts to finding a link between all the people who had been sent sinister floral offerings. As far as Simmy could see, they were all very different. An elderly lady, a young farmer's wife, a middle-aged man and another young woman, living in scattered villages roughly centred on Coniston. There would have to be probing questions as to their work, contacts, movements and activities, which even at first glance struck Simmy as horribly intrusive. They had all seemed perfectly nice people, undeserving of the disruption and distress that had befallen them and which was very likely to get worse.

The sight of the Old Man looming out of the frosty morning mist to her left made her shiver. It was an eerie mountain at the best of times, perhaps because of its name, which suggested consciousness of some kind. The people of Coniston probably felt protected as if by a guardian angel, but as a visitor, Simmy perceived it more as a watchful and mildly threatening presence. She remembered that Kathy's daughter was performing some sort of experiment on its slopes, and wondered whether she was all right.

The mountain rose to a sharp point, dominating the smaller ones surrounding it. There was wispy cloud veiling it in horizontal bars, the whole scene drained of colour, leaving nothing but white and pale grey. She remembered that her first sight of it, in March of the previous year, had been all of brown and orange. In summer it blazed in a hundred shades of green. Her father had expounded on the copper mining which killed all the fish in the lake, and the charcoal burning that went on until well into the twentieth century. Despite appearances, the western fells had been sites of some industry since Roman times – something that Kathy's daughter was somehow focusing on, if Simmy had correctly understood the somewhat garbled story.

The two delivery addresses were at opposite ends of the village, neither of them close to the scene of the previous day's murder. With any luck, she could avoid setting eyes on any police personnel, and postpone reporting the Newby Bridge puzzle until she got back to the shop. She wanted no further impediments to opening its doors to would-be customers.

She also very much wanted the deliveries to go smoothly. The first turned out to be blessedly straightforward. A woman with a small baby answered the door and took the flowers with a broad smile and effusive thanks. The second was to a much older woman who appeared to be rather unwell. She held a thick scarf across her throat, and opened the door a bare three inches. 'Yes?'

'Flowers for Mrs Thomas,' said Simmy.

'Really?' A thin hand reached for them and took them through the gap. Simmy hovered, heart beating in apprehension. But all was well. 'Oh, the silly boy! It's my son, Robin. Sent me a Valentine. Isn't that ridiculous! Any other son would wait for Mother's Day.'

'How nice,' said Simmy.

'Of course, we both know I might not be here that long. Now, if you don't mind, I must close the door. The cold makes me catch my breath, you see.'

Mother's Day was little over a month away. There was something very grim in the thought that the woman might not even have that long to live. She certainly did look extremely frail. But what a devoted son he must be, doing his best to cheer her, apparently with considerable success. The relief at having brought the hoped-for delight to all but one of the morning's customers was considerable.

Yewdale Fells rose to the east as she turned back, planning to retrace her route southwards. A spectacular scene in its own right, it was generally overshadowed by the Old Man. The clouds had left a clear gap through which the rugged slopes could be clearly seen. The folds and gashes in the hillside threw odd shadows, some of them suggesting patterns in the brief moment of clarity. Simmy had heard that it was a difficult climb through gorse and bracken, with old mines and quarries to be negotiated along the way. This summer, she promised herself yet again, she really would get organised and do some serious exploring. But first she must concentrate on the day ahead. If she hurried, she might get back to the shop by half past eleven, in time for any lunchtime shoppers.

Before she had even passed the Coniston car park, however, she was intercepted. Not by DI Moxon lurking in wait for her, but by a distraught woman flagging her down on the pavement. The bright lettering on the side of the van plainly announced her identity, of course. It was intended to, after all. But now she very much wished she could become anonymous and unobtrusively slip back to work without attracting attention.

With a sigh, she braked. The woman ran out into the street and round to the driver's window. 'Oh, thank God! What a miracle, you being here!' she gasped. 'I've been so upset, thinking of poor Maggie taking my flowers the wrong way. And here you are, so I can explain it to you.'

Maggie? Which one was she, wondered Simmy. 'Um . . . ?' she said.

'Maggie Aston. On the farm. She says she *threw* them at you. I never *dreamt* she'd do that. I should have put my name, of course, but I assumed she'd understand. And all the time, she thought it was Trevor apologising for an affair or something. How embarrassing for you. I'm so sorry.'

'No problem,' said Simmy, feeling bemused. On first impression, it seemed that particular flower delivery could be removed from the case. 'These things happen,' she added meaninglessly.

'But you must have felt so *awful*,' the woman persisted. 'What a dreadful waste of flowers.'

Simmy silently agreed, but could hardly say so aloud. 'Is everything forgiven now, then?' she asked.

The woman flushed violently. 'You must think I'm a complete idiot. I know I exaggerated in that message. The thing is, I did do something very bad and I wanted Maggie to forgive me. I thought she would hate me for ever and I couldn't *bear* that. So flowers seemed a good way of admitting my fault. A confession, in a way.'

Again Simmy was inhibited in her desire to ask what the crime had been. 'I see,' she lied.

'Well, I expect it'll come right in the end. Things usually do.'

Simmy wasn't sure she agreed with this. She gently revved the engine, having carefully not turned off the ignition. 'I'm sorry,' she began, 'but—'

'Oh, yes. It'll be a busy day for you. My aunt was a florist and she nearly went mad on Valentine's Day. Even worse for Mother's Day, of course. That's a nightmare.'

*Thanks* thought Simmy.

'Off you go, then,' the woman encouraged. 'I'm a bit busy myself, actually. I do the cleaning for some of the holiday homes hereabouts. But I can't go down there.' She ducked her chin at the little road leading down to where Moxon had stood guard over a dead body the previous evening. 'They won't let anybody pass.' She lowered her voice. 'Something very nasty happened, apparently. It was on the news just a little while ago.'

Simmy had no intention of getting into that subject. Let Ben accuse her of a wicked lack of curiosity, if he wanted to – she was adamant. 'Bye, then,' she said and closed the window. Before the woman could say another word, she was off down the main street and southwards past Torver as the quickest way home. The sky was clearing, which was not entirely good news, because it lowered the temperature. But she saw no sign of ice on the roads and made reasonably good time. Her thoughts flitted from one unexplained event to another, hoping to arrive at a reassuring conclusion that nothing that was happening had anything to do with her.

So the murder was public knowledge, at least in a generalised way. The apologetic woman had called it 'something nasty', so perhaps it had not been disclosed that a man had been violently killed. Even so, there was little doubt that Ben and Melanie would quickly get to hear of it and approach her for more information. Their natures were both infinitely more inquisitive than Simmy's was. Ben never wasted any time in drawing conclusions and connections, aided by Internet searches and an impressive intelligence.

She could not evade the fact that her morning drive had produced at least one new factor in the story, and probably two. Wherever she went, people forced knowledge on her against her will and completely unsolicited. She garnered names and links without the slightest effort. It was as if fate was conspiring against her, and yet she had learnt over the past four or five months that it was much more rational than that. A florist put herself in the line of fire simply by being associated with major life events where emotions were heightened and families forced to confront disagreeable truths. This forcing was occasionally violent, leading to further violence and even murder.

As for the *real* Mr Hayter, his daughter Daisy had reported him missing, which implied an absence of wife or girlfriend. Furthermore, the *false* Mr

Hayter also known as Mr Braithwaite, had a son who was Moxon's godchild, and who clearly did not live with his father. She entertained a picture of the two men living quietly together, separated or divorced from the mothers of their children, and enjoying a sparse social life. Into this calm oasis a bombshell must have been thrown, perhaps in the shape of an anonymous bunch of flowers. And now they were both dead. The mystery that brought Simmy nothing but pain and frustration would no doubt give rise to an excited curiosity in young Ben Harkness. He would do his best to drag details, facts, reported conversations out of Simmy. But he would be disappointed – all she could offer where the second body was concerned were impressions – that no wailing wife or daughter had been in evidence; no white-faced brother or son. The body had presented a neglected abandoned aura, with nobody but police officers attending it. Belatedly, Simmy felt sorry for the man. Until then she had been aware only of her own reactions, her stoicism in confronting her first dead face full on. Only now did she experience a flush of sadness at the pain he must have endured and the sudden extinction of a life that should have run for another twenty or thirty years.

She reached the shop at eleven forty-five, and quickly turned the Closed sign to Open. Within minutes four people had crowded in. One of them was her mother. 'Where have you been?' she demanded. 'I was hoping for a mug of coffee, an hour ago. I had to go to Julie's instead.'

Julie ran a hairdressing salon in the centre of Windermere and was Simmy's closest local friend. 'Did you get your hair cut while you were there?'

'Of course not. But I did make an appointment for next week. And we had a nice chat.'

Simmy winced at the thought of the interruption Angie had probably caused.

A couple in their thirties were hoping to discuss wedding flowers, which given the date struck Simmy as somewhat thoughtless. She gave them a stack of brochures and leaflets and made an appointment for the coming week. And a familiar elderly woman hovered meekly behind everyone else, obviously hoping for a quiet word with Simmy.

'Mum, I can't talk now. I'll try and drop in over the weekend, but as I told you already, I'm more likely to just slob about on Sunday, getting over this week. It's all every bit as chaotic today as I thought it'd be.' *And I should phone the police*, she remembered. There was an ominous feeling that real chaos was on its way, especially if Ben showed up as he often did on a Friday afternoon.

Angie left with an impatient sigh and Simmy turned to the old lady. 'Mrs Crabtree,' she said. 'How can I help you?'

'You remember me?' It evidently came as a great surprise.

'Of course. I've been thinking about you.'

'The police came to my house this morning. Two women in uniform. I dread to think what the neighbours made of it.'

'I'm sorry. I expect they explained more about the run of unpleasant messages sent with flowers, including yours. They do need to catch the person doing it.'

'Well, I was very little use to them, because the whole business proves to be entirely innocent.'

'Oh?' Simmy's spirits rose at this reassurance and she smiled broadly at her visitor.

'Yes – you see, my niece, April, called to say her mother – my sister Pattie – sent the flowers, because she'd got the idea I was moving. Poor Pattie's losing it, I'm afraid. She can be perfectly lucid one moment and away on another planet the next. She took it into her head to send me a bunch of flowers, and only told April about it this morning.'

'I see,' said Simmy uncertainly. 'So she's not so bad that she can't write a letter to order some flowers – unlike your son and daughter?'

Mrs Crabtree laughed. 'You remember that, as well! Pattie was a highly competent professional woman all her life. She could write a letter in her sleep, even now. She keeps postage stamps and writing materials in a lovely old walnut bureau that once belonged to our grandmother.'

'In that case,' Simmy asked slowly, 'why have you come here? I mean – if everything's all right, after all?'

Mrs Crabtree smiled. 'I had a feeling you might be worried. You looked so concerned at my distress.'

'You could have phoned.'

'I could, yes. But I liked you and wanted to see you again. I know you had some trouble at the end of last year, and this business was probably the last thing you wanted.'

'That's very sweet of you.'

The woman tossed her head in denial. 'Not at all.'

'Well . . . would you like a hot drink while you're here? It looks chilly out there.'

'That would be lovely. Coffee, if possible, thank you.'

Settling her guest awkwardly on the small chair by the till, Simmy quickly went to prepare the drink. In the absence of any customers, they enjoyed fifteen minutes of comfortable chat.

'I suppose letters were the standard way of communicating, not very long ago,' Simmy mused.

'Indeed. I miss them very much. Although I'm not so different from my sister, to be honest. I still send one or two a week. I admit to writing opinionated missives to the papers now and then, but I've never said anything to offend. I just talk about the old days and the way people keep on making the same mistakes over and over again.' She gave Simmy an assessing look. 'You might not be old enough yet, but when you get to my age, you start to see the way nothing ever changes. It's depressing, really.'

Mrs Crabtree looked to be a few years shy of seventy – scarcely old enough to qualify for 'elderly', when so many people lived into their nineties. Where Simmy had initially seen her as soft and slightly pathetic, she now revised this perception to include a sharp and restless mind. 'What did you do for a living?' she asked, expecting the answer to be teaching or nursing.

'I was a civil servant.'

Not far off, Simmy thought. 'Oh! I have a friend in the civil service. She's visiting me at the moment, actually.'

'It's a big employer, the state – though not as big as it used to be. There was a time when it employed three-quarters of a million people. It's less than half a million now,' she added regretfully. 'What department is your friend in?'

'Oh . . . um . . . Revenue and Customs, I think. She doesn't talk about it much.'

Mrs Crabtree smiled. 'No, I don't suppose she does. I was MoD, and I hardly talked about it at all. One thing you do learn there is discretion.'

'I'm sure,' said Simmy, wondering whether there could be any possible connection between a hush-hush job and a malicious bunch of flowers, with the story of the dysfunctional sister nothing more than a smokescreen.

'I retired eight years ago. It all seems like another world to me now.'

'But you keep up with the news. I mean – if you write to the papers, you must have a good grasp of everything that's going on.'

'Oh, not really. I stick to local matters.'

'So – don't you think it's a good thing that the police are taking the flowers seriously? I mean, you were quite upset when you thought someone was trying to force you to move house. That's not a nice thing to do, is it?'

Mrs Crabtree shuddered. 'It's my Achilles heel,' she admitted. 'Or I would never have been so emotional about the flowers. I know it would have made more sense to move to a bigger town, where I could walk to shops and all the other things you need. But there's a good bus service where I am, and I expect to go on driving for at least another ten years.'

'You drove here today? Over Hawkshead Hill in these icy conditions?'

'I did.'

'You're a better man than I am, then. I came the southerly way just now.'

'From where?' The woman frowned her confusion.

'I had to go to Coniston this morning, with some flowers for Valentine's Day. I hate icy roads. The thought of a skid terrifies me.'

'You won't skid if you use the gears properly. And if you do, just steer into it.'

'Easier said than done,' said Simmy. 'I have a feeling my feet would just take over and ignore anything my head tried to tell them.'

Mrs Crabtree laughed and then met Simmy's eyes with a very straight look. 'A man was killed in Coniston yesterday, according to the policewomen. They didn't say so directly, but I concluded they think it's connected with you and those flowers you brought me. It gave me reason to worry about you.'

Simmy's heart lurched. She should have learnt by now, she told herself, that professional women of a certain age were very often uncomfortably direct in what they said. Perhaps, she sometimes thought, it arose from an aversion to wasting time. Beating about the bush could delay an effective exchange for weeks or even years. This one was transforming into a woman of steel before her very eyes. The look she gave Simmy was verging on the accusing. 'Oh, no,' she protested. 'I really don't think . . .'

'If you *do* think a minute, you'll see how it is.'

'But how do you *know*? I mean – did they tell you his name? Is he somebody you knew?' She groaned softly. 'Or does everybody know everybody around here?' Having met Melanie's grandmother

144

a few months earlier and been treated to a spate of gossip about a lot of people, she already knew the answer to that question. Anyone who had grown up and gone to school in the area, and who had continued to live and work there all their lives, did indeed know almost everybody.

'Coniston isn't far from Hawkshead,' was all she got in reply.

A customer finally interrupted them and Mrs Crabtree made her departure, showing every sign of having said what she had come to say. Simmy found herself unsure of exactly what that had been. Had the woman made the intrepid drive into Windermere solely to reassure the florist – or did she have other business there? In any case, it had had the effect of delaying the call to DI Moxon, to tell him about the girl in Newby Bridge – or *not* in Newby Bridge, to be more accurate. The new customer required full attention for ten more minutes, requesting an instant bouquet of flowers all in a narrow spectrum between pink and mauve, choosing and rejecting from the many blooms Simmy had available.

It was almost one o'clock when she found herself alone at last. With a powerful sense of reluctance she called Moxon.

'Mrs Brown,' he said, as always. It was never a question. He then waited quietly for her to say her piece.

'Yes. I thought you'd like to know I've had

another peculiar flower delivery. It was Newby Bridge this time.' And she told him the story, including the vague description of a man in a long dark coat who paid for the flowers in cash. 'And a couple of other things happened as well. I was in Coniston again this morning and a woman flagged me down and confessed to being the sender of one lot of flowers. The farm one. Then Mrs Crabtree came into the shop just now—'

'Wait, wait,' he begged. 'I can't keep up with all this. Did you say "confessed"?'

'Yes. Maybe "admitted" would be more accurate. No – she wanted to confess to me, of her own free will. Admitting implies I was already questioning her, doesn't it?' She paused to examine the definitions of the two words. 'She told me she was an idiot not to have signed the card. She'd done something to upset Maggie Aston and thought it would be obvious who the flowers were from.'

'Did she send the others as well? Who *is* she?'

'Oh, no, I'm sure she didn't. That wouldn't make any sense. She's a cleaner – works for people with second homes. She knew about the murder, or at least that something horrible had happened.'

'Name?'

'I don't know.'

'All right. And on top of that, one of the people you delivered flowers to has been to talk to you?'

'Right. Mrs Crabtree. She lives in Hawkshead.

146

She's not nearly so meek and mild as I first thought.'

'I've got a report here. She was interviewed this morning.'

'I suppose that's really my fault for overreacting. The flowers were completely unconnected to anything you're investigating. Her sister sent them. I must have wasted police time. Sorry about that.'

'Is that what she came to tell you?'

'Sort of. She rambled a bit about her family and her job, which I don't think was relevant at all. When she heard about the murder in Coniston, I think she must have assumed that you thought there was a connection with the flowers, so she came to make sure I knew there wasn't. It was rather sweet of her, I thought.'

'Hmm. And you believed her?'

'Of course I did. She's just a nice lady who wants to keep things right.'

He sighed very audibly. 'I worry about you, Persimmon Brown. I really do.' He said *Per*simmon, as almost everyone did, despite her trying to teach them otherwise. Her mother was almost the only person who got it right, with 'P'simmon', but then she was the one who established it in the first place. By definition, whatever she said must be correct.

'I worry about myself,' she agreed. 'All I ever wanted was to be the bringer of happiness with beautiful blossoms and instead I get drawn into one horrible crime after another.' She took a breath.

'What about your friend Tim? It sounds as if you're still on the case.'

'I don't anticipate any change. I've explained my position to the chief superintendent, and he doesn't seem too bothered.' He spoke carelessly, like an ordinary person having an idle conversation.

'If it was me, I think I'd be quite glad to be set aside. You can go and investigate illegal fishing on Esthwaite or something instead.'

'It's not you though, is it. Tim Braithwaite deserves a thorough investigation, and even if I say it myself, I am undoubtedly the best person to do it. Everybody understands that.'

Simmy didn't know what to say; he sounded so confiding, she could not simply dismiss him with claims of busyness. 'Did the girl – Daisy, is it? – know him well? Is she going to be doubly upset, losing him as well as her father?'

'That's a good question. She was in and out of the house a lot, seeing her dad. And Tim's son Jasper knew her too. He was quite keen on her at one time. I think they even got engaged for a short time. She's a very pretty girl. I think most of the lads in the area fancied her, at one time or another. She's too good for the chap she's marrying, according to most people who know them. Tim was never entirely sure what to make of her, but I think he would have been happy for Jasper to settle down with her. I can't really guess what she'll be feeling now.'

'Is the wedding going ahead, after all this?'

'I've no idea. I assume it must be. A wedding isn't an easy thing to cancel these days, is it?'

Had it ever been, Simmy wondered, thinking idiotically of Lorna Doone getting shot on the threshold of the church. Only such extreme measures could avert the cumbersome juggernaut that was a wedding, in most periods of history. She went back to what she supposed was the main topic on Moxon's mind. 'Do you think Mr Hayter somehow killed Mr Braithwaite and then himself? Could it have been a fight over a woman?'

Moxon moaned gently. 'Nothing so simple. Hayter died at least twenty-four hours earlier than Tim, according to the pathologist's initial observations.'

Simmy could hear the voice of Ben Harkness plucking wild theories out of the air and voiced one or two of what she imagined they might be. 'But perhaps he left something poisonous for him to drink or injured him somehow so it took a day for him to die? I suppose that's all a bit fanciful.'

'It is,' he agreed, with a hint of sharpness. 'It's my friend we're talking about, remember.'

*And if you're going to be so sensitive about it, you're best taken off the case,* she thought, but did not say aloud. 'Sorry,' she muttered, feeling misunderstood. 'I'll go now. I just thought you should know about what happened this morning.

Maybe I needn't have gone to the trouble. I don't suppose it's the least bit important.'

'I've written it all down,' he said. 'Obviously *something's* going on, with all these malicious flowers flying about.'

'Literally, in the case of Maggie Aston.'

'The woman at the farm,' he said, with a slight question in his voice.

'Right.' She paused. 'But now we have innocent explanations for those *and* Mrs Crabtree's. That's good, isn't it?'

'I never really thought they were all from some sort of master criminal,' he said drily.

'Didn't you? Ben did. I should warn you, I'm going to tell Ben and Melanie about this new thing. Ben really does come up with some clever ideas, after all.'

He tutted softly. 'That boy is so off the scale when it comes to unauthorised interference, I hardly know what to do with him.'

'You'd be mad to exclude him. Look at how helpful he was last time. He's got all the right instincts – he's more or less an apprentice detective already. He's totally serious, you know. The fact that he's been accepted unprovisionally on one of the only courses in forensic archaeology shows that other people think he's good at it. He's probably going to revolutionise the whole police forensics system in a few years' time.'

'Well, don't let him anywhere near any actual people, okay? I can't stop him hypothesising, but I don't want to see hide or hair of him until this is all sorted out.'

'He understands that.'

'I'm pleased to hear it.'

'And I might remind you that Melanie has her uses, as well.'

'Melanie Todd is a different matter entirely. Last I heard she was still going out with Joe Wheeler, who seems incapable of keeping his mouth shut.'

Simmy remembered the text message about a second death and found herself agreeing with Moxon. The ginger-haired police constable's appeal for Melanie remained incomprehensible. Ben's brother Wilf would be a far better prospect; most of Melanie's friends assumed it was sheer perversity that motivated her in sticking with Joe.

She made a wordless sound, to avoid committing herself to an opinion.

'Somebody ought to come and see you in person,' he added worriedly. 'We'll need a description of this cleaner person, for a start. And more about the Newby Bridge thing. I can probably manage it just before you close.'

'I could come to you,' she offered, without enthusiasm. 'After I've shut up shop.'

'That would be helpful.'

Simmy gnashed her teeth a little as she realised

she would be late home and therefore neglecting Kathy. She ought to make an effort to provide a meal, or take her out to a characterful local hostelry. 'All right,' she said. 'About quarter to six, then.'

The shop bell rang before he could say more and she put the phone down. Two people were standing there – a man and a woman. She knew the man and gave him a wide smile. The woman, she supposed, was just a customer.

'Caught you at last!' said Ninian Tripp. 'It's been *weeks* since I saw you.'

But the other person rushed forward and drowned him out. 'Simmy! Remember me? Joanna Colhoun. Kathy's daughter. You've got to help me – I think my mum's got herself into some serious trouble.'

# CHAPTER NINE

'Whoa! Slow down,' Simmy ordered, as Joanna started some tangled tale of missed communications and sudden surprises. 'Where's Kathy now?'

'That's just it. I have no idea. She called me this morning before nine, and we agreed to meet in Coniston for an early lunch. I had no idea she was up here, checking up after me. I wasn't very nice to her. I'm terribly *busy*, you see. There's such a lot to *do*, and not nearly enough time for it all. But I said I'd try to be down in the village to meet her a bit before mid-day, and then Baz said I had to stay where I was, and get all the data onto the laptop. Mum said she'd explore for a while so I left her to her own devices. I mean – she should have *said* she was coming.'

'She was worried about you. You'd gone quiet, after saying you were having some problems. Just what is it you're doing up there, anyway?'

'I can't explain it now. Baz has a theory about climate data, basically, and we're trying to test it out. But there's more to it than that. Those old copper mines are really awesome, you know. We've been trying to find time to explore them as well.'

Simmy did a double take at this apparent non sequitur, and chose to stick to the main issue. 'So what's the problem with Kathy? She can't have been gone for long. It's not two yet.'

'Long enough,' said Joanna ominously. 'In fact, it's *hours*, now. She sent a text at half past eleven, that said, "Car misbehaving. Am awaiting RAC." And then when I tried to call her back, the phone was dead. Not even voicemail. I mean – she needs the phone for the RAC man to tell her when he's coming. They call you back constantly, to make sure you're happy.'

'The car seemed fine yesterday.' Simmy visualised the rather impressive blue Subaru, with 2011 plates. 'It's almost new, isn't it?'

'She bought it new. Cost a fortune. It's probably something electrical,' said Joanna vaguely. 'There's so much to go wrong, isn't there.'

Simmy chewed her lip thoughtfully. 'It does sound strange,' she agreed. 'Knowing Kathy, she's probably got some fabulous up-to-the-minute phone, that she keeps on all the time.'

'Right. They never just *die*. It must be broken, like the car. I thought maybe she'd come back here to have lunch with you and you'd gone on the lake or somewhere and she'd dropped the phone. Something like that. She told me about you and the shop and the drama of last night.' She rubbed her forehead, as if in pain. 'I'm really scared, to be honest. If there's a murderer out there, I'm right to worry, aren't I? Especially given what's been happening to me and Baz and the others. Somebody's really trying to stop what we're doing. They seem to think we're about to uncover some deep dark secret.'

'And are you?'

'If we are, it's nothing for anybody to worry about now.'

Ninian was standing aside, listening lazily to what was being said. Simmy turned to him for a contribution. 'What do you think?' she prompted.

'Me? I'm not here to *think*, am I? I think someone's gone missing for a couple of hours, and someone else is in a flap about it.' He smiled. 'Happens quite a lot around here. Always has. She'll have been taken by goblins, I shouldn't wonder.'

Simmy laughed, knowing she shouldn't. It was a reference to *The Princess and the Goblin*, by George MacDonald. In the week after Christmas, when she had been recovering from an injury, Ninian

155

had brought her books and stayed to talk, day after day. They had discovered a shared delight in that particular book from childhood. A friendship had been forged, or so Simmy had thought. But when her shop had reopened in the New Year and winter had settled firmly onto the fells and pikes of Cumbria, Ninian had fallen quiet, presumably in hibernation in his secluded little cottage above Bowness, and Simmy had scarcely seen him for weeks.

'What?' said Joanna. She suddenly looked dreadfully young – even younger than Ben, who was at least four years her junior. A transparent suspicion that she was being teased by Ninian made her sulky.

'Sorry,' said Simmy. 'That was mean of us. But really, I think Kathy can take care of herself. There's no reason at all to worry about her. She might have got the car fixed and be off exploring somewhere.'

'No, no.' Joanna clenched her fists. 'She wouldn't send that text and then just go silent. Nobody would do that. Would they?'

Simmy was forced to agree. 'Probably not. Okay, Jo. I can see you're really in a tizz about it. I can call the police, if you like. I've been . . . involved with them this week, anyway.'

The girl grimaced. 'Actually . . . I'm not sure . . . the thing is . . . Baz isn't going to want police people interfering with the project. There's been enough bother already, without that.' She shifted uneasily and her cheeks flushed pink. 'I can't really explain.'

'You're not trespassing, are you?' Simmy tried to remember the details of what Kathy had told her the day before. 'Wasn't there something about you being driven off by local landowners?'

'No, that wasn't it at all. It's common land. We're not disturbing anything. We did intend to pitch a tent on the site, but ended up in a guest house.'

'In Bowness, right? Isn't that a terribly long way from Coniston? Couldn't you find anywhere closer?'

'We're not in Bowness now. That was just the first night, while we got organised.' Again she seemed uncomfortable.

'Something else is going on,' Simmy realised. 'Something about you and this Baz person.' The obvious explanation hit her between the eyes. 'You've fallen for him. Is that it?' She remembered Kathy saying something of the sort.

Joanna smiled hesitantly and confirmed everything Simmy had been thinking. 'You could say that. We've been in the same digs for a few days, and last night – well, you know. It's not a problem. But the thing is, it's totally against the college rules. We don't want my mum to know too much about it just yet. I mean, she knows

I'm keen on him, because I talked about him all through the Christmas vac, but she'd never dream he'd . . . reciprocate. I know it's not very sensible. But Baz is so . . .' she sighed and cast her eyes upwards. 'Charismatic,' she finished.

'Listen, Jo,' Simmy said, trying to sound parental. 'I don't think your love life is the important thing just now. If we can't tell the police about Kathy, there isn't much else we can do, is there?'

'Phone the RAC and ask them if they've had a call out to a misbehaving car in Coniston,' suggested Ninian. 'Tell them the registration number.'

'Do you know it?' Simmy asked Joanna.

The girl shook her head. 'Do you?'

'Only the eleven part. But if we say her name and the make of car, that ought to be enough.'

'They'll be busy, this time of year,' said Ninian, clearly making an effort to compensate for his flippancy.

'I don't know the number for the RAC,' said Jo helplessly.

Simmy wished passionately that Melanie or Ben were there to take charge. Ben in particular seemed to have magical ways of discovering contact details for every known organisation. Why Joanna Colhoun was not equally competent was a question to tackle later. 'We can google it, presumably,' she said.

They crowded around Simmy's computer,

and found a number. Simmy called it, and after explaining the story in detail, was told there was nothing they could do to help, because all client information was confidential. They could only speak to somebody on the mobile number originally provided.

'But that phone's dead,' Simmy said. 'Whatever happens, it'll be a different number.'

'We would ask for security details and membership number, then.'

'Her mother's maiden name is Clements,' said Joanna, catching some of the conversation, speaking more in despair than in any hope that this would be regarded as relevant.

A customer arrived in the middle of the phone call, wanting a 'sheaf' of lilies and tulips. 'Not a bouquet. A *sheaf*,' the woman insisted. Simmy was forced to hand the phone to Joanna and go into the back room to collect the required blooms. She fashioned a perfect fan-shaped sheaf, with wires to hold it in place, and generous greenery to hide them. It took fifteen minutes, during which she rolled her eyes at Joanna and Ninian and left them to their own devices.

When the woman finally left, the phone was back in its place and Joanna was looking very tense. 'So?' Simmy asked.

'Nothing of any use. All they would say was that someone will have responded by now and either got the car going or taken Mum and it to a garage. But they wouldn't actually confirm that there was any such call-out in the first place.'

'I suppose that's the most you can hope for, when you think about it. I mean – they have sort of implied it was genuine, haven't they? What more can they say?'

'A lot! They could tell me *which* garage, for a start.'

'Just be patient,' said Simmy. 'Kathy's going to walk in here any minute, you'll see. She'll have dropped the phone and broken it, so she'll come here and use mine. Except she won't need to, because you're here already.'

'But I can't stay. Baz needs me to finish the data inputting and check the equipment again at three. I'm never going to make it. He's going to be mad at me when he knows I've been here.'

'Have you got a car?'

'One of the team brought me, because we did need some shopping. He's waiting for me down the street. We'll go on the ferry. Look, this is my mobile number. Call me, will you, the minute you hear anything? I'll keep trying Mum and watch out for her. She might come looking for me at Coniston, I suppose.' She looked close to tears helplessly needing to be in several places at once. The confusing mixture of childishness and real competence left Simmy unsure how to behave. 'But

160

will you be all right?' she asked.

'*I* will, of course. It's not me that's gone missing, is it?'

Ninian had gone quiet again, passively watching and listening. Simmy wished she had his knack of staying out of the action. Instead, she seemed to take centre stage for every local drama, however hard she tried not to.

She changed the subject. 'When do you have to be back at college?'

'Monday. That's why there's such a rush. We need everything finished by Sunday night.' She looked mournful. 'And Baz has to get back to work. He says if we can publish our findings quickly, it'll make his reputation and nothing else is going to matter.'

'You've been here a week? Is that right?'

'Nine days. But the experiment's been going for a year. A lot of other students are involved as well. Look – I can't stop to explain it now. I'm horribly late as it is.'

And she dashed out of the shop, leaving her phone number on a scrap of paper. Ninian and Simmy looked at each other. 'Makes you feel old, doesn't it?' he said wistfully.

'We *are* old. We could be her parents. My friend *is* her parent.'

'She seems a clever girl. Interesting hair.'

Ninian's artistic eye had unerringly registered Joanna's most distinctive feature – her hair was long and kinky, the colour of treacle toffee. It rippled down her back and framed her face in a very pre-Raphaelite sort of way. Simmy had thought it looked rather unsuitable for a scientist working on a cold fellside. 'Yes,' she said.

'Are you okay?' he asked her, with a probing look. 'You seem frazzled.'

'Valentine's,' she said. 'And a murder in Coniston. And a lot of malicious flower sending. And now Kathy going missing. Frazzled doesn't really cover it.'

'You ought to hole up in a faraway cottage like me.'

'I thought that's exactly what I *had* done. Troutbeck isn't on the way to anywhere, after all. The snag is that I have to earn a living, and that involves interacting with people and walking the mean streets of Windermere.'

He laughed. 'You're wonderful with words, Sim. Did you know that?'

She huffed weakly, shaking her head. 'I don't think so.'

'Have you had any lunch?'

'Um . . . no, I don't think so. It all seemed to run away with me. It's teatime, nearly. I'll go and put the kettle on. I think we've got some buns out there, if Melanie hasn't taken them.'

'Tea and a bun sounds wonderful. I'll guard the shop while you boil the kettle.'

'Ben's liable to show up any minute. He slopes off early from school on Fridays, and if he's heard any of the latest news, he'll be keen to catch up.'

'Oh, *Ben*,' said Ninian, as if the boy were a constant irritant to him.

'He's a genius, you know. Whatever he does, he turns out to be brilliant at it. Look at that model in the window.'

'The model is extraordinary,' Ninian conceded. 'But it's showing a bit of wear and tear. I see another bit's fallen off since I last looked. And your young friend is also a talented actor, which I admit surprised me. Geeks like him aren't usually able to step outside themselves well enough to play a part with any conviction. They're not supposed to understand how other people function.'

'He's not that sort of geek. And I'm not sure that's true anyway. There was a boy at our school who came top in every subject, with the same effortlessness as Ben, and he was always the star of the school play as well. He's a barrister now, defending the indefensible, last I heard. Pushing through outrageous developments and that sort of thing.'

'Yuck. So we should watch out for Ben joining the dark side, then?'

Simmy just laughed and went out to the back room, where a small corner had been allocated to kettle, mugs and a tin for buns and biscuits.

As predicted, Ben Harkness burst into the shop at five to three, his school bag over his shoulder as always, and the universal dusty look of a schoolboy on a Friday afternoon.

'You smell of the chalkface,' said Ninian.

'They don't use chalk these days. Besides, how can you smell me amongst all these flowers?'

'Sensitive nose.'

'Where's Simmy?'

'I'm here.' She came through with a tray containing three mugs of tea and a heap of little cupcakes that she had bought three days earlier and then forgotten.

Ben eyed her accusingly. 'You were in Coniston last night, identifying a murder victim,' he said. 'And you never told me.'

'Doesn't sound as if I needed to. Who's your mole this time?'

'Same as before. Wilf's friend Scott. He's still working at the mortuary. This is the first murder since . . . you know. They're all talking about you, according to Scott, and how Moxo's got such a soft spot for you. Apparently he can't believe his luck that this one involves you as well.'

'And *apparently*, you've got no idea what you're talking about,' snarled Ninian furiously. 'Think, man, before you say stuff like that.'

Ben flushed but continued undaunted. 'Anyway,

I googled this Braithwaite bloke, as soon as I heard, and he's really something. Top scientist at some place in Carlisle, seconded to the Met Office in Exeter for a couple of years, with a team of physicists. The thing is – he's produced a set of very embarrassing figures, to show that carbon dioxide isn't actually a greenhouse gas at all. It's all there online. He posted his findings without authorisation, and there's been a lot of ruffled feathers. So no wonder he got himself knocked off. Right? Must be thousands of people wanting to shut him up.'

'Would that change anything, if his findings have already been published?' asked Ninian.

'Maybe not – but think how enraged they must be, if there's a chance he's right. Funny I'd not come across him before now, though.'

'Could be he really is a crackpot, and nobody's taken him seriously. I mean – how can anybody seriously argue that $CO_2$ isn't a greenhouse gas?'

Ben paused, visibly struggling to retain an open mind. 'I don't know. He could be totally wrong,' he conceded. 'But I doubt it. There's others saying much the same thing.'

'Which rather undermines your theory about his death, wouldn't you say? Or do you think there's going to be a campaign of slaughter aimed at everyone who questions the carbon hypothesis?'

'I think the whole thing is a disgusting corrupt

mess,' Ben said, with juvenile passion. 'And I just bet it's what lies behind this particular killing. You wait and see. Don't you think so, Simmy?'

They both looked at the florist, who was standing transfixed, staring at the door and the person who had just walked in.

# CHAPTER TEN

Kathy Colhoun was feeling very cross indeed as she stomped uphill somewhere above Coniston. She had parked her car near a small bridge and walked blindly towards the peak that filled the sky ahead of her. It had all gone wrong with Joanna, even worse than she'd feared. The girl had been furious with her for showing up unannounced and demanding to know what was going on. She had snapped at her mother down the phone and finished up by shouting at her that she was much too busy to talk to her, and she'd have to amuse herself at least until lunchtime. Wounded, Kathy had calmly replied that she would take herself on a fell walk for the morning.

She had driven to Coniston and found a place to park on a quiet little road. Then she walked uphill for twenty or thirty minutes, pausing to look back at the rapidly expanding vista below her.

Coniston Water sparkled to the east, the wooded slopes beyond interspersed with fields. Her mood mellowed and she began to plan her route more carefully, aiming for a ridge beckoning from much higher up the shoulder of the Old Man. The track was clear – indeed so well laid was it that a vehicle had evidently managed to use it. To her right, in a hollow, stood a blue Transit van, irritatingly out of place.

And then, some twenty or thirty yards away, a man emerged out of a hole in the ground, like Alice's white rabbit in reverse. Kathy's squeal of surprise alerted him and before she knew it he had grabbed her arm in a painful grip and demanded to know who she was and what she was doing, in a voice shaking with some sort of desperation.

'I'm walking on the fells,' she said. 'Like a hundred other people.'

'Not today, they're not. There's only you. Look around and see for yourself.'

'Anybody could come over that ridge at any moment. If you want to keep something secret out here, you're an idiot. What's down that hole, anyway?' Already she had suspicions as to who he must be, and her simmering rage returned with new force. 'I bet I know who you are,' she said recklessly. 'You must be Baz. I've heard a great deal about you. In fact, I've been looking for you.'

'Who the hell are you, then?' His voice was a snarl. He glanced repeatedly at the hole from which he had emerged, as if expecting something else to pop out of it.

Kathy was stridently piling up her accusations. 'It's obvious you're up to no good. What have you got hidden down there? What's this "trouble" I've been hearing about? What have you been doing with my daughter?'

'Daughter?' He stared at her.

'Joanna. Listen – I'm taking her back with me today. She's been here too long already on this stupid experiment or whatever it is. I shouldn't wonder if it was all some elaborate scheme to get her up here so you could . . .' Words failed her. You couldn't say *Have your wicked way with her* these days.

The man was struggling to keep up. 'Jo? You're *Jo's* mother?'

'Too right I am.'

'You can't take her back. We haven't finished.'

'Finished what?' She fixed him with a stare worthy of any basilisk as she challenged him to explain.

He flushed. 'The experiment. We have to get it all done by the end of tomorrow.'

'So where are they, your precious team? Still half undressed and eating bacon and eggs? Not much sign of urgent work there. Or did you mean "finished" in another sense?'

169

'Shut up. You don't know anything about it. Jo and I . . . we . . .'

'Oh, please. Don't give me that. Valentine's must have gone to your head. You must be seven or eight years older than her. It's exploitation from a position of power. You're her *tutor*, you bastard. What do you think the college is going to say when I tell them?'

'Shut up,' he repeated, turning pale. 'You can't tell them. I'll lose my job.'

'You should have thought of that sooner.'

Again his eyes flickered towards the entrance to the tunnel or shaft or whatever it was, and an idea was visibly born. 'I just need two more days, and then you can do what you like. Once we've got all the data properly recorded, it isn't going to matter so much. Jo's an adult. She can speak for herself. But if you rock the boat now . . . I can't allow you to do it. I absolutely can't. I've been five years setting all this up. I'm not throwing it away now.'

Kathy felt no fear, but a niggling sense of sympathy for his distress was trying to push itself forward. She quelled it firmly. 'If you'd only had the sense just to smile and say "Hello" when I first saw you, I'd have thought nothing of it. Probably forgotten the whole thing in five minutes. But now it's all much too late. You can't hope to stop me. And I've got no choice but to remove Jo from your clutches. She's not safe out here.'

Kathy had never feared men, since none of them was capable of the noisy tyranny she had known from her father. After him, all others were wimps. Just the same, there was an uncomfortable impasse going on with this one. If it came to a struggle, he might prove the stronger. His desperation made him unpredictable. And he was right – there really was nobody else out here on this chilly February day.

'People are expecting me,' she bluffed. 'They know where I am, so if I don't show up soon, they'll come looking for me.'

'What people?'

It felt much too risky to admit to the arrangement to meet Joanna, so she invented a variation on the truth. 'Friends. I've got a lunch date with three friends in Coniston. I should be there in about half an hour.'

'You won't make it. I don't believe you.'

'Yes I will. My car's just down at that bridge – whatever it's called. It's less than a mile away. In fact I'm going back now. Don't even think of stopping me.'

It was worth a try, but it had the exact wrong effect. He was still holding her arm, and now his grip tightened. 'I *will* stop you,' he grated. 'I don't have any choice.'

He looked once again at the hole he'd emerged from, clearly considering the possibility of pushing her down it. But the plan evidently had some defects and he shook his head.

Then it came to him. 'Phone them! Tell them you've had car trouble or something. You won't make the lunch date. Then I'm going to lock you in the van while I get on with my work.'

This struck Kathy as a very convenient suggestion. 'All right,' she said, bringing the phone out of her pocket.

'No. Wait. They'll ask a lot of questions, and you might say something before I can stop you. Send a text. Don't say where you are. Show it to me first.'

She thought quickly, trying to remember exactly how much information a phone showed on its screen when a text was being sent. Quite a lot, she feared. But if she thumbed it in quickly, he wouldn't be able to stop her. So she composed a message that she hoped would arouse at least some concern in the recipient. 'Car misbehaving. Am awaiting RAC.'

'Will that do?' she asked him, pushing it into his face. 'That'll stop them looking for me, won't it?'

He nodded. 'Send it, then.'

With rapid movements, she sent it to Joanna, hoping feverishly that he wouldn't be able to read the tiny words and numbers.

As it turned out, he didn't bother to look, but instead simply snatched the expensive gadget and threw it on the ground. Then he stamped on it repeatedly. It was like watching someone savaging a puppy. Kathy whimpered. 'You didn't have to do that.'

'I did, actually. Never trust a woman with a mobile. Now you'll have to come with me.'

'Where to?' She knew the question was fatuous, the answer unlikely to be helpful, and yet she asked it automatically. It was something to do with trying to maintain a degree of normality, hoping that this impossible situation would transform itself into an ordinary exchange between two civilised people.

He gave no answer at all, but pulled her by the arm down the slope of the hillside. She tried to look at him, to assess his mental state. If she kicked him hard, or gave him a violent push, he might well let go. Then she could do her best to outrun him. It was certainly worth a try. But he seemed to read her mind, because that was when he drew the knife from a sheath on his belt.

'What are you doing with that? Don't you know it's illegal to carry a lethal weapon like that?' she demanded, still not quite afraid. This was another fatuous question, but she had locked onto a hope that he was sufficiently rational to realise that he had just overstepped a very significant line. It was a plain, pointed knife, seven or eight inches long, with a black handle. She had one very like it in her kitchen, which cut through raw meat like butter. Her hopes receded. No ordinary person would fashion a sheath for it and take it outside with them. Her daughter had obviously fallen in love with an unstable lunatic. 'If anybody sees it, they'll report you to the police,' she added defiantly and uselessly.

'What do you think I'm going to do with it?' he said, and slashed the air.

That was when she felt frightened.

# CHAPTER ELEVEN

It was a very tall, slender, handsome black man. Simmy knew immediately who he must be, but not why he should appear so emotional. His eyes bulged, and he held one arm in front of him, the fist tightly curled.

It was the boyfriend from Newby Bridge. Rapidly, Simmy reviewed the events of the morning. She had not delivered the flowers intended for his address. They were still in the back of her van. Miss Drury, his girlfriend, was working somewhere in Coniston, and believed herself to be the victim of a nasty prank designed to sour things between herself and this man. A fourth nasty prank that week, in fact.

'Aye aye,' muttered Ninian. 'Looks like trouble.'

'Sshh,' said Ben, shrinking towards the back of the shop, eyes wide.

'Can I help you?' Simmy asked, trying not to sound nervous.

'My name is Solomon Samalar. I saw your van,' the man said, in an accent more suggestive of Eton than Mogadishu. 'You came to my house with flowers this morning.'

'I did. But there was no reply when I rang the bell.'

He ignored this, and took a step forward. 'They were for Selena, is that right?'

'Miss Drury,' she nodded, abandoning any attempt to protect the wretched girl. Looked at in a certain way, she had already been remiss in taking money for the order and then failing to deliver the flowers. Any further misbehaviour in the form of fibbing or concealing was definitely not a good idea.

'So where are they now? The flowers?'

'In my van. I spoke to Miss Drury and she said she didn't want them. I was left in an awkward position,' she added defensively. Only then did she remember that she had told the police about the order. This man might find that an even more infuriating act on her part.

'I will take them,' he said, lowering his fist, but standing very tall.

'Not addressed to you, mate,' said Ninian, who was successfully presenting a thoroughly unthreatening demeanour. Simmy almost allowed herself to describe him as *cringing*. But his words were brave, she supposed. Ben had practically disappeared from view behind some ornamental grasses.

'Addressed to *my* house, sir. And not delivered as promised. Am I not right?' he asked Simmy.

'Technically, yes,' she agreed. 'But you see – it's really not that simple. I'm very much afraid that there's something rather unpleasant going on, with people sending flowers in order to create trouble and upset. It looks as if yours are one of these malicious orders. The police—'

'Police?' He spoke in a whisper that carried disbelief and rage in equal measure. 'The *police*?'

'Well, yes. There was a murder, you see, in Coniston, which might somehow be connected to these flowers for people . . . I mean, it's all a real muddle, but—'

'Trouble and upset,' he repeated, more calmly. 'Is that what you said?'

'Yes. It's really quite horrible, using flowers in such a way, when they're meant to bring happiness. I'm quite upset about it myself. I hate delivering worry and confusion to people. I never know when the next one will be, you see. They all appear so innocent – new job, new house, apology and so forth. But they all carry an underlying message that frightens people. And yours . . . Miss Drury's, I mean . . . turned out to be another of them. They came from someone she doesn't know, apparently.

Designed to make you think she has another boyfriend, or something like that. You really need to understand that it's all a way of getting at her for some reason.'

His features relaxed somewhat as he tried to take it all in. 'Another boyfriend? You're telling me that some stranger is trying to make me jealous? To disrupt the relationship I have with Selena? Someone who knows her, evidently? And wishes her ill. Did you see this person?'

'Yes,' Simmy admitted. 'But all I remember is a man in a long dark coat. My assistant dealt with him, but she's not here just now.'

'And did this mysterious man order flowers for the other people who have been troubled and upset?'

'We're not sure. It doesn't seem very likely. Two more came in different ways – one was in the post and the other was sort of *thrown* in here. That was the one for Maggie Aston, I think.'

'Did they give their details? Names? Addresses? How did they pay?'

He was as importunate as DI Moxon, and Simmy was loath to cooperate any further. 'It's all under investigation,' she said.

'By the police?' There was none of the alarm or annoyance that she was expecting. Instead, Mr Samalar smiled. 'So others have been as enraged by this malice as I was myself.'

'Not exactly.' She bit her lip.

'Don't say any more, Sim,' Ben advised. 'The inspector wouldn't want you to.'

'And who might you be?' the man asked the youngster. Then he looked at Ninian. 'And you? I took you for a customer, but perhaps I have it wrong?'

'They're both friends of mine,' Simmy explained.

'And the boy is a detective? A police apprentice of some sort?'

Simmy laughed. 'That's not too far from the truth of it. He does have plans for a career in crime detection, or whatever it's called these days.'

Her laughter, albeit slightly choked and brief, did a lot to relieve the strain. The tall man smiled faintly. 'I'm grateful to you for the explanation,' he said, bowing his head with an old-fashioned dignity. 'You must forgive me for being angry.'

Ben found courage to take two steps forward. 'But *why* were you? What got you so worked up? You saw Simmy's van at your place – so what? And why'd you take so long to get here? Her address and phone number are on the side of the van.'

The man tilted his head and looked down at his questioner. 'I only saw the name, Persimmon Petals, from the window of my upstairs study. I was on the telephone and did not hear the doorbell ring. I saw this lady carry flowers from my front gate to her vehicle and put them in the back. I could not understand it, so I telephoned Selena to ask whether

179

she had made an order for some reason and whether I should try to recover the blooms. Her reaction was very out of character. She stammered and prevaricated, which I found confusing and a little suspicious. She told me to think no more about it, because it was obviously a mistake, and you had come to the wrong house. So I had some lunch and thought it over, and found myself unable to credit what Selena had told me. Hence my presence here now.'

Nobody spoke after this speech, but all looked at each other with little nods and raised eyebrows. The pinging doorbell came as a relief, and the presence of a small elderly man with a hesitant manner sent Simmy into full professional mode.

'Can I help you?' she trilled.

'Yes, I hope so. It has just come to my notice that today is St Valentine's Day, and I was wondering whether you might have a bouquet of red roses that I could buy? I have a lady friend who would be delighted to receive something of that sort. I realise I've left it rather late.' He smiled self-mockingly, his cheeks pink with embarrassment.

'Of course,' Simmy assured him. 'How many would you like?'

'How many would you recommend?'

'Well, most people have ten, or sometimes a dozen.'

'A dozen,' he said decisively.

With a light tread, Simmy went out to the back room and collected the blooms. There was something solid and sensible in amongst the romantic frivolity generally associated with red roses. It was business. Compared to a murky murder enquiry, where everything was half understood and constantly changing, this simple transaction was a gust of fresh air. She wrapped and presented the flowers with a smile. 'I hope she likes them,' she said.

'Oh, she will. Thank you very much.' And the satisfied customer took his leave.

As did the Somali, apparently realising he had nothing left to say. Simmy watched him turn left along the street, walking with long strides, his head held high. He was about forty, she guessed, and expensively dressed. His house had been substantial. Was he in Britain legally? Was he conducting some shady international dealings involving refugees and human trafficking? *Stop it*, she told herself, aware that yet again she was taking on Ben's sort of thinking.

Ben himself was almost hopping with excitement. 'Wow! Exotic or what!' he crowed. 'What a brilliant bloke! I thought he was going to hit you.'

Ninian coughed. 'He would never have dared,' he protested.

'Not *you*. Simmy.'

'You can understand his suspicion,' said Simmy.

'The girlfriend was worried he'd react like that – and he did.'

'You'll need to tell me the whole story,' said Ben. He settled onto the chair beside the till and extracted a large notepad and pen from his bag. 'I'm going to make a diagram of everything that's happened this week, and see if we can find a pattern to it.'

Simmy and Ninian sighed in unison. The potter reached behind his head and tightened the band that held his hair in its ponytail. Then he squared his shoulders. 'Not me,' he said. 'I need to get home before dark, or I'll get waylaid by highwaymen.'

'Or stolen by goblins,' said Simmy. The joke fell disappointingly flat. At some point the atmosphere had changed and the thread connecting them had lost its shine.

'Bye, then,' said Ben carelessly.

'Melanie sold one of the vases,' Simmy remembered.

'Yes, she told me, and she gave me the cash out of a tin under your counter. Very efficient young lady, your Melanie.'

'Indeed she is.'

'I'll try and get down again tomorrow with a replacement pot, shall I? I've got a rather handsome dark-blue thing you might like.'

'Fine,' she said. 'The others have been admired. I expect we'll sell them all, once the tourist season gets going.'

His smile was uncertain, as if afraid she might say something else that he might not want to hear. And then he went, leaving Ben with pen poised, eyes eagerly expectant.

'So?' he prompted.

'Oh, Ben. Are you sure we ought to be doing this? Can't we just leave it all to the police? I'm going there after work, to explain what happened this morning. They'll be able to connect it all up just as well as we can.'

He shook his head. 'What *did* happen this morning?'

'The flowers for Miss Drury at Newby Bridge, for a start. You'll have got the gist of that already. Then I went to Coniston and a woman flagged me down – I *wish* people would stop doing that – and told me she sent the flowers to Mrs Aston at the farm. It was like a dramatic confession to some awful crime. She really seemed quite upset. And she knows about the murder, which isn't surprising. I gather it's been on the news. Oh, and Kathy's gone missing.'

Ben looked up from his pad. 'Pardon?'

'Yes. That's why the Coniston stuff all seems so long ago. A lot more's happened since then. Kathy's daughter, Joanna, came in at two o'clock and said her mum sent a text about her car breaking down, and she was waiting for the RAC man. Then her phone went dead and we don't know where she is.'

'Have you told Moxo?'

'No. Joanna says she wants to keep the police out of it. She's doing something dodgy up on the slopes of the Old Man, and her friend Baz would not take kindly to police attention. Something like that.'

'Something dodgy? Like what?'

'Measuring rainfall or temperature or something. Kathy gave me a garbled version of it yesterday. Something about going against mainstream thinking about the climate, because the statistics weren't properly obtained. Sounds a bit heavy for a bunch of undergraduates.'

He gave her a reproachful look, reminding her that he may be a mere sixth-former, but that nothing was too heavy for *him*. 'Well, that connects to the Braithwaite man, doesn't it? Like – *obviously*.' His patronising tone was probably deserved, Simmy decided. 'What if these students have got some data that supports – or contradicts . . .' he frowned for a moment, 'what he's been saying? Either way there's likely to be trouble. If they're worried about the police, that suggests there might already *be* some trouble.' He tapped his teeth with the pen. 'The thing is – how, if at all, does this connect to these nasty flower messages?'

'It doesn't, Ben. They've already been explained. Mrs Crabtree's got a daft sister – have I told you about that?'

Ben tapped his teeth with the pencil. 'I think not. The sister sent the flowers, did she?'

'So it would seem. And there's Mrs Aston's remorseful friend and Selena Drury's ex-boyfriend to explain the others. So the bottom line is that none of them's got anything to do with violent deaths.'

'Except Mr Hayter, who might have killed himself because of it.'

'Please don't say that,' she begged. 'Just when I was feeling better about it all.'

'I'm still not convinced by these explanations, all turning up in a rush. Has anything like this happened here before?'

'Anything like what, exactly?'

'People getting flowers with messages that didn't fit. That upset them.'

'Well – there *was* Mrs Joseph in Ambleside. And see where *that* landed us.' She shuddered and rubbed the freshly-healed injury that had kept her from driving for so long.

'This is a bit like that, I suppose,' he mused. 'But only a bit. Nobody was trying to scare old Mrs J.'

'Selena Drury wasn't scared. In fact, *none* of them were. They were bewildered or cross, mainly.'

'They might have got scared later, when they'd had time to think about it.'

'Possibly. But none of them matters now. The *really* urgent thing is Kathy.'

Ben waved this aside, and tilted his head,

thinking hard. 'What if there's a big group of people with some history between them, and there was an agreement that sending flowers with an inappropriate message was some sort of trigger to action? What if it signalled that the Braithwaite man should be killed for some reason? So one of them went and did it. It would be a brilliant way of communicating without leaving any trail. And what if the Hayter chap couldn't stomach it, so he topped himself to get out of the whole business?'

'Stop it, Ben. This is going too far.'

The boy ignored her. 'Or could be they got the wrong chap. Which means they didn't know each other personally. They're a loose group, say. Or maybe the man who was killed wasn't one of them, but presented some sort of threat. So they activated a prearranged plan, designed to eradicate anybody they didn't like. Maybe Hayter was meant to do the dirty deed, and chickened out, so one of the others stepped in.'

As so often before, Simmy was drawn in, in spite of herself. 'But I gave the flowers to the wrong man in the first place. Braithwaite instead of Hayter. Maybe by doing that I wrecked some delicate detail and *caused* the two deaths.'

'Yes! Braithwaite should never have known anything about the flower messaging, so he had to die.'

'Stop, stop!' she begged him. 'This is getting silly.

I don't like the implication that it might be all my fault, when it definitely isn't. Everybody's made it quite clear that the flowers were wrong in one way or another. They would never have done that if it had been some kind of signal. They'd just nod and thank me, and act according to whatever the message indicated.'

'That's probably true,' he agreed, with a flicker of admiration at her clever thinking.

'So, please stop all these flights of fancy. You were running away with yourself and I got caught up. I don't like it.'

'No, they're not flights of fancy. We're finding hypotheses that fit the facts. It's what you have to do. Then you check to see if the hypothesis holds.'

'And does my friend Kathy fit in here somewhere?'

'That would constitute a big coincidence, which is never comfortable. We don't like coincidences. The only link would be you.' He chewed the pen. 'And not in a good way. The only theory I can think of to fit that would be if Kathy was the killer, who already knew most of these people, without telling you about it, and chose you as her florist because she already knew you.'

Simmy's heart thumped. 'Watch it! That's not funny.'

'You have to consider every option,' he defended. 'It would make sense.'

'Of course it wouldn't. She wasn't even *here*

187

when that man was killed.' She took a moment to order her thoughts. 'I know Kathy might have been roaming around Bowness or Windermere or some other place during Thursday afternoon, but that was a long time after Mr Braithwaite must have been attacked.'

Ben nodded patiently. 'Do we know exactly when he *was* killed, anyway? I don't think Scott's said anything helpful about that.'

Simmy tried to remember what Moxon had told her. 'Wait a minute. All I can remember is that it was after Mr Hayter died. So I suppose that means between Tuesday and early Thursday.'

Ben frowned. 'Why not Thursday afternoon?'

'Well, he was . . .' she swallowed and tried again. 'He was *very* dead when I saw him. I just had the impression he'd been lying there for more than a few hours. Moxon was upset about it. He was a friend of his, you see He's godfather to Mr Braithwaite's son. He's called Jasper. I must say I didn't think he was being very professional about it, actually, although you can't really blame him.'

'I would think it might even endear him to you,' teased the boy. 'But you obviously picked up a whole load of information. Do you know what killed him, as well?'

'A knife. He was lying on his back, so I suppose it was done from in front – assuming they hadn't moved him. They might well have done, of course.

Moxon said he was stabbed between his ribs.'

'Well, people have ribs back and front,' Ben pointed out. 'Was there a lot of blood?'

'Hardly any, as far as I could see. Most of him was covered up. Can we stop the detailed questions now, please? It's not helping.'

'Sorry.'

'Let's just stick to the important part, which is that it can't possibly have been Kathy. She only got here yesterday. And even if he'd only been dead a few hours, she didn't have time to get to Coniston and back in the little time she was gone from here. It takes ages, whichever way you go. Besides, the idea is utterly ludicrous. She was with me when I got called to identify him. And why on earth would a housewife from Worcester murder anybody?'

'Who can say? I told you, you have to explore every option.'

'All you're doing is distracting me from worrying about her, as I ought to. Look – it's almost dark out there and there's no sign of her. What if she's fallen into a crevasse somewhere on the fells? She'll die of cold before we find her.' Suddenly, panic swelled in her chest, choking her. 'Gosh, Ben, how can we just carry on as if everything was all right?'

'Steady on! I only knew she was lost ten minutes ago. She's *your* friend. And if you won't tell the police, there's not much we can do, is there? I for one refuse to go crawling about on the Old Man in the freezing dark. My mother would kill me.'

'So would mine,' she flashed. 'Me, I mean, not you.'

He snorted, half laugh, half impatience. 'So?' he demanded.

'I don't know. Joanna's so young, I can't let her take it all on her shoulders. What if she takes it into her head to go and start searching for Kathy?' She gave herself a shake. 'Of course I have to tell the police. I'm going to shut the shop early and go there now.'

'Wait a minute. Let me just finish this. Look.' He drew four circles, radiating out from the centre of the page, which had a square containing the name 'Braithwaite'. 'Here's Mr Hayter. And here's the Hawkshead lady – what's her name?'

'Mrs Crabtree. She was in here today. I forgot to tell you.'

'I need to put how all the different orders were delivered. Can you remember?'

'Of course I can. Mr Hayter's was a hand-delivered letter, which I found on Monday morning. Mrs Crabtree's came in the post. Mrs Aston's was chucked in by a person you and Melanie thought was female, but aren't sure. That was on Wednesday. Miss Drury's was another hand-delivered one, quite a while ago now – I can't remember which day it was. A man dashed in and said he had to catch a train. Four different people, Ben. I'm certain about that.'

He wrote it all down, checking names and addresses with care.

'You can cross Mrs Crabtree off,' said Simmy.

'Never mind her, then – at least for now. Here's the farm woman. Aston, did you say? And lastly the people at Newby Bridge. All got unexpected flowers, with nasty messages.'

'No – Mr Hayter didn't. They were addressed to him, but his housemate took them, letting me think he was Mr Hayter. It just boils down to that one, Ben. The others don't matter.' Ben added notes to all the circles: *wrong man*, to the first; *came into the shop* to the second; *sender confessed* to the third, and *smart black boyfriend* to the last. 'I don't like to dismiss them all too lightly,' he worried. 'I can't believe there's no link between them somewhere.'

'But they're all so *different*. The stories are different. There are no proper connections between any of them.'

'Coniston seems to be one,' he argued, plainly unable to abandon the idea of a network between at least some of the people on his diagram. 'Except the Crabtree lady's in Hawkshead. Tell me what she said.'

'She worked for the MoD, which I suppose is the Ministry of Defence, retired ages ago, is a good driver. And she said Hawkshead isn't far from Coniston. She heard about the murder, because the police called on her this morning.'

'Blimey, Sim! Ministry of Defence!'

'She isn't involved with them at all now. Sticks to local matters. Probably book groups and stuff like that.'

'Probably anti-wind farm action groups,' said Ben darkly. 'Sounds the right sort of person for that.'

'Very likely. So what? Do you think all this business is political?'

'I think there's some kind of group in the picture somewhere, yes I do.'

'Why? Don't you believe the explanations I've given you for Aston and Crabtree?'

'I'm keeping an open mind,' he said pompously. 'It's perfectly possible that they told you lies, precisely so you'll stop thinking there's any connection between them and the murder.'

Simmy moaned. 'That's ridiculous,' she complained. 'You have to believe people.'

'I don't think so. It's obvious there's something going on, and we still have a massive list of unanswered questions. Why did they all choose you, for one?'

'Coincidence.'

'Possibly. But I still suspect there's a link between all of them. It's not family business, so what is it? These people aren't all cousins to each other. They didn't go to school together. They must be linked in some way, and that just leaves groups.'

Simmy forced herself to think. 'Men and

women, oldish and youngish, scattered around the area. One's a farmer's wife – except I still don't think we should count her, because somebody already confessed very convincingly to sending those flowers. How can we ever hope to find a connection?'

'That's a job for the police. But, you know something? I think you must be right – I don't think the same person sent the other flowers, anyway. But they might have known each other. It might all be part of a big picture.'

Simmy took her coat from the hook on the back of the door into the cool room. 'I'm going, Ben. I need to talk to DI Moxon about Kathy as well as all this other stuff. I'll tell him your ideas about a group of some sort.'

'Can't I come with you?'

'Oh! Well, I don't see why not, if you're not supposed to be somewhere.'

'The cop shop's on my way home, anyhow.'

'So it is.' Ben lived in Bowness, a ten-minute walk from Simmy's shop.

DI Moxon's expression registered a complicated mixture of resignation and reproach with a dash of gratification, when he saw Ben. 'I might have known,' he said. 'Have you brought me one of your famous dossiers again?'

'Work in progress,' said Ben, bringing his

notepad out of the bag on his shoulder. 'Mostly just names, ages and relevant observations.'

'I ought to send you straight home, you know. However you look at it, you're too young for this business. I'll have your parents after me.'

'Just pretend Simmy's my mum,' said Ben easily. 'She can be *in loco parentis* then.'

'I'm horribly afraid you're going to find him rather useful – again,' Simmy warned. 'He's full of theories.'

'I don't doubt it. I have no illusions about the effectiveness of a well-trained young mind. It's just . . .' he spread his hands to suggest defeat, '. . . he makes me feel sluggish and thick by comparison.'

Simmy avoided Ben's eye, and merely smiled sympathetically. 'Me too,' she muttered.

'Look on it as work experience,' Ben advised. 'If it makes you happier.'

Moxon arranged them all around a table holding a computer and a ring binder, and invited Simmy to describe in the fullest possible detail the events of the day. 'First,' she said, with a renewed rush of anxiety, 'I have to tell you that my friend, Kathy Colhoun, has gone missing this afternoon. I should have told you sooner, but her daughter . . . well, her daughter wanted to have a proper look for her first.' She winced inwardly at this untruth, annoyed at the need to maintain a sort of protective shield between the Colhouns and the police. 'But now I haven't heard anything for three hours, so I suppose she hasn't found her and something more official ought to be done. It does all seem quite worrying,' she finished, with true British understatement.

'Missing?' He repeated the operative word slowly, and eyed Simmy closely, trying to assess the seriousness of this new twist. 'Where was she last seen?'

Simmy remembered that the dead Mr Hayter had also been reported missing by a worried daughter, and her own anxiety level rose considerably. 'At my house, I suppose, at eight o'clock this morning. Then she phoned Joanna about half past nine, and Jo said she was too busy to meet her until lunchtime, or words to that effect. So Kathy went off on her own and then Jo got a text saying Kathy's car was misbehaving and she'd called the RAC. Then the phone went dead, and there's been no more news. We got through to the RAC but they wouldn't tell us anything.'

Moxon made a noise, part groan, part sigh. 'She's a grown woman, right? In good health, mentally and physically?'

'Absolutely.'

'How old is she? And the daughter?'

'She's forty-five. Joanna's twenty-two. She's still at college. A group of them are up here doing scientific stuff on the slopes of the Old Man of Coniston.

Kathy got a bit worried about them and came here to see what was happening. She's an old friend of mine from Worcester. She's staying with me.' A fresh spasm of worry gripped her insides. 'There must be something wrong, because she knows we're meant to be spending this evening together.'

'With you and not the daughter?'

Simmy paused, trying to remember what the plan had been. 'I think so, yes.'

'So you would definitely be told if and when she was found?'

Again, Simmy paused. 'Yes. Kathy's got my mobile number.'

'But her phone has gone dead. Does she know your number by heart?'

'Probably not.'

'So she might not be able to contact you?'

'She could find my landline numbers – at home or in the shop. She's perfectly competent.'

Ben sat impatiently tapping his fingers on the table through all this. He was plainly unconcerned about a grown woman who had got herself lost, unless it could be demonstrated that she was involved in the murder of Mr Braithwaite. Moxon seemed to have a similar attitude. 'Well, should we perhaps go through the other things first?' he said. 'A woman who approached you in Coniston, and another strange delivery of flowers in Newby Bridge?'

'And a visit to the shop by Mrs Crabtree,' Simmy added.

'Right, right. One thing at a time. Start with the woman in Coniston. What exactly did she say?'

'I can't remember *exactly*. A lot's happened since then. She said she hadn't meant to upset Mrs Aston with the flowers and she realised what a fool she'd been not to sign the card. She thought it would be obvious who they were from. It was a grovelling apology for something she did to Maggie.'

'You don't know what that was?'

Simmy shook her head. 'Something awful, she said.'

Moxon and Ben looked at each other, in a very man-to-man sort of way. 'How did she know Mrs Aston had rejected the flowers?' asked the detective.

'She'd spoken to her. Maggie told her she'd thrown the flowers across the yard. She said I must have felt bad about the waste. Which I did.'

'It's an odd story. What awful thing could one woman do to another, anyway? How old was this person?'

'Fifty or so, I would guess. And Maggie Aston is mid thirties. I have no idea what the connection is between them, but there must be a logical explanation. Perhaps they're both in the WI and the older one blocked Maggie's bid for the Chair.' Simmy felt rather pleased with herself at this inspired piece of invention. She was generally the one stuck for any creative thoughts.

'We'll have to find out who she is. Can you describe anything else about her?'

'Hang on. Why do you need to see her? Don't you think all these flowers are nothing but a red herring? Even Mrs Crabtree says now it's completely innocent. Her sister sent them, apparently.'

'Humour me,' he insisted. 'After all, we still have no idea who sent the flowers to Jack Hayter. This woman . . .' he prompted.

'Well, all right. She works as a cleaner – did I already say that? Not very tall, a bit plump, brown hair, dyed, I suppose. Local accent, but not very marked. Light-coloured eyes, rather deep-set. She had a blue coat on. She knew there'd been some sort of incident down at Mr Hayter's house. Said she'd heard it on the news. Didn't mention murder or even a death. Just "something nasty".'

'Should be easy enough to find her,' said Ben. 'Ask at the post office in Coniston and they'll know right away. There can't be many cleaners with blue coats.'

'Even easier than that – ask Maggie Aston,' said Simmy, with a touch of smugness.

Moxon nodded with a wry smile. 'Somebody will be with her now, actually. If she confirms this cleaning woman's story, that'll be enough to take her out of the case.'

'You can cross Mrs Crabtree off as well,' Simmy reminded him.

'Maybe. Now we need to have a talk with this third lady.' He consulted his notes. 'Miss Drury.'

'Selena. I forgot to mention that her partner came into the shop this afternoon. He was fairly annoyed, but we managed to calm him down.'

Again Moxon groaned, and ran his fingers through his hair in disbelief. 'You're joking!'

'Sorry. I suppose it has been quite an eventful day, one way and another.'

The detective turned to a new clean page in his notebook. 'At this rate, I'll have to get you to brief the whole team. I'm not going to be able to carry it all in my poor old head. But let's give it a go. Selena Drury, is that right?' He wrote the name at the top of the page. 'Address? Name of the partner? Any other observations?'

Simmy felt a rare burst of anger. 'Actually, I can't tell you anything else. I told you the address already. It's in Newby Bridge. His name is Solomon something. It began with an S. Look – I want to go and look for Kathy, not sit here doing your job for you.'

Ben shot Simmy a horrified look at her rudeness. 'He's black,' he said. 'Tall. Dignified. Speaks with a posh accent.'

Moxon nodded with transparent restraint. 'Thank you,' he said.

'Sorry,' Simmy muttered.

'Don't mention it. I can see you're under a strain. And I admit you are at least partly doing my job for me. I know it's not deliberate, but you do very effectively position yourself at the heart of these things.'

'It's the job,' Ben explained. 'We worked that out a while ago. All these high moments in people's lives, where they send each other flowers.'

'It's different this time,' said Simmy tightly. 'They're *using* me. It feels very personal and I don't like it.'

Moxon visibly had a thought. 'And you're worried that the disappearance of your friend is directed at you as well? Is that it?'

'No! My God – that never occurred to me. That would be insane, when I haven't done anything to anybody. Why would they do something like that?'

'A diversion,' said Ben, holding up a finger to indicate a significant point. 'Don't you think?' he asked the detective.

Moxon said nothing. He seemed to think he had already said too much.

'How did the Braithwaite man die?' Ben asked, to Simmy's surprise. Hadn't the boy believed what she'd already told him? 'Are you allowed to tell us that?'

'"Allowed",' he repeated, wonderingly. 'I'm a detective inspector. I don't normally think in terms of what I'm allowed to do.'

'But there's quite a few ranks above you,' Ben pointed out. 'The detective superintendent, for a start. This must be his case, officially, not yours. Isn't he the SIO? And more than that – if the victim was a friend of yours, doesn't that mean you've got a conflict of interest? Or at least that you're too closely involved to keep an objective mind?'

'We're a small team here, Ben. We all work together. Nobody pulls rank or tells the others what they're allowed to do. We muck in and share the load. So long as I make it clear what my relationship was with Tim and his family, nobody's going to stop me taking part in the investigations.'

'Great,' Ben approved, quite unfazed by the implied reprimand. 'So how was it done? The murder, I mean.'

'A sharp instrument into his back.' Moxon couldn't prevent a rictus of pain from crossing his face. 'Between the ribs and into his heart.'

'Did he die instantly? Takes some force, that, you know. A lot of tough muscle tissue to get through. Not to mention finding the right angle, and avoiding the ribs.'

'I dare say that's right.'

'For heaven's sake, Ben!' Simmy burst out. 'Don't you *ever* consider people's feelings? You're talking about the inspector's *friend*. He's godfather to the man's son.'

Ben sagged melodramatically. 'So?' He addressed the detective. 'You don't mind, do you?'

'I can bear it,' said Moxon.

'Right. Good. Does the son live locally?'

'Ambleside. He's training to be a vet.'

'Where's his mother?'

Moxon sighed. 'Last I heard, she was in Glasgow. They divorced ten years ago.'

'So the son lives with his dad?'

'No – he lives in Ambleside. He's twenty-three and his name's Jasper. I don't often see him these days, but I had to tell him about his father last night, which was extremely upsetting for me, because the two of them were always rather at odds. I've noticed, you see . . .' He looked at Simmy, as if hoping she would understand, 'that the grief and pain can be a lot worse when things weren't right between you and the person who's died. Something to do with unfinished business and not having a chance to get things straight.'

Ben waited a beat, before saying, 'But you're bearing up, right?'

Moxon smiled, seeming to be genuinely amused by the boy's briskness. 'I think so.'

'So, can I ask just a few more questions? For instance – you said "instrument". Did you mean "implement"?'

'Is there a difference? Does it matter?'

'I just like to be sure of the terminology. It can be

important, you know. I don't want to get it wrong. I am trying to *learn*, you see.'

'Please, *please*, shut up, Ben,' pleaded Simmy. 'Listen – I really *must* see what's happened to Kathy . . .'

'How?' asked Moxon gently. 'It's dark out there and you have no idea where to start.'

'I can phone Joanna, for one thing.'

'The best thing you can do is go home, and just wait for her to call you. I know that's much more difficult than it sounds, but it really is the best course to take. From what I can gather, she came here on a mission that she hasn't fully explained to you.'

'She would never just leave me to worry like this. And not just me, but her own daughter. Joanna was really scared. What if she's—'

'Don't start what-iffing,' he begged. Again he scanned the notes in front of him. 'I'm not sure we're really finished here, but you've given me some new factors to go on. I'm grateful to you – really. It's all a great muddle at the moment, for everybody. But we'll sort it all out, I promise you. We've alerted the recipients of the flowers to be careful about who they let into their houses.'

'Not Selena Drury, you haven't. I've only just told you about her.'

He shook his head in mild admonishment. 'You told us this afternoon, remember. Somebody will have spoken to her by now, I shouldn't wonder.'

'How, when she's working somewhere miles away on the fells?'

He frowned. 'Leave it to us, all right? Nobody else is going to get hurt. The chances are, the killing had nothing at all to do with these other people, anyway. It looks connected, but it most probably isn't.'

'The woman who made the confession about sending the flowers,' said Ben suddenly. 'Isn't that extremely peculiar, accosting Simmy in the street, when you think about it? Why would she do that?'

'Because she was worried I'd be upset about the waste,' said Simmy.

'But the waste was hers. I mean, her money. She doesn't sound very well off. Was she asking for a refund, do you think?'

'Definitely not,' said Simmy. 'No way. How could she possibly think . . .' She was breathless with outrage at the idea. 'After I'd traipsed all the way up to that farm.'

'Ben's right, though,' mused Moxon. 'She does stick out, somehow, doesn't she? As if she needed to make a special point. And why use a Windermere florist, when Ambleside is much closer?'

'And Coniston closer again. We keep wondering that,' Simmy agreed. 'But she made her point, loud and clear, didn't she? Even so, it doesn't seem especially odd to me. She might think I'd refuse to take any more orders from her, or something. So she wanted to keep on the right side of me.'

Man and boy gave her long sceptical looks. 'The order was anonymous – right?' said Moxon. 'So if you didn't know who she was, how could you boycott her in the future?'

'Daft idea, Sim,' Ben confirmed. 'And the old Crabtree person, too, come to that. She's another one who went out of her way to set your mind at rest.'

'Seems as if they might both have had a reason for speaking to you,' Moxon continued. 'After all, wasn't it an incredibly lucky coincidence for the one in Coniston, seeing you at that exact moment, just where she happened to be? Remind me what you were doing there, anyway.'

'Delivering flowers,' said Simmy wearily. 'What do you think?'

'Who to?'

'A woman who hasn't much longer to live. Her son sent her a Valentine bouquet, because they're not sure she'll make Mother's Day. It sounds very sad.'

'Maybe this cleaning woman does for her as well, and knew there'd be flowers coming,' said Ben. 'So she lay in wait for you so she could make her confession.'

'We keep calling it a "confession",' Moxon noted. 'That's strange, isn't it? Given the circumstances.'

'You think that I think she killed Mr Braithwaite?'

Simmy asked. 'Because I really don't. It never crossed my mind. I'm perfectly sure that none of these people have anything whatever to do with it.'

'All the same, I'd like to find out who she is before much longer. She feels important.' He slapped both hands on the table and levered himself out of the chair. 'Action!' he announced. 'Thank you for coming, both of you. Now you can go. Don't worry about your friend, Mrs Brown. If there's no word from her by morning, we'll get cracking on a search. Okay?'

*Mrs Brown*, thought Simmy, half amused and half irritated. *Well, fair enough. I still don't know what his first name is.* Which seemed surprising, after nearly six months' acquaintance.

Ben walked home and Simmy drove back to Troutbeck. The light on her landline phone was flashing. When she accessed the message, she heard: 'Simmy? It's Kathy. I don't want you to worry about me, but I've got into a bit of a pickle. I won't be back tonight. Sorry. I can't stop now, it's a payphone and I haven't got enough change to call your mobile. Look – please don't panic. I'm not in any danger. And whatever you do, don't contact the police. See you tomorrow, I hope.'

Simmy stared at the phone in an agony of turbulent emotion. Questions danced through her head, with little prospect of any answers. Had Kathy also called Joanna? Was she somehow being coerced into making the phone call? What hope was there of finding her? And what harm might she, Simmy, have done by telling the police her friend was missing?

She sat down with a thump on the chair in her hallway and tried to think logically. If Kathy had been forced to use a payphone, she must have a reason to avoid asking someone for help. Otherwise, surely she would have knocked on a door or gone into a shop and asked to use a normal telephone. She could even have stopped any passing individual and borrowed their mobile. Payphones were vanishingly rare, after all. She knew from her mother that guest houses and self-catering holiday homes sometimes installed them for visitors, but out in the open, there could not be a working one left apart from perhaps on railway stations. Had Kathy got herself to one of the local stations, then?

Answers slowly came into focus. Kathy might well not know Joanna's mobile number in her head, but did manage to retain Simmy's landline number, having phoned her so recently. With such efficient electronic memories doing all the work, who bothered to commit them to their own brains any more? If Kathy's phone had died, she could well be left helplessly unable to retrieve any but a shorter landline number that did happen to be easily memorised. 304506 was a sequence that Simmy had discovered stuck easily in many people's minds.

The area code would have been displayed on the payphone handset.

Quickly, before anyone else could call her, she keyed 1471, in the hope of discovering the number of the phone Kathy had used. Miraculously, the recorded voice told her a number she did not recognise, and she wrote it down. The police, she assumed, could readily locate the spot by tracing the number.

But Kathy had insisted the police should not be alerted. This led to a new line of questions and slowly formed theories as to why that might be. Kathy was a civil servant and might not want any smudge on her character. Even being logged by the police as a missing person might eventually lead to embarrassing publicity. That would be an understandable and innocent explanation and Simmy badly wanted her friend to be innocent. She also wanted her to be safe. The big question was – could she believe the reassurances in the phone message? 'A bit of a pickle' sounded worrying. Taking into account traditional British understatement, which had always been a point of entertainment for the two friends, it was perfectly possible that it meant two broken legs and a severed artery. But it could equally well refer to the troublesome car or the malfunctioning mobile. And her friend *had* got herself to a working payphone, which was a major achievement in itself. It was also rather peculiar, and the more she thought about it the more peculiar it seemed. For a start, the closest railway station to Coniston was at Windermere. And if Kathy could get that far, she could surely manage the final quarter of a mile to Simmy's shop. However strenuously she tried to believe otherwise, she could not shake off the conviction that her friend was not all right. There were no credible explanations that included her being fit and free. Everything pointed to her being some sort of captive, allowed a quick phone call from a public box to allay suspicions.

But that sort of thing didn't happen to ordinary innocent women in the small towns of southern Cumbria in broad daylight.

Did it?

Reluctantly, Simmy acknowledged that now and then it did. Something even worse had already happened in Coniston, with the killing of Mr Braithwaite. And she came to the conclusion that she could not afford to obey Kathy's ban on calling the police – especially as she had already told them her friend was missing. Yet again, she was going to have to phone DI Moxon and try to explain a further worrying twist to the already tangled case.

But first – of course – she could try the number herself. Somebody might hear it and answer, which might at least tell her where it was. She keyed it in and heard the ringing tone. It rang for ten or twelve unanswered peals, with no answer service cutting in.

Eventually she put it down and phoned the detective inspector.

He answered more slowly than usual, just as she was trying to compose a message to leave as a recording. 'Simmy Brown,' he said, the use of her first name a surprising deviation from the norm. 'Again.'

He was annoyed with her, she realised. Perhaps he had held the ringing phone in his hand for three or four long peals before sighing and then responding. He had had enough of her, with her endless string of encounters with individuals associated with the Coniston case.

'Sorry,' she said.

'Don't be. Has something happened?'

'Actually, yes. There's a message on my home phone from Kathy. She says she's in a pickle, and I'm not to call the police, whatever I do.'

'I see,' he said, plainly untruthfully. 'And you ignored her instruction.'

'Because it doesn't make sense. I've got the number she called from. I tried ringing it and there was no reply. She said it was a payphone. I mean – there *aren't* any payphones these days, are there? You can find out where it is, can't you? It's not a Windermere code.'

'Let me have it then.' When she'd done so, he immediately said, 'Looks like Cockermouth to me. That's a fair way from here. Can you think of a reason why she might be there?'

'Absolutely not. So can you trace the number to the actual phone?'

'Of course.' She could hear a keyboard tapping. 'It's a pub in the main street. The Cock and Bull. And it's not a payphone.'

'Pardon?'

'It's an ordinary phone.'

'Oh.' She tried to think logically. 'So she lied to me. Why would she do that? Somebody must be forcing her. She must have been *kidnapped*. And why didn't anybody answer it just now?'

She heard his deep sigh. 'I doubt she's been kidnapped. Perhaps she just wanted to keep you from worrying, while she does something of her own that she'd rather you didn't know about. Did she sound frightened or hurt in any way?'

'No. Not really.'

'Well, I suggest we just hang on for a while longer. You know where she is now. In the morning you can go up there and see for yourself.'

'What about her car and the RAC?'

'It can all wait until the morning,' he insisted. 'I'm at home now, hoping for a few hours' sleep. This isn't a serious enough matter for a police hunt tonight. We're investigating a homicide, you see.' He did sound tired, she realised. Tired, cross and just a bit patronising. 'I can tell you're worried and I'm sorry. But I don't believe there are grounds for concern. All right?'

'Hmm,' she said. 'I suppose so. But she *did* tell me not to call the police,' she blurted. 'That's what worried me.'

'Maybe she meant it at face value. A way of assuring you she's all right.'

'No. That wasn't it at all. But thanks. I'll try to get through the night without troubling you again.'

'Good girl,' he said. And that really *was* patronising.

# CHAPTER TWELVE

Melanie Todd often found Fridays frustrating because she had a full timetable at college, and that meant she couldn't work in Simmy's shop. Unfortunately Fridays were often quite eventful at Persimmon Petals. Twice before she had found herself sidelined during the climax of a murder investigation, and she was very much afraid it was happening again.

At five o'clock, she was on her way home in the temperamental car she shared with her brother, convinced that Simmy had been having all sorts of excitement in Hawkshead or Coniston or Newby Bridge. During Simmy's recovery from her injury at Christmas Melanie had shouldered more of the responsibility of the shop, and had found herself increasingly engaged, both emotionally and professionally. Six months earlier, she had scorned the frippery of flowers, only taking the job because the hours suited her. Since then she had discovered that there was a great deal more to floristry than she would ever have guessed. For a start, there had been all that *feeling*. People often cried as they composed messages of sympathy for a funeral wreath. Or they blushed and giggled over words of love that obviously reflected deep commitment. They told stories of long-awaited babies and unwise marriages. It was one long revelation to Melanie, who had until then focused exclusively on making an escape from her turbulent family by forging a career for herself in hotel management.

Hotels were exciting, too, of course. Her long-term ambition had not changed. But the prospect of leaving Simmy's employ in another three or four months' time was more and more unpleasant. She liked to think she had brought a degree of order and discipline to the business, insisting on proper spreadsheets for the finances and using the flowers strictly in rotation. She hated the thought of a new young assistant taking her place and messing everything up.

Valentine's Day had proved, on the whole, rather a washout. Joe had sent a boring card, which the idiot had actually *signed*. Wilf Harkness had sent nothing, much to her disappointment. Wilf was an ongoing problem, for which she could blame nobody but herself. They had briefly gone out together, over a year ago now, and somehow she had managed to give him the idea that she wanted nothing more to do with him. When Joe Wheeler had made his move, she had hoped it would galvanise Wilf into renewed efforts to get back to her. Instead he had receded out of sight, leaving a clear field to Joe. Not until Ben had hinted at his brother's continuing interest had she come to see herself as in a dilemma. At Ben's school play, a few days before Christmas, Wilf had made eyes at her and chatted briefly, but nothing more than that. So she stayed with Joe, fully conscious that he was second best. If it hadn't been for his useful police connections and his reliable car, she'd have packed him in months ago.

They always went out on a Friday evening, and this one ought to be at least a bit special, given the date. The fact of a murder investigation underway was sure to add some spice to the occasion. If Wilf couldn't get his act together to send her a card or even a text or something, then sod him. She'd stick with Joe for a while longer and make the best of it.

She was ready by six, and was in the noisy family sitting room, two younger sisters fighting over the TV remote, and her brother loudly on his phone to some girl or other. Their father – or stepfather in Melanie and Gary's case – was singing tunelessly in the kitchen. The dog was whining to go out, ignored by everyone. Melanie knew the wretched animal was doomed to be returned to the rescue place the

215

first time it peed on the floor or chewed something precious. Her mum was always getting a new pet and then sending it back within weeks. She ought to be blacklisted, by rights, but she always managed to convince the people she'd give the creature a good home.

Then little Maxie wandered in, holding a Nintendo DS and wailing. 'It's brogen,' he wept. 'The DS is *brogen*.'

'Come here,' said Melanie with a sigh. 'Let's see.'

Maxie was five, the tail-ender that had been the final straw for their mum. The other kids had effectively reared him, changing nappies, feeding him and mopping up his many tantrums and troubles. Their mother had sunk hopelessly into an uncoping lethargy that wasn't quite depression or bipolar or OCD, but a weird combination all of her own. She could be bright and funny on occasion, but her default condition was a vague smile as she flipped through a magazine or simply stared out of the window. The family conspired to pretend that all was well – and this extended to the regular acquisition of abandoned dogs, which Mum genuinely loved, at least to start with. Their stepfather was a soft, selfish man who sat about waiting to be fed, often with Maxie on his lap or one of the girls leaning against him, telling him a long story about school. He earned reasonable money as a plumber and was good with his hands. Melanie did not dislike him, since he was harmless, but she had never managed to feel any affection for him. Her own father was a different matter – resentful at his many failures and pathologically obstructive of anything his children wanted to do. Gary and Melanie had long ago lost hope that he would ever be of use to either of them.

'It just needs charging, I think,' Melanie told her little brother. 'Let's see if we can find the lead for it, shall we?'

But then the doorbell made its usual discordant jangle and Melanie went to answer it. Joe stood there, as he always did, half afraid to venture into the midst of the swirling family. 'Clo – find Maxie's charger thing, will you?' Melanie ordered one of the sisters, before pushing Joe ahead of her out into the street.

She pulled the door shut behind her and closed her eyes. 'God, it never gets any better in there. I'm twenty, for God's sake – time I had a place of my own.'

Joe eyed her worriedly. 'Um . . . I'm not sure . . .' he stammered.

'Don't be stupid – I'm not asking *you* to do anything. I can sort myself out, thanks very much. You know that.'

He changed the subject. 'Did you get the valentine?'

'Oh – was that from you? I never would have guessed.'

'But I put my name on it.' He paused, catching her eye. 'Ah! I get it. Very funny.'

'They're meant to be anonymous, you idiot. That's what's romantic about them. The thought of a secret admirer and all that stuff.'

'Well, then,' shrugged Joe vaguely. 'What's your problem? Why would you want a secret admirer when you've got me?'

There was at least a hint of self-mockery in his words, she told herself. Nobody could be such a plonker as to mean it literally. 'Where are we going, then?' she asked.

'How about hopping down to Kendal? There's that Balti place in Wildman Street. My mate Kev says it's great.'

Melanie weighed it up. 'Okay,' she said. The drive would make a change, and an Indian place probably wouldn't be fully booked with Valentine couples. 'On condition you don't order the hottest thing on the menu and then barf on the way home. Like last time.'

'There was something bad in it,' he defended.

'Just the same . . .'

'Okay. I'll have something milder, if it matters to you.'

Joe was a decent lad, she reminded herself. He'd never take a bribe or get involved in dodgy goods. He liked working in the police, being kind to old ladies and lost dogs. He sometimes got overexcited when there was anything more serious going on, but basically he did as he was told and made himself agreeable to his colleagues. His ginger hair and freckles made him look young and oddly old-fashioned. Some people called him 'Ron' after Harry Potter's sidekick. Others would use 'Wheels' as a nickname, both because of his surname and his devotion to his car.

They chatted idly for the first few miles, and then Joe said, 'Your boss lady's been in again – did she tell you?'

'What? Today? I haven't seen her. Did something else happen?'

'Just a bit. Seems she's got a friend from the south staying, and she's gone missing. Moxo logged the report, but said no action needed till tomorrow soonest. Thing is, everyone's doing the headless-chicken thing about this Coniston business, and there's nobody free to go searching for a grown woman. Different if it was a kiddie, obviously.'

'You're telling me that Kathy thingummy has got herself lost? When? How?'

'Search me. I just saw it on the computer, with Ms P. Brown the one reporting it in. Thought it must be your lady – with the Troutbeck address, an' all.'

'Simmy had wall-to-wall deliveries for most of today. All morning, anyhow. She wasn't meant to go gallivanting with her friend.' Melanie frowned in puzzlement. Yet again something big had happened on a Friday, just when she wasn't there.

'You can ask her all about it in the morning,' he said curtly, apparently regretting ever mentioning the matter. As a humble uniformed constable, his access to the inner workings of murder investigations was severely limited – a fact he tried to conceal from Melanie. Any small nugget of information was treated like gold dust and conveyed to his girlfriend as if central to the whole process.

There were still a couple of tables free in the Balti and they settled down to study the menu. 'You paying?' she checked before ordering.

'I surely am. How can you even ask?'

Her natural caution where money was concerned prevented her from choosing anything too costly, but she didn't stint herself. Pappadoms *and* nan bread, she insisted, to go with the rogan josh.

As they waited for the meal to arrive Melanie looked around her. Kendal was far enough from Windermere for there to be little chance of seeing anybody she knew, but it was a habit with her to examine all the other diners and try to see what they were eating. A man sitting two tables away with his back to her seemed familiar, hair tied back in a ponytail and wearing a red quilted jacket that looked handmade. Opposite him was a very attractive woman whose hair was dyed a dramatic coppery shade. Melanie had never seen her before.

Ninian! It was Ninian Tripp the potter, who

220

was meant to be soft on Simmy. What was he doing with this classy-looking creature? Her clothes were obviously expensive, her make-up immaculate. To Joe's detriment, Melanie spent the next ten minutes trying to hear what the couple were saying, and to figure out the precise nature of their relationship. By the time the first course was finished, she could bear it no longer. 'Just popping to the loo,' she told Joe, and then wove her way between tables in entirely the wrong direction, so as to bring herself face to face with Ninian.

'Hey! Is that you?' she cried, in a piece of appalling acting. 'Fancy that.'

He frowned up at her, clearly unable to place her. 'Melanie,' she prompted him. 'From the flower shop.'

'Oh, yes. Of course. Sorry.' He seemed distracted, his eyes returning constantly to the face of his companion. 'Melanie. Hello.'

'I'm with my boyfriend, Joe. Valentine's meal, see.' She waited expectantly, glancing at the pretty woman.

'Nice,' said Ninian.

'I'm Selena Drury,' said the woman, with a little laugh. 'No point expecting him to introduce me. He's hopeless at all that sort of stuff.'

'Pleased to meet you,' said Melanie, with raised eyebrows. 'From Kendal, are you?'

'Sort of,' she agreed. 'You could say I'm between

221

houses at the moment. I'm in Coniston most of the time.'

'You weren't in the shop today,' Ninian observed. 'So you won't know who Selena is. This isn't how it looks. She's my sister's oldest friend, as it happens. But she's had some dealings with your employer today, and needed someone to talk it over with. So she's taken me out for a slap-up meal.' He beamed gratefully at the woman across the table.

Melanie could think of nothing to say, other than 'Dealings? What dealings?'

'It's a long story, and I'm sure your boyfriend wouldn't want to sit there by himself while I told it. Besides, Selena and I were in the middle of something. You can ask Simmy to explain it all tomorrow. It's been a very busy day for her. You've got a lot of catching up to do.'

She had no choice but to return to her table and try to focus on Joe. He hadn't even noticed what she'd been doing, being occupied by selecting a dessert. 'There isn't much of a choice,' he grumbled.

'It's not about the puddings in a place like this,' she snapped. 'Haven't you had enough already?'

He looked up in surprise. 'What's up with you?'

'Fine cop you are. I've just been talking to two people from Windermere – well, he lives near Bowness, actually and she says she's between houses, whatever that means – who've been involved in this murder of yours, and you never even noticed.'

'I thought you were in the loo.'

Only then did she realise she'd never got that far, and that she really ought to have done. She sighed. 'Ninian Tripp and a woman called Selena something. They're talking about stuff that happened today, to do with Simmy and the shop. I missed the whole thing, damn it. Again. Everything happens on a Friday.'

Joe ordered mango sorbet and Irish coffee. Melanie got up again and went off to the Ladies, in a very un-Valentine mood.

# CHAPTER THIRTEEN

Simmy slept badly, tormented by dreams in one of which Ben fell down a deep chasm on the side of a mountain and DI Moxon hauled him out on the end of a rope. Following closely on that one was another in which Simmy's mother berated her for wearing her best shoes to walk through a snowy field to reach her car, which had one door dangling off.

Nothing about Kathy, she noted when she woke up at seven-thirty. At least, nothing she could remember.

The lack of urgent cooperation by the police was worse than frustrating. It implied that she was overreacting, and that was humiliating. If they would only instigate a search for the Subaru, as well as visit the Cockermouth pub where Kathy had used the phone, then everything might have quickly come right. As it was, she, Simmy, felt she had little choice but to go to the pub herself and see if Kathy was there. But she had a shop to run, and Saturday mornings often saw a good deal of business. She might leave Melanie in charge, of course, but would have to explain the whole story first. And Melanie preferred not to be left alone without a good reason. She liked to chat between customers, and there was undeniably plenty for them to discuss.

It would have to wait until after they closed at one, she decided with a sigh. Perhaps by then everything would have come right by itself.

Melanie was in the shop before her, at the indecently early hour of eight forty-five. 'Blimey!' said Simmy. 'Why so keen?'

The girl gave her one of her accusing looks. 'I missed out again,' she said bitterly. 'Why does everything have to happen on a Friday?'

Simmy tried to remember all the events of the previous day, and was forced to concede that there had been a lot. 'Good question,' she smiled. 'It'll take all morning to bring you up to date.'

'You can start with a woman called Selena Jury.'

'Drury. Do you know her?'

'I met her last night in a restaurant in Kendal. She was with Ninian Tripp.'

Simmy took many seconds to absorb this news. 'She can't have been,' she concluded flatly.

'Well she was. She's an old friend of his sister, he says. And something happened to her yesterday. Here in the shop, apparently.'

225

'No. It was in Newby Bridge – sort of. Someone pretending to be a boyfriend sent flowers to her real boyfriend's address. Obviously aiming to cause trouble.'

'Like the others.'

'Very much like the others, yes. Although a woman in Coniston says she sent the ones to Maggie Aston, and Mrs Crabtree says it was her sister who's a bit demented, so perhaps they don't count any more. So that only leaves two, I suppose. Hayter and Drury, and we think Drury has an innocent explanation as well. But now my friend Kathy's gone missing and I need to get to Cockermouth and try to find her.' But still at the front of her mind was an image of Ninian spending Valentine's evening over a romantic meal with a woman. She already thought she knew what her dreams would bring that night. Most likely she would be gouging eyes out or using a silver fork to stab the creature through the heart.

Melanie slumped dramatically as if impossibly overburdened. 'All that in one day!' she moaned.

'There's probably more that I've forgotten. At least I got all the Valentine roses delivered and nobody's complained. Except Solomon from Somalia, of course.'

'That's a joke, right?' Melanie's false eye seemed to glitter ominously.

'No, I'm afraid not. Selena Drury is in a relationship with a man called Solomon, who she said is a Somali. He speaks perfect English and seems to be doing very nicely for himself. He saw me trying to deliver her flowers, but never came out of the house while I was there. Later on, he came here and I had to tell him what'd been going on.'

'Which was?'

'I just told you. Someone pretending to be a boyfriend sent them. Another lover.'

'But she doesn't live with this Solomon. She told me she was between houses, but was based mainly in Coniston.'

'Yes, that's more or less what she told me. She sounded cross but not panicked at all. I thought they both seemed grown up enough to deal with it. Except . . .' she frowned, 'she should have been out with him last night, not Ninian.'

'I'm only guessing here,' said Melanie, 'but I'd say they aren't dealing with it too well, actually. If she felt the need to run to Ninian for comfort, that suggests things aren't so good with the boyfriend, doesn't it?'

Simmy chewed her lip. 'He didn't look the type to make a big thing of Valentine's Day. He probably thinks it's just a stupid commercial frivolity, not worthy of his attention. He was a very *serious* sort of chap.'

'Hmm. Well you can't say that about Ninian.'

'Or Joe?'

'Joe's fairly serious in his way.' Melanie sighed.

'When he does try to be fun, it's mostly to do with football or drinking.'

They fell silent, thinking about men and the difficulties they presented in so many ways. Then Melanie shook herself. 'What's this about Kathy? Where did she go?'

Simmy did her best to summarise the sequence of events since the previous morning. 'DI Moxon doesn't seem at all worried about her. I suppose if she can make a phone call and tell me lies about it, she can't be in too much trouble.'

'I'd have thought the opposite, actually. Why would she lie to you if she wasn't being forced to? It's irresponsible of the police just to brush it away like that. But listen – I've got a mate in Cockermouth. She's called Mary Ann and she works in a hotel there. We can get her to go round to that pub at lunchtime and see what's what. She'll be up for that.'

'You've never mentioned her before.' Melanie's social circle was an ongoing mystery to Simmy. The people she described as friends mainly appeared to be little more than acquaintances, with no single name recurring often enough to suggest a genuine intimate.

'I bet I have. She was on my course, but didn't finish. Her sister got her a place with a big hotel chain, doing the website or database or something. She's already got all the qualifications for that stuff, so didn't see any point in carrying on with management. She's from Dumfries originally.'

It rang no bells with Simmy, but she was more or less willing to let this Mary Ann deputise for her if it saved a long drive up to Cockermouth. 'Okay, then,' she agreed. 'If she wouldn't mind.'

But before anything could be done about it, there was a knocking at the street door, which was still locked. Simmy looked at her watch. 'Still only five to nine,' she said. 'What's the rush?'

'Someone forgot to send a Valentine,' said Melanie. 'And wants to pretend it's all our fault.'

But when Simmy went to the door she recognised the long mane of hair belonging to Joanna Colhoun. Beside her was a young man Simmy had not seen before. She turned the sign to Open and unbolted the door.

'Sorry!' Joanna panted breathlessly. 'We thought you'd be open by now. This is Baz.'

Simmy gave him a brief look. He was dark-haired, with blue eyes and a long sharp nose. He looked too old to be a student, but rather young to be a tutor. 'Hello,' she said, 'Your mother . . .' addressing the girl.

'Oh, yes. That's why we came. She's all right, you see. Panic over. She sent a message to my dad. She's really sorry to have messed you about so much. You must be really pissed about it. The thing is, apparently, she managed to get her car started again before the RAC man turned up, and just drove to the nearest main road, in case it conked out again. But the really mad part is . . .' here she laughed merrily, 'she *ran over* her phone. Don't ask me how, but she did. Smashed it to bits. But she didn't think it was a problem until she realised she couldn't remember anybody's number. Not even mine. She says she was starving hungry by then, so headed up towards Keswick, with the car flashing all sorts of warning lights at her, thinking she'd find a pub and a garage and a phone all at the same time.'

'Your dad phoned and told you all this, did he? He actually spoke to Kathy?'

Joanna looked questioningly at Baz. 'He did, didn't he?'

Her beloved put an arm around her and squeezed. 'That's right, sweetie. And your dad's been trying to get hold of you, but there wasn't a signal.'

'So how did all these messages get passed around?' Simmy asked.

'Um . . . I think Dad called our guest house in Coniston, and the woman gave him Baz's mobile number. Something like that.'

'As it happens,' Simmy disclosed, 'Kathy called me last night, from somewhere in Cockermouth.'

'What? She can't have done. I mean – why didn't you contact me and tell me she was okay? I was really worried all night.'

'I assumed she *had*,' said Simmy, not quite

truthfully. She had not in fact considered Joanna's anxiety at all, much to her shame.

Again, the girl turned great spaniel eyes onto Baz. 'What does it mean?' she whimpered.

'God knows,' he said. 'When you meet up with her, it'll all be explained.'

'Yes. But where is she *now*?'

'She'll be fine,' said Baz blandly. 'She's getting her car sorted and buying a new phone. And she knows you're still busy, doesn't she? After what you said to her yesterday.'

'Oh, don't.' Joanna shuddered. 'I was so *horrible* to her.' She gave him a gentle prod. 'That was *your* fault, you know. You told me nobody should know . . . oh! Sorry.' She went pink and clamped her mouth shut.

'Well, she was definitely in Cockermouth yesterday,' said Simmy, determined to stay well out of any romantic implications. 'Even though she didn't say where she was. It took the police computer to find out that it was a pub in the main street there.'

Baz pushed forward. 'Police?' he rasped.

'Yes. You probably haven't heard that there was a murder this week in Coniston, and I've been marginally involved. I know Joanna said it wasn't worth worrying them about your mother, but I didn't agree.' She straightened her spine and lifted her chin, as if to say *And I'm the responsible adult around here, after all.*

231

The young man backed down, with a little nod. 'Okay,' he said. 'No problem. We can just call them and say it's all sorted now.'

Joanna gave him a surprised look. 'But you said—'

He gave her a quelling glance. 'No probs, Jo. We'll be off tomorrow anyway, so we don't have to worry.'

'Did you finish your project, then?' asked Simmy.

'More or less. It's not really something that can ever be "finished" as such. It's permanently ongoing. We've got some decent data to play with, anyhow. Makes a change from all those bloody computer models.'

Simmy was lost and glanced at Melanie to see if she was equally bemused. The girl was straightening some irises in a bucket, pretending to ignore the conversation. 'Right,' said Simmy vaguely.

'So, that's it, then.' Baz clapped his hands together. 'All settled, nothing else to worry about. Can't think why Jo's old lady had to come up here in the first place, to be honest. All she's done is cause a lot of bother for nothing.'

'I think she was worried about Jo,' said Simmy, still feeling decidedly cool towards this insensitive young man. Her irritation extended to Joanna as well. The whole exercise felt irresponsible and dangerous, made worse by its secretive nature. 'Perhaps if you'd explained more clearly what you were doing, none of this confusion would have happened.'

'There's no mystery about it,' flashed Baz. 'We're measuring rainfall, temperature, hours of sunlight, $CO_2$ levels and wind speed, over a period of a year in an identical spot to the one where an amateur scientist made the same measurements in 1887. It will provide a very useful comparison. There are other student groups involved, so we can spread the work through the year. But somebody's blabbed about it on Facebook and now the whole thing's got blown all out of proportion.'

'Gosh! That sounds complicated,' said Simmy.

'There's no substitute for real data, you see,' said Joanna earnestly. 'It has to be taken into account. If we get cracking first thing on Monday, setting the record straight, they'll soon be thanking us.'

'Good,' Simmy agreed. 'Although—'

'Oh, we realise it's just a snapshot, a tiny detail in the whole picture. But it's a lot better than most of what's been used up to now. A *whole year* of statistics, then and now, from the same place. It's got to be useful.'

Simmy was entirely unqualified to comment. 'Well, it sounds very worthwhile,' she said feebly.

Baz smiled tolerantly and ushered his friend back towards the door. 'We need to go now,' he said. 'See you sometime. Jo and I have a lot to do.' The girl giggled revealingly.

'Be careful,' said Simmy, with a sudden pang of concern.

'No worries,' Baz laughed and they were gone.

Melanie said nothing for a whole minute. Then, 'So we can forget about Kathy, can we?' she remarked. 'Which is good, because I think this Jury person is a lot more interesting.'

'Drury. I'm not sure she is, really. And I don't think we can forget about Kathy for a moment. That story was rubbish. Nobody ever runs over their own phone, for a start. She'd never have gone aimlessly driving round like that, either. I don't like that Baz one little bit.'

'So I noticed. But he's very nice-looking. Sort of Johnny Deppish, when he was young.'

'I wish I could just forget everything and go back to bed, to be honest. I got through Valentine's all right. What more can anybody want from me?'

'Don't ask me.' Melanie sounded cross, causing Simmy to suppress a sigh. The girl burst out, 'I give up. I don't know who half these people are, so why should I waste my time bothering with them? You and Ben always charge ahead without keeping me in the loop. I'd be better off forgetting all about murders and stuff and just minding my own business. And I suppose we don't need Mary Ann now, after all.'

'Think yourself lucky,' Simmy said. 'I wish I could forget it all myself.' Then she had a thought.

'But you'll have to speak to Moxon or someone anyway. They want a description of the person who ordered the flowers for Selena Drury.'

'What?'

'You took the order, sometime last week. You were talking about it on Wednesday. That man who dashed in and said he was rushing for a train. Remember? He was wearing a long coat. I hardly saw him.'

'Oh, yes. That seems ages ago. How do you spell the name?'

'D-R-U-R-Y. The house is called Primrose Paddock in Newby Bridge. A dozen red roses, to be delivered during the 14th February. Paid in cash.'

Melanie closed her eyes and rubbed her forehead with a thumb. 'Primrose Paddock? It was ages ago. What does Moxon want to know about it?'

'Anything you can tell him, I guess. For a start, it would help to be sure what day that was.' Simmy riffled through a stack of paper. 'I should have looked for it yesterday. I suppose it must have been Monday afternoon. Or possibly last Saturday. Ah – here it is. February 8th. Saturday.'

'We were busy. I was juggling all those online orders and we caught that kid trying to nick a card. Wasn't that Saturday?'

It was disconcertingly difficult to cast her mind back a week. A boy of about nine had made a pathetically poor job of stealing a greetings card from a stand, and had wept when apprehended. It was his mother's birthday and he couldn't afford the hefty £2.50 that a card would cost. Simmy had made him put it back, but taken the matter no further. 'Draw her one yourself,' she advised him. 'That'll mean just as much.'

Unconvinced, he had trailed out of the shop, leaving Melanie and Simmy to comment on how unusual it was to see a child that age out on his own these days.

'Must have been,' she agreed. 'But that's not very helpful, is it?'

Melanie closed her eyes in painful thought. 'A long coat, did you say? Did he have a hat as well?'

'I barely even glimpsed him, but I'm fairly sure there was no hat. The coat was brown, I think. Might have been a mac. Not terribly long, really, but he was tall, so it made a solid patch of colour. I can visualise him standing right here, bending down to give you the details. I didn't see his face.'

'Just about everything has gone out of my head,' said Melanie worriedly. 'I must be getting old.'

Simmy laughed. 'It comes to us all,' she said.

'Oh, well,' Melanie shrugged. 'I don't expect it matters.'

'Ben thinks there's some sort of group with a big secret. According to his theory, Mr Braithwaite must have been in it and did something to annoy them, so one of them killed him. Then these people getting flowers were either being warned off, or somehow informed of what was happening, through the messages attached to them. Something like that, anyway,' she finished weakly. 'Doesn't make a lot of sense. Just another of his elaborate theories.'

'Mrs Crabtree, Maggie Aston and Whatshername Drury are all in some mysterious group? Like what?' Melanie's scepticism was palpable. 'And what kind of back-to-front way would it be to contact them – sending flowers?'

'He thinks it would escape notice from any surveillance system, I suppose. Emails, phone calls, texts and all that are monitored, aren't they?'

Melanie gave a scornful laugh. 'Only if they're members of some suspicious mosque or neo-fascist political party. Nobody reads every email that's sent, do they?'

'I doubt it.' It was a familiar subject, often sparked by Simmy's mother's attitude towards state intervention in ordinary lives. She would very likely approve of any message-sending method that slipped under the radar. 'But maybe this group, if it exists, is already known to the authorities, so they have to be extra careful.'

'There's no such group,' said Melanie with utter certainty. 'The idea's insane.'

'Oh, well. We'll just leave it all to the police, then. That suits me very nicely. And it's a relief that nobody needs to check out Cockermouth pubs in search of Kathy, either. Normal life can resume, with any luck.'

'That's pretty weird about Kathy, though. Driving all over the county in a car that might conk out at any moment, for no good reason – what's that all about?'

'She can tell us when she shows up. *If* she shows up. She's probably feeling pretty silly.'

'Worse than silly, the way she's messed you about.'

'I'm hoping she'll spend this afternoon with me and we can have a good old natter. She'll be going home again tomorrow, presumably, so she can get back to work on Monday.'

It was still only half past nine, with three hours more to get through before the shop could be closed for the remainder of the weekend. Simmy felt unusually vulnerable, there in the main street of Windermere where anybody could find her. Solomon Samalar had turned out to be readily mollified, but there was a real possibility that the person who killed Mr Braithwaite might get the idea that Simmy presented a threat to his safety and decide to silence her. It had, after all, happened before – or something like it. Melanie too had been accosted by a violently angry man at the centre of a murder. Nothing was really safe, when it came right down to it. After all, she admitted to herself for the five thousandth time, if her perfect baby girl could die for want of a properly functioning placenta, then anything could happen.

'They've all accosted me, one way or another,' she realised suddenly.

'Pardon?' Melanie blinked her perplexity. 'All who?'

'Well, all except Mr Hayter and Mr Braithwaite,' she amended. 'But the others have. Mrs Crabtree came in person to tell me off for giving her name to the police. The woman who sent the flowers to Mrs Aston flagged me down in the middle of Coniston. And Selena Drury's boyfriend tracked me down yesterday. They all seem determined to demonstrate that I'm in the middle of the whole stupid business. I know now how the maypole must feel when all those children are dancing in a circle, wrapping streamers tightly round it. They're weaving a pattern I can't see, using me as the central post somehow.'

'Fanciful,' Melanie judged. 'Very fanciful. Do you think one of those three might be the murderer, then?'

'Not Mrs Crabtree, surely. Although – she did seem to have a steely sort of character, under the old-lady image. And the cleaning person seemed much too ditzy to kill anybody. Don't you have to be strong to shove a knife into a grown man's heart?'

'Depends on whether you know what you're doing, I imagine.'

'And Mr Samalar is too . . . dignified. I can't see him killing anybody, either.'

'Dignified!' Melanie hooted scornfully. 'What difference would that make?'

'I don't know. It's hard to explain. I just didn't think . . .'

'Anybody can commit murder, Sim. You of all people ought to know that by now.'

'Don't say that,' she begged, seeing again the cold waxen features of the dead Mr Braithwaite. 'I don't think it's true, anyway. At least, not with a knife. You'd have to be completely desperate or crazy to do something like that.'

'It's the eternal question, isn't it?' said Melanie with a heavy emphasis. 'Joe talks about it sometimes, when he's managing to be interesting for a change.'

Simmy shook herself. 'We're meant to be working,' she said. 'I haven't even checked for new orders yet.'

'There won't be anything. It's going to be dead all next week, just you see.'

'People still have birthdays and anniversaries.' She went to the computer and switched it on. 'Can you make us some coffee?' she asked the girl, as she got comfortable on the small chair. There were times when standing for long still brought about a deep ache in bones that were not yet fully healed. She still regarded herself as slightly fragile, moving more slowly and carefully than before the injury.

Melanie was in the back room when the screen presented a list of emails. 'Oh!'

Simmy's squeal was loud enough to bring her assistant to her side. 'What?'

'Look! It's from Kathy.' Simmy clicked to read the message. 'Listen to this. "Ignore all previous phone calls, etc. I was under duress. Hope I've got your email right. Can you come and meet me at the Yewdale Hotel today 12.30pm? If I'm not there, wait for me. Wear walking boots." For heaven's sake!' Simmy smacked a fist on the table in frustration. 'What the *hell* is this all about? She wants to take me fell walking in February! It's freezing out there. She must have gone completely mad.'

'You're right about the cold, anyway,' Melanie confirmed. 'And getting colder, they say. The Yewdale Hotel in Coniston, is it? I went there not long ago, for an assignment. They're good.'

'Right. It's where Moxon made us go on Thursday, when I had to look at the dead body. I suppose Kathy's trying to tell me that this has something to do with the murder. "Under duress" she says. So how come she can send an email?'

'You can't be sure it's from her, of course. Anybody can *pretend* to be her.'

'It's her address, look. That's the one she always uses. And mine's easy to remember, after all. If it's not her, it's somebody who has access to her account and knows her password. It's a game, Mel. She's playing some stupid game.'

'Has she done anything like this before?'

Simmy slumped. 'No, of course not. She's a civil servant. She's very sensible as a rule. But the bossy tone is her all right. She's in no doubt that I'll do as she says. She's always been like that. But this time I'm not going to cooperate. If she can get to the Yewdale, she can jolly well get here, and explain herself to me in a civilised fashion.'

Melanie looked unconvinced. 'Mr Hayter killed himself somewhere on the side of the Old Man, didn't he? So maybe there is something going on out there that she wants to show you.'

'And it's where her daughter and that dozy Baz have been working.'

'But it doesn't connect to the Jury – *Drury* – person, or the farm woman or Mrs Crabtree, does it?'

'How would we know? Maybe they all belong to a walking club and saw something suspicious going on. That's what Ben would say, anyhow.'

'And the flowers you delivered were a way of warning them to keep quiet?'

'Something like that – although it doesn't seem to have worked. None of them showed any sign of knowing what it meant.'

'Can I come with you?' Melanie burst out. 'And can we tell Ben? We can *all* go.'

'You're joking. No way am I going out there at all, on the strength of some childish email message. If she wants to tell me something, she can come here and do it face to face.'

'You said that already.'

'Well, I mean it.'

Melanie pulled a face. 'It's not the same as the phone messages, though, is it? This says to ignore all previous messages. And from what Joanna said, she hasn't actually spoken to her mother directly since yesterday. It sounded as if it had all come through her father via that Baz. A whole chain of Chinese whispers. What if somebody's deliberately pretending to be Kathy, just to stop us all from searching for her. What is he like, anyway, the Baz chap? Seducing students is a complete no-no. He's living dangerously, if you ask me.'

Simmy said nothing, feeling painfully torn and resentful. She frowned over Melanie's words. 'I probably should have said something about that.'

'Not your problem, Sim. Let her parents sort it out.'

'That would be the easy option,' Simmy agreed.

'Yeah. So first find her mother, right? And for that, you'll have to go to the hotel in Coniston.'

'I might have to, because I still can't quite believe that Kathy's okay. This email is so weird.'

'You've got to go to the Yewdale. You know you have.'

Simmy felt deeply inadequate. 'Let's just see, shall we? We've got all morning to get through first.' Then her main preoccupation reasserted herself. 'What was she like? Selena Drury, I mean.'

'What? Oh! Very classy. Expensive clothes, posh accent. Made poor old Ninian look quite scruffy, I must say. Why are you worrying about *her*?' Then she realised. 'Oh, my God – you're *jealous*. Oh, Simmy, how sweet! Listen – you don't have to worry. You can have Ninian any time you like. He's just waiting for you to click your fingers and he'll be right there. Honestly. He's not interested in anybody else, believe me.'

'Shut up.' Simmy blushed infuriatingly. 'It's not that at all. I just—'

She was saved by the shop doorbell. A middle-aged woman came in hesitantly. 'Are you open for sending flowers?' she asked.

'Yes, of course,' said Simmy. 'What did you have in mind?'

'Something for a friend who's just come out of hospital. Did you know you can't send flowers to patients any more? Not while they're in hospital. Isn't that a scandal!'

'It's ridiculous,' said Simmy with feeling.

'And bad for business,' muttered Melanie.

'Anyway, she's home now, so I can send what I like. Could you do something cheerful for her?'

Simmy immersed herself in the selection of

244

colourful spring blooms for the next five minutes. When the woman proffered three ten-pound notes, having recited the recipient's address, something rang an alarm in her head. 'Can I take your name and address as well?' she asked. 'Just for our records?'

'Oh – that seems a bit unnecessary. You'll be sending me advertisements and badgering me on the phone, I shouldn't wonder. I'd much rather not give them. I don't think you can insist, you know.'

For a fleeting second, Simmy wished she had a CCTV camera in the shop, to capture the woman on film. Then she felt the force of her own misguided thinking, and smiled an apology. 'You're quite right – I shouldn't have asked. Of course you don't have to tell me anything.'

'It's a sign of the times,' nodded the woman. 'I used to just go along with it, but just lately I've got a bit more assertive. Now I don't even give my phone number when I order things online.' She leant forward to whisper, 'I just make up a string of numbers. The computer doesn't know any different, you see.' She chuckled. 'We really can't let them rule our lives, now can we?' She shook the cash in her hand. 'And I've been paying for as much as I can with cash. It's ever so much easier, when you think about it.'

Here was a woman after Simmy's mother's own heart, and she wished Angie could hear her. 'And good luck to you,' she said warmly. 'I'll take the flowers to your friend later this morning, if that's all right?'

'Thank you, dear. I would go myself, but it's more of a surprise if you do it. And I have to be somewhere else today, anyway. Now you've got the card safe, haven't you – with my message on it?'

She had written, 'Get better quickly, Sal. See you soon. Lots of love, Lynn.'

'Yes, it's quite safe,' Simmy assured her.

When she'd gone, Melanie grinned. 'Nice try,' she said. 'At least we could both identify her again if we had to.'

'She's a perfectly ordinary innocent person. I feel awful for acting as if she was anything else.'

'Sign of the times,' remarked Melanie. 'Just as she said.'

The doorbell rang again, and another middle-aged woman came in. This time, the face was unmistakably familiar to Simmy.

# CHAPTER FOURTEEN

'I know her,' Simmy breathed to Melanie, before greeting the woman with a smile. 'Hello again,' she said.

'You remember me? I wasn't sure you would.'

'It was only yesterday,' said Simmy, thinking it felt much longer ago than that. 'You stopped me in Coniston.'

'That's right.' The woman gave her a penetrating stare. 'And you never told me about poor Jack Hayter or dear Tim Braithwaite. I feel sure you knew what had happened to both of them, and you let me go on wondering without saying a word. Of course I realised there was something very nasty going on, but I never *dreamt* . . .' She clutched her own throat dramatically. 'That poor man!'

Melanie was making low questioning sounds behind her, so Simmy made an awkward introduction. 'This is the lady who sent the flowers to Mrs Aston, on the farm,' she explained. 'She wanted to put me straight about it, so she stopped me when she saw my van yesterday.'

'Right,' said Melanie slowly. 'Pleased to meet you.'

'Pamela. My name's Pamela Johnson,' said the woman with some impatience. 'And I have to say I'm not very impressed at all. I've had the police chasing round trying to find me, which I might say is *very embarrassing*. Everybody in Coniston knows about it by now, and they'll be wondering what I've got to hide.'

'You knew them? Mr Hayter and Mr Braithwaite?' Simmy cut through the whining complaints. 'So the police would have wanted to speak to you in any event, surely? It's nothing to do with me at all.'

'That's as maybe. But they would never have known about me and Maggie Aston if you hadn't told them.' Triumph flickered on her face, as if a significant point had been scored.

'So what?' said Melanie. 'Does that have anything to do with the two men?'

'How well did you know them?' Simmy interrupted. 'Did you do their cleaning, as well?'

'As well as what?' The three of them were firing questions at each other, giving little time for replies. The air was spiky with accusation and misunderstanding. Pamela Johnson seemed to resent everything that was said to her, shaking her head as if nothing of relevance had yet been dealt with. 'You're not *listening* to me.'

'All right,' said Simmy, taking a deep breath. 'What are you trying to say?'

'I came to complain about the way you reported me to the police, when I did nothing wrong.' It came out loud and clear. 'I think it's a disgrace, I do really.'

'I didn't *report* you. I'm sorry if it's made things difficult for you, but what *I'm* trying to say is that they would very likely have wanted to speak to you anyway, if you knew the two men who died. They'll be asking everybody in Coniston for background information on them, I expect. It can't only be you they've spoken to.'

'I wouldn't know about that,' said Pamela Johnson mulishly.

'*Did* you do their cleaning?' asked Melanie.

'As it happens, I did. Not regular, mind you – just when they were having people round. They liked to have the stairs given a proper going-over, and the curtains washed and the rugs shaken, in the old-fashioned style. Very old-fashioned they were, in some ways.'

'So it must have been an awful shock to hear they were both dead,' Melanie persisted. Simmy had already observed that the woman showed little sign of grief or upset at the loss of her employers.

'Oh, well – yes, of course. But they weren't what you could call *friendly*. I'll miss the work, and they were nice enough in their way.' She wriggled her shoulders. 'A shock, yes. But shock doesn't last long, now does it? Funny, that – the way a person can so quickly get to grips with all kinds of surprises, in no time at all. Course, it's different if it's one of your own. That's a *very* different matter.'

'Yes,' said Simmy, thinking there was some real truth in the woman's words. 'But when somebody's murdered in your own little village – that must take some getting used to.'

Pamela Johnson gave this some thought. 'They'll not be greatly missed. Men like that – they attract the wrong sort of people, don't they? They're not like the rest of us, just getting on with our lives as best we can, never getting excited or fighting. It's just one drama after another with that sort.'

Simmy recalled Ben's googling results. 'But Mr Hayter entered his vegetables in the show. He sounds thoroughly ordinary.'

The woman laughed scornfully. 'A few runner beans don't buy popularity, I can tell you.'

'But you remember them, all these years later? That's amazing.'

'There was some trouble,' said Pamela shortly. 'Not so easily forgotten.'

'So, what sort of men were they?' Melanie demanded to know. 'Are you saying they were gay?'

'That's what everybody said.'

'Did they share a bedroom?'

'Mind your mouth, miss! Just you watch what you're asking.'

'Did they?'

'Seems not. But that could've just been for show. Keeping up appearances, sort of thing.'

'Did you ever see them doing anything to suggest they were a couple?'

'Like what? I never saw them kiss and cuddle, if that's what you mean. But two men living together – what else are people to think?'

'They had lady visitors, didn't they?' Simmy ignored a small inner voice that suggested she should not share facts disclosed to her by DI Moxon. The whole direction of the woman's words was irritating her beyond endurance.

'*One* lady visitor, every few months. Sixty, if she was a day. They told me she was Mr Braithwaite's sister.'

'When you first came in, you called him *dear* Tim Braithwaite. That sounded as if you liked him. So why are you trying to blacken his character now?'

Flustered and cross, Pamela Johnson snapped, 'He *was* a dear, some of the time. All I'm saying is, that sort of a lifestyle can get a man into trouble. Maybe I went a bit too far just now, but you did push me, you know you did.'

'Mr Hayter has a daughter and Mr Braithwaite

has a son, called Jasper. Both the men have been married. I know that doesn't prove anything, but I really think you ought to take care in what you say. The police see no reason to believe they were a couple. Even if they were, that's no reason for the village to think the same way you seem to. Why would it be so shameful to admit you're shocked and sad that they're both dead?'

'Because life has to go on,' Pamela shot back. 'And we need to find an explanation for what's happened, before it can do that. Those men were incomers, with all sorts of London connections and business things we don't understand. Jack Hayter killed himself, right? So he had worries of some sort. Money or a scandal. Then someone came to Coniston, bold as brass, and murdered Tim. Left him outside in the cold for anyone to find him. Might have been a kiddie, or someone with a weak heart. Did they think of that? I saw him myself on Monday evening, coming out of the pub. Looked perfectly all right, and then – *bang!* He's dead. As you say, a real shock. Believe me, my dear – nobody's being bigoted or doing a hate crime, or whatever they call it. We're just getting by the best way we know how.'

'You saw him on Monday? So you *will* have been a help to the police. That's crucial information.'

'Don't see why. Everybody in the pub would have seen him as well.'

'Was he drunk?'

'Not a bit. Seemed just as normal to me.'

'What did you do to Maggie Aston?' Simmy changed the subject so suddenly that Melanie as well as Pamela looked stunned. Two mouths hung open in unison.

'You said that's what you came to talk about, so let's talk about it.'

'I-I told the police, so I don't see why I have to tell you.'

'You don't, of course,' said Simmy coolly.

'Oh, I suppose I should. It was her little boy, Edward. I help out at his nursery a couple of days a week, and a little while ago I accidentally spilt some hot water on him. He was ever so upset and it left an awful blister on his arm. I was in real trouble, and they said I'd have to stop coming. It was always a bit iffy, you see, because I'm not qualified. I knew it couldn't last. But in all the unpleasantness, little Edward got forgotten. So I decided to send the flowers. I told the police the whole story.'

'But Maggie didn't realise the flowers came from you. Wouldn't it have been sensible to put your name on the message?'

'I just assumed she'd know.'

'Couldn't it be possible that she *did* know, but still hasn't forgiven you?'

'Oh, no. I spoke to her and she said it was all right. She'd decided to stop work and stay at home with Edward, and thanked me for helping her come to that decision. She hadn't been enjoying the job anyway, and her husband's started a nice little sideline breeding Border terriers, so money's not as tight as it was.'

As an answer, it was gratifyingly comprehensive. 'Border terriers? Are they particularly pricy, then?' asked Melanie. 'My mum tried breeding dogs once, when I was five, but the pups all died. Mug's game, if you ask me. You just get landed with a load of unwanted dogs because their tails curl in the wrong place.'

'Not according to Maggie,' said Pamela. 'They had seven pups in the first litter and sold them all at seven-fifty each. That's nearly six months' earnings, if you take out the nursery fees and petrol and all that.'

'*Seven hundred and fifty quid for a dog?*' Melanie's voice rose in disbelief. 'You're joking.'

'What was Maggie's job?' Simmy asked. She was still hoping to find some link between all the people in the case. DI Moxon had once told her she was good at seeing the big picture, and ever since then she had tried to do just that.

'Some sort of admin assistant for the National Trust. What we used to call a secretary, I suppose.'

It was evident that the conversation had dried up. After an awkward hiatus, Pamela turned to go. But first she fired one last shot. 'Just be more careful who you betray to the police. Things aren't always what they seem, remember.'

Wordlessly, Simmy watched her leave. Then she pulled a face at Melanie. 'At least we've almost got the full set now. Apart from the ones for Mr Hayter, somebody from all those strange flowers has been in.'

'Speak for yourself,' grumbled Melanie. 'This Pamela person is the only one *I've* seen.'

'You haven't missed much – although I did quite like Mrs Crabtree.'

'"Betray" is a bit strong,' Melanie sympathised, accurately pinpointing the word that Simmy was still struggling with.

'I thought so. It never even crossed my mind that she'd be annoyed about it. Same as Mrs Crabtree, actually. She came in to complain about the very same thing. Either everyone round here is involved in some huge criminal enterprise, or they distrust the police on an epic scale.'

'The second one,' nodded Melanie. 'Nobody wants to get themselves on that database, do they? They're convinced that every name that a cop writes down is kept for ever.'

'They're probably right. My mother would say so, at least. But you'd think when there's a *murder*, they'd want to help.'

'Not if they don't see it as their problem. You heard her. They've convinced themselves that a pair of old queens got themselves bumped off for murky reasons that don't concern the locals at all.'

'Are we allowed to say "queens"?'

Melanie did her alarming eye roll. 'There's a lot worse I could say. Not that it worries me at all.'

'Some of your best friends are gay,' said Simmy with a laugh.

But Melanie merely frowned and said, 'No, they're not.'

'It's a thing . . . oh, never mind. What time is it?' She answered her own question with a glance at her watch. 'Ten to ten. Right. Must be time for a coffee.'

'Yes, boss. Coming right up.'

Twenty minutes passed uneventfully, with Simmy alternately worrying about Kathy and pondering on small-town prejudices. Inevitably she thought of her mother as her chief source of information on the habits and opinions of Cumbrian people. Angie belonged to a few local organisations and engaged in regular discussions on a multitude of subjects. Her own opinions were defiantly individual and outspoken. Instinctively she avoided buzzwords such as *homophobia* or *hate crime*, rightly pointing out that neither of those particular examples made the slightest sense. 'They're deliberately selected to influence people's thinking,' she would explain. 'If you sow the idea that dislike of gay people arises from a person's own psychological problems, you make enormous progress in changing the cultural viewpoint,' she said once. 'I mean – that's not necessarily a bad thing in the long run, but it's sneaky, all the same. It's playing dirty, because it's based on a very uncertain premise. It closes off so many other perfectly valid attitudes. Essentially it works against free speech, not to mention free thought.'

'Just shows the power of language,' Russell had added. 'You're right, of course.' And he had added several more examples to the list. Simmy had listened in awe as her parents effortlessly critiqued a great range of contemporary positions, all of which carried fear of being seen as different at their heart. 'No place for the individual in this society,' Angie finished glumly. 'If you say something on Twitter that's disapproved of, you'll have the police knocking on your door within the hour.'

Which did, Simmy supposed, explain Pamela Johnson's annoyance at being brought to the attention of the authorities. It also perhaps explained why she had come in person, to express herself in spoken words which were not recorded in any way.

'Phew!' she sighed. 'Things have all got a bit deep this morning, haven't they?'

'How do you mean?'

'Surveillance society in its many guises. Even

here in a humble flower shop in a faraway corner of northern England, the tentacles of the state have penetrated.'

'Steady on!' Melanie protested. 'Where did that come from?' She narrowed her eyes. 'Is it a quote from Shakespeare or something?'

'No,' laughed Simmy. 'Just my mother.'

# CHAPTER FIFTEEN

Ben's Saturday morning began irritatingly early, with his brother Wilf waking him at seven. They shared a room, to the disgruntlement of them both, although they conceded that there was no other option, where a family of seven had to fit into a four-bedroomed house. Ben, like Melanie, was the second child of five – but in his case they all had the same two parents.

Wilf was nearly twenty-one and working his way towards becoming a chef. Always a keen cook, he had prepared entire family meals from the age of twelve, with creamy smooth sauces and legendary mashed potato. He worked irregular shifts at Storrs Hall hotel, south of Bowness and regarded his younger brother with an impatient sort of admiration. Ben had always been the bright one, sailing through school exams with ease and spending most of his waking hours on impossibly complicated computer games. His encounter with Simmy and a local killing four months earlier had almost instantly sparked an ambition to work in forensics. Within weeks he had landed an unconditional place in a top university at a freakishly young age, with the prospect of a postgraduate course in America.

'Why are you up?' Ben asked his brother now. 'Are you doing breakfasts?'

'Sorry. No – I'm going up to Coniston. Scott's organised a day on the fells. There's a gang of us going. I told you.'

'You didn't,' mumbled Ben. 'It's February, you know. Cold. Windy. Dangerous.'

'That's how we like it. No grockles.'

'What?'

'That's what they call them in Devon. I don't think we've got a similar word up here.'

'Ergghh,' moaned Ben. 'Just go, will you.'

'Actually, Scott got the idea from that murder on Thursday. He thought we might stumble across some clues, daft bugger. He gets more like you all the time.'

Ben finally opened his eyes. 'Clues? What sort of clues?'

'I have no idea. But the other bloke topped himself somewhere on the Old Man, didn't he? I think Scott has some idea of re-enacting what might have happened.'

'Then he's thicker than I thought,' scorned Ben, and pulled the duvet back over his head.

But he couldn't get back to sleep. Instead he visualised the group including his brother and Scott Reynolds tramping about on the icy fells, pretending to be Sherlock Holmes and probably managing nothing more than scaring some sheep. That wasn't the way to solve murder investigations, he thought crossly. You had to work with whatever evidence and testimony you had, and test out a variety of theories. At least, that was one method. You also had to listen out for careless talk, and keep a very open mind. Most criminals were caught because they boasted to so-called mates about what they'd done. Boring but true, and not much credit to the CID. All they had to do was to link up fingerprints or DNA and there it all was, done and dusted. Which was why Ben had elected to work in forensics, rather than waste his whole working life trudging around asking for witnesses, who half the time couldn't remember the most important details anyway.

Getting to know Simmy and Melanie had been revelatory in many ways. The female angle on detection work was both infuriating and fascinating. Simmy's squeamishness was often hard to understand, because the truth was, she had more courage than she gave herself credit for.

She valued a clear conscience above all things, he realised, and would put herself at risk if it meant she was doing the right thing. Melanie was more complicated – seen by other teenagers as a freak, much as Ben was himself. Not because of her missing eye, but because she was determined to climb out of the disorganised mess that was her family, using her own wits and ambition to propel her. Melanie and Ben had both learnt early that the opinions of one's classmates could not be allowed to matter.

But when it came to solving crimes Melanie's main usefulness, ironically, came from the very roots that she was trying to pull up. She knew the background connections of scores of local people, mainly through her grandmother's remarkable memory for personal histories. When murder arose from murky past events and ancient antipathies, Melanie and her gran were real founts of knowledge.

The Coniston thing was annoying because he had not learnt anything of significance about the *way* either of the men had died. He guessed there was a lot that Simmy knew, which he'd missed out on – and that seemed a waste, because Simmy only wanted to stay out of it all. She probably felt guilty about the flowers she took to Mr Hayter-stroke-Braithwaite, but this time there was obviously nothing she could do to make amends, since both men were dead.

He had two substantial A-level assignments to be done over the weekend: one on a tricky piece of biochemistry and the other a translation of a long chunk of Catullus. He'd added Latin as an extra subject on a whim, given that he was deemed to be excellent at languages, but it was turning out to be harder than expected. The whole mindset was new to him, with every word needing to be examined to see what case it was in, in order for the sense to become clear. It was laborious, with no scope for short cuts. There were no teachers at the comprehensive equal to the task of instructing him, either, so he was muddling through an online course, with Mr Brent as a sort of mentor, making sure he stuck to the schedule.

But there was acres of time before Monday morning, and he could easily fit in a visit to Simmy's shop as well as a bit of homework after breakfast. He might even spend an hour or so analysing the known facts about the Coniston case and seeing if anything new jumped out at him. So he rolled out of bed, got dressed, and sat down at the desk in the corner of his side of the room. It held a computer, notebooks, maps, and stacks of printouts from various websites. On the floor were untidy heaps of textbooks. Somewhere in the muddle was the flow chart he had started the day before with Simmy.

He was acutely aware of the danger of jumping to conclusions, having been lectured on the subject by DI Moxon more than once. Coincidences were possible but unlikely, and nothing anybody said could be believed. Even if not deliberately lying, they got things wrong or jumped to conclusions of their own.

All of which led him to conclude that there was really no reason to think that Mrs Crabtree, Mrs Aston or Miss Drury had anything at all to do with the killing of Mr Braithwaite. The fourth order for flowers however – which had perhaps sparked everything off in the first place – was still unexplained. And regardless of logic, he still could not dismiss the strong instinct that said there were connections between all four of them. It was originally because Simmy had been instrumental in delivering upsetting flowers to all four of them that anybody thought there might be a link. Even though it seemed that three could be eliminated, he still wasn't entirely persuaded. His wild idea about them all being part of a secret group, with a system of sending flowers as a means of communicating, now seemed childish; the sort of thing that would elicit a stern word from Moxo, and make Ben feel ten years old – and yet it stubbornly persisted as a faintly possible theory.

But if coincidence were to be discounted, then

that must surely mean that there really *were* links between at least some of the people on his flow chart. It was no good – he needed a lot more data before anything would even begin to make sense. Perhaps Scott would disclose a few more details to Wilf during their freezing trek on the fells.

Or perhaps he should call in on DI Moxon on the pretext of checking that the police did at least know everything that he and Simmy knew.

It was only just after eight when he went down to breakfast, and the kitchen was deserted. His mother was an architect, working mainly from home, and his father taught languages at a different secondary school to the one his children attended. Ben's three younger sisters seldom got up before ten at the weekend. Most likely, everyone was still asleep. Seizing his chance, he fried bacon, sausages, eggs and mushrooms, musing to himself that Simmy's mum must spend her life cooking up huge breakfasts for her guests, thinking nothing of it. As it was, the eggs were done long before the sausages were halfway cooked, the yolks gone hard and the whites with crispy black edges. He decided to eat each item as it was ready, which at least had the virtue of passing the time before he could decently set out on the short walk to the police station.

Before he could embark on the sausages, his youngest sister, Natalie, bounced in, wearing yellow pyjamas. 'Hey!' she shouted. 'Are you taking all the food? I want some.'

She was the younger of the twins by fifteen minutes, and Tanya never let her forget it. Zoe, almost fifteen, was balanced between two brothers and twin sisters, finding the position intolerable. They were all noisy and clever and very demanding.

'Help yourself,' he said, waving his fork at the fridge.

'I want some of yours.' She reached out and snatched a rasher of bacon, narrowly evading the fork that tried to stab her hand. 'That would have really *hurt*,' she said, with wide-open eyes.

'Serve you right, you thief. Next time I'll get you.'

'You're so horrible, Ben. Why can't you be kind and nice like Wilf?'

'It's not in my character,' he said, inwardly wincing at his own words. Basically, he believed, he was actually a perfectly benign and patient person. It was simply that young sisters were a trial that nobody with a morsel of self-respect could endure quietly. Which suggested that Wilf was a doormat, a martyr and a wimp for putting up with them.

He gobbled down the rest of his breakfast, shielding it ferociously from the deplorable Natalie. Then he went back up to his room in a sour mood. Why couldn't he have been an only child, he wondered for the thousandth time. Wilf wasn't so bad, he supposed – his parents could have stopped after two, then, and saved the world a whole lot of grief.

For want of anything else to do before he could decently call in on DI Moxon, he sat down to have a look at the Catullus. It was reasonably interesting stuff, once you got into it, with some very direct rude language in it. Most of the vocabulary was familiar to him. The man wrote over a hundred poems, in which he managed to cover most of human experience, but the ones to his friends in which he threatened buggery were a bit strong. Mr Brent agreed, and suggested Ben concentrate on something slightly blander. Ben had a sneaking admiration for poetry and had turned his hand to writing some of his own, once in a while.

In defiance of his teacher's advice, he was working on 'A Warning: to Aurelius'. He scrupulously avoided other people's translations until he'd arrived at one of his own, which turned the whole exercise into something of a game.

He had reached the ninth line, where things became decidedly graphic – *'uerum a te metuo tuoque pene'* – and was very thankful not to be studying the poem in a class full of sniggering boys. Even the dimmest one was likely to find an easy translation of the word *'pene'*. 'Yes, Higgins,' the teacher would sigh. 'It does mean what you think it means.' The poet was warning his friend off his own 'boy' in the most straightforward fashion. It wasn't a very subtle matter, after all. The last two lines, as far as Ben could tell at a quick glance, were a very graphic threat as to the revenge Catullus would wreak if Aurelius ignored the warning.

Sex, romance, pairing up – it was all unknown territory to Ben personally. Girls shied away from him, on the whole, nervous of his fearsome intelligence. People became stupidly jealous for no reason. They leapt to paranoid conclusions on the basis of a look or a word. They suffered agonies through misunderstandings that could easily be settled by a direct question. It was all a major distraction from the important things in life, as far as he could see. And yet here was Catullus two thousand years after his lifetime, still studied and admired because he wrote down, in plain language, the basic emotions that humans struggled with.

'Hmm,' he muttered to himself, and wrote 'I'm scared of you and your dick' as his translation of line nine. Then he checked two existing translations, on websites he'd bookmarked a week ago. 'You are the one I fear, you and your penis' seemed seriously clunky to him. And 'truly my fear is of you and your cock' struck him as unduly convoluted. 'Onwards,' Ben told himself, moving to line ten. This one was simpler, with line eleven the really crude one. *'infesto pueris bonis malisque'* required careful attention to the cases, but *'quem tu qua lubet, ut lubet moueto'* had a wicked poetry to it which called for a translation that would do it justice.

At nine-thirty, he lifted his head from the work and looked at his bedside clock. Furiously, he grabbed his murder flow chart and ran downstairs. Throwing on his thickest hooded jacket, he left the house without further delay.

The police station was on the southern edge of Windermere, or the northern edge of Bowness. It was only a few minutes' walk from his house. Just before he got there, he saw two people going in. One of them was impossible to mistake.

The tall figure of Solomon Samalar was strolling in a relaxed sort of way through the entrance, with a much smaller younger woman at his side, who looked very downcast. As if drawn by a string, Ben followed.

Inside, the man spoke to a police officer on the desk. 'I believe Inspector Moxon is expecting me. My name is Samalar.' He made no reference to the woman, who leant forward and said something softly, which Ben couldn't hear. The officer nodded, and lifted up a phone. Ben hovered in the doorway, suddenly aware of the ambivalence of his position. While a police station was to some extent a public place, it was not customary to enter one without due purpose. Simply following someone and trying to hear what they said did not constitute a valid reason for being there. And if Moxo was interviewing these people, he'd have no time for Ben. With an awkward little shrug – which he didn't think anybody saw – he turned and went back into the street.

Nothing for it, then, but to carry on northwards to Simmy's shop. It was another ten minutes at least, past the Baddeley clock tower and into the town centre. Melanie would be there and the three of them could share all their findings and impressions about the case. They could reinvigorate the old gang, as he thought of them, and possibly plan some kind of action. The fact that Wilf had gone up to Coniston without him, with the express intention of looking for clues, niggled at him. That was *his* sort of thing, not his brother's. Wilf was a cook, not a detective.

It really was a very cold day, with a nasty wind blowing. He pulled the hood over his ears and wished he'd brought some gloves. His feet were cold, as well, in somewhat inadequate trainers. Why didn't men wear fur-lined boots like women did, he wondered? The many follies of fashion had always been an annoyance to him. As a small boy he had loved dressing in frilly nylon frocks that the nursery kept in the dressing-up box. He still thought women had a far better deal when it came to clothes.

It was shortly after ten o'clock when he got to Persimmon Petals. There were three women in the shop – Simmy, Melanie and Simmy's mother. Ben felt a leap of anticipation at the sight of Angie. He liked her, from what he had seen and heard of her, especially at Christmas. The fact that Simmy had a mother not totally unlike his own gave him an additional sense of fellowship with her. Angie was straight-talking, sure of herself and dependable in a crisis. His own mother was not entirely reliable on this last count. Her work mattered enormously to her, and there had been several times when she gave it priority over her family. Her attitude tended to be that where there were five children, they could surely watch out for each other, without troubling her too much.

'Morning, Mr Harkness,' Angie said now, with a friendly smile. 'Cold for the time of year.'

'Certainly is,' he agreed. 'My toes are frozen.'

It wasn't very warm in the shop, either. Flowers objected to excessive heat and while the back room was kept deliberately cool, the shop was never very much better.

'Well, I'm not staying. Don't get into any mischief, will you – you three. There was quite enough of that at Christmas. Maybe see you tomorrow, P'simmon. Come for tea, if you can. I've got a great big fruit cake that one of my returners brought.'

'Sounds tempting,' said Simmy. 'But I keep telling you not to count on me. I'm even more determined

271

to stay in bed all day tomorrow, after this excessively energetic week.'

Angie nodded carelessly, and went out. They watched as she turned up her collar and ducked her head as the wind bit at her on the pavement. 'Think what it must be like on the fells,' she called back, before the door closed behind her.

'Returners?' queried Melanie.

'People who keep coming back for the B&B. She's got lots of them. They think of themselves as sort of family and bring presents. I have no idea who most of them are, although I've gleaned a few names.'

'Guess who I've just seen, going into the cop shop,' Ben burst out. Then, before giving them a chance to speak, he went on, 'That Solomon chap, and a woman. Seems he had an appointment to talk to old Moxo. Didn't look too bothered about it.'

Simmy and Melanie looked at him with very different expressions. Melanie's eyes widened with excitement, plainly happy to be getting straight to something interesting. Simmy's eyes actually closed for a few seconds and her head shook gently from side to side. 'Oh, Lord,' she sighed. 'Do we have to?'

'Was it the Drury woman?' Melanie asked. 'Middle height, dyed hair, kind of copper colour? Mid thirties sort of age.'

'Nope,' said Ben with certainty. 'This one was about twenty-six, five foot one and curly fair hair.'

'Wow! Who on earth could that have been, then?'

'It looked as if he didn't know her too well. Friendly, but no more than that. He left her to introduce herself.'

'You were in there as well?' Simmy demanded. 'Why?'

'I followed them,' he said brazenly.

'And then what?'

'I came out again. I don't think anybody noticed me.'

Simmy tutted and Ben smirked at her.

'There's been a development this morning,' said Melanie importantly. 'Sim's friend Kathy's up at Coniston somewhere and wants her to meet there at 12.30.'

'So she's not missing any more, then?' To his shame he had completely forgotten about Kathy. Grown women getting lost didn't really fit with his flow chart, and he had never entertained the idea that Kathy might be involved in the Coniston murder. All the same, now he thought about it, there was a very odd coincidence going on. 'Why's she in Coniston?' Then he remembered. 'Oh – her daughter's working there, isn't she? That must be it.'

'Actually, no, not really. Joanna came in early today, with the chap who's in charge of their project – whatever it is – and told me a totally different story.'

'Different from what?'

Simmy rubbed her forehead. 'I can't remember how much you know from yesterday,' she admitted. 'It was all such a whirl, with you, Ninian, Moxon and that man from Newby Bridge all coming and going. Not to mention Joanna Colhoun and Mrs Crabtree. I know you weren't here for them.' She had a thought. 'Could the girl you saw just now be Joanna, I wonder? Long fair hair, kinky rather than curly. Maybe it was . . . although I don't see why she would be with Mr Samalar.'

'This was definitely curly hair. And Joanna's younger than twenty-five, isn't she? This one looks a bit like Scarlett Johansson.'

Melanie snorted. 'Gorgeous, then.'

'If you like,' shrugged Ben, still carrying thoughts of Catullus and men engaging in sex with boys.

Simmy was still running through everything that had taken place since she last saw Ben. 'Yesterday seems *ages* ago now. The past twenty-four hours would fill a whole book, with all the things that happened and people I've seen. Even my mother's been in twice during that time. I can't think why.'

'She's worried about you,' said Melanie. 'After last time.'

Outside, the wind had virtually cleared the streets of shoppers. The prospect of any customers was receding rapidly. 'You don't really need to be here,' Simmy told Melanie. 'It's going to be a very slow morning.'

'I'm staying,' said Melanie firmly. 'If it's as quiet as all that, you can go up to Coniston now and see if you can find Kathy. Except,' she added, 'I want to go with you.'

'So do I,' said Ben.

'I'm not closing up yet. It's not even half past ten. We'll have to stick it out until twelve at the earliest, which still gives us just enough time to do what Kathy wants.'

Melanie and Ben exchanged astonished looks. 'You'll let us both come, then?' said the boy. 'Gosh!'

'Last I heard, you were refusing to go at all,' said Melanie.

'You persuaded me. And you can both come with me on condition you, Ben, tell your parents where you're going. And you, Mel – will they be wondering where you are?' Melanie was assumed to be an independent adult by her parents, but her family relied on her so heavily that her movements were often quite constrained.

'No problem,' she said. 'They'll be glad to have me out of the way.'

'Me too,' echoed Ben. 'And I did half my homework before breakfast.'

'I don't believe you,' said Melanie.

'Okay – it was *after* breakfast – which I had before eight o'clock, actually.'

'But I'm not sure I want you hanging about here all morning,' Simmy added. 'Especially not if you're going to go on about murder all the time.'

He puffed out his cheeks in protest. 'So where do you want me to go? It's freezing out there.'

She hesitated, but before she could answer, the door flew open and her mother rushed back in. 'P'simmon! You'd better come. Something's going on out here that probably concerns you.'

# CHAPTER SIXTEEN

Quelling her instinct to panic, Simmy followed her mother outside, expecting to see crumpled cars in the road, or perhaps people fighting. Instead, there was a white-faced girl leaning against the wall of a shop a few yards along the street. 'She says she knows you,' Angie panted. 'I found her just about to faint, down by the lights. We were walking up here, but she can't seem to get any further than this. I don't know what's the matter with her, but at least you can take her in and give her somewhere to sit. And a drink. We might have to call an ambulance if she doesn't get any better.'

It was Joanna. 'Where's Baz?' Simmy asked.

The girl merely shook her head and whimpered. Her lips were blue. 'Come on, then,' said Simmy. 'If we take a side each, we can walk you to the shop. It's only a few yards away.'

Angie and Simmy almost carried Joanna to the shop, and dropped her into the upright chair at the back, where people would sometimes sit and chat with Simmy. It had no arms, and the girl had difficulty staying upright. 'What on earth happened to her?' Simmy wanted to know.

'Pity you can't call her mother,' said Melanie.

'What? You *do* know her, then?' Angie said. 'She was mumbling your name when I found her, so I assumed she was trying to reach you.'

'She's Kathy's daughter. You know – my friend Kathy from Worcester. She's staying up here for the weekend because Joanna's doing some college work at Coniston. It's all got a bit complicated,' she finished weakly. 'Jo! What happened to you? What's the matter?' She put her face close to the girl's and spoke loudly.

'Thank goodness for that,' said Angie. 'If her mother's here, she can take over.' She looked around the shop. 'So where is she?'

Joanna showed no sign of hearing anything that was said, letting her head droop forward like an unwatered flower. Her long hair fell over her face.

'Has she got a weak heart?' Angie wanted to know. 'I don't like those blue lips.'

'Melanie, can you call an ambulance?' Simmy asked her assistant. 'She's practically unconscious.'

Ben was standing well back, aware of his limitations when it came to medical matters. He might be taking A-level biology, but he had no idea what to do in a case like this.

'Listen – I need to be somewhere,' said Angie. 'You can manage from here, can't you?'

Simmy merely flapped a hand at her mother and kept her eyes on Joanna's face. Did young girls have heart attacks? Or heart *failure*? Was it just a drastic case of shock? Or some sort of allergic reaction to something? The last seemed the most probable. 'Maybe there's a card in her bag saying she's got some sort of condition,' she muttered. 'Has she *got* a bag?'

'What?' Only Ben had heard her. 'No – doesn't look like it. Try her pockets.'

'But I *know* her,' Simmy insisted to herself. 'I'd know if she was diabetic or hyper-allergic. Kathy would have told me.' All the same, she pushed probing fingers into the pockets of the girl's coat, finding nothing but a tissue and a phone.

'Give that to me,' said Ben. 'She might have an app to do with allergies or whatever, that would give us a clue.'

Simmy's knowledge of apps was sketchy at best, despite Melanie's efforts to educate her on the subject. She handed the phone to Ben.

Melanie was speaking with impressive composure to an operator. 'Ambulance. It's a girl, early twenties, almost unconscious. We have no idea what happened to her. She was outside in the street and more or less fainted, as far as we can tell. She hasn't said anything.' And then a series of yes/no replies, during which she checked with Simmy for some further information. 'Is her skin clammy? . . . Are her eyes open? . . . Is she breathing regularly?'

Apparently the answers were sufficiently alarming for a swift response. 'No, there's no reason to think she was attacked . . . although there was a man with her, and he seems to have disappeared.'

Until then, Simmy hadn't given Baz a single thought. Could this have something to do with him? It was impossible to see how.

'They'll be five or six minutes,' Melanie reported. 'Probably there'll be police as well.'

'For heaven's sake, why?'

'Incident in the street,' Ben supplied. 'That's their responsibility. And they'll want to know exactly what happened.'

'I don't see why,' Simmy grumbled again. 'It's obvious that no laws have been broken.'

'Unless she's been poisoned,' said the irrepressible boy.

'The most likely thing is a diabetic coma,' said Melanie. 'Don't you think?'

'If it is diabetes, she's only recently developed it. Isn't she terribly young for that?'

Melanie shrugged. 'Little kids have it sometimes.'

'She'd have a card, and an emergency bar of

chocolate,' said Simmy. 'Wouldn't she? What about a thing for the insulin?' She was angry with herself for her own ignorance, and gave Joanna a little shake. 'Jo! Can you hear me? Are you diabetic? Can you nod or shake your head?'

Joanna roused slightly, but her eyes were unfocused and her breathing laboured. She shook her head minimally, but said nothing.

'Was that a no?' Simmy consulted the others.

'Looked like it. I don't think you go cold and clammy like that with diabetes,' said Ben dubiously. 'I read that somewhere.'

Without any warning siren, there was suddenly an ambulance parked right outside the shop. A man and a woman walked in briskly, their yellow jackets brash and artificial amongst the softer colours of the flowers. The woman literally pushed Simmy out of the way to get to Joanna.

'Anaphylactic,' muttered the man. 'Severe.'

The woman opened a box she carried with her, and took something out. 'Epinephrine,' she said, and pulled up one of Joanna's sleeves. 'Hey! Look at this.'

Everyone leant forward and Simmy caught sight of a tattoo, which she could not decipher. 'The symbol for allergy and latex,' the medic announced. 'That's it, then.'

She administered an injection and dabbed at the spot. 'Vitals?' she asked the man.

He was doing something with a portable electronic gadget, from which he read several numbers. 'Okay, we're off,' said the woman. 'I'll get the chair.'

Joanna was transferred into a wheelchair and onto a lift at the back of the ambulance. As far as Simmy could see, her condition was not much improved. She automatically followed, assuming she would be needed in some capacity. The male medic produced another electronic gadget. 'What's her name? Next of kin? Address?' Simmy supplied all three answers, though minus the Colhoun family's postcode. 'She's been staying up here for a week or so. Her mother's here as well. I'll find her and tell her to contact you. Where are you taking her?'

'Kendal or Barrow. We'll get instructions when we phone it in.'

Simmy closed her eyes for a moment against a rush of recent memories. 'Okay,' she said.

'We'll need your number, as a contact.'

She gave him landlines for home and work, plus mobile for good measure. 'I hope you can get her right,' she said fatuously. 'Thank you.'

They sped off without a friendly word, and she struggled to think charitably of them. The initial push had been quite unnecessary, and quite hard to forgive.

'What's all this then?' came a familiar voice from behind her.

'Nothing for you to worry about,' she said, before she'd even turned round. 'She's allergic to latex, apparently.'

'Simmy,' he said softly, with a very human reproach in his voice. She waited, but nothing more was said. When she looked at him, it was with the tiniest worm of distaste for his long head and lank hair. His eyes were slightly magnified by his spectacles and looked moist. He wore a thick jacket that could do with a clean.

'They needn't have sent you,' she said, trying to be kind. 'You must have better things to do.'

Then Ben came out of the shop at a trot, grinning at the detective and obviously eager to speak. 'Hey!' he began. 'Who was that girl with the African bloke? I saw them this morning.'

Moxon's nostrils tightened as he wrenched his gaze from Simmy's face. 'Pardon?' he said.

'*You* know. They must have gone to tell you something about the murder. That's obvious. So who *was* she?'

'Truly, son, it doesn't concern you. You can't just demand to know details of an investigation like this. It's about as out of order as you can get.'

Ben was unimpressed. 'Yes, I know. But this is me. And Simmy. After all, you've shown up here – again. Doesn't that mean we're involved? What harm can it do to tell us?'

Moxon sighed. 'Not much, probably. All right – it was Miss Daisy Hayter, soon to be Mrs James Goff.'

'Daughter of the man who killed himself!' flashed Ben. 'So how does she know the Solomon character?'

The second sigh was much deeper. 'Her fiancé used to be in a relationship with Selena Drury, who is now with Mr Samalar. They came to explain to me that the Valentine flowers sent to Miss Drury were from Mr Goff, who was having a kind of pre-wedding panic, and wanted to be absolutely sure he was doing the right thing.'

'Duh!' scoffed Ben. 'What a plonker!'

'That's not for me to say. The only relevant point is that the mystery is now resolved, and has nothing at all to do with the murder.'

'Doesn't it?' Ben frowned. 'Don't you think the fact that Daisy's so closely linked with it might mean something? After all, she is the daughter of the housemate of the murder victim.'

'Hang on,' said Melanie. 'This is very interesting. If the girl's father's dead, does that mean they'll postpone the wedding? And might the bridegroom be having serious second thoughts about it? Sounds to me as if they've swopped partners. Solomon and Daisy, Goff and Selena,' she summarised with a chuckle.

Moxon gave her a frown of some severity. 'What would any of that have to do with Mr Braithwaite?'

'I have no idea. Probably nothing. But I don't see how you can just scrub them off your list of suspects.'

'Maybe the prospect of losing his daughter to the man called Goff drove Mr Hayter to suicide,' said Ben. 'But I don't agree with the inspector – it does seem to me to connect to the murder.'

'Let's hope not,' said Simmy. 'After all, the flowers for Selena were sent *after* both men died, so they can't have been directly linked, can they?'

'Precisely,' said Moxon emphatically.

'And they were ordered well before the deaths,' Melanie pointed out.

'You're right. I was thinking what a rotten thing to do,' Simmy said slowly. 'I mean – when your fiancée's suddenly lost her father and needs all the love and support you can give, to send Valentine flowers to a former girlfriend at her present partner's address would be terrible. It's fairly sick, anyway, but not as awful as it could have been, if we're really right about the timing. She probably doesn't want to marry him now, even so. I know I wouldn't.' She thought of the way her husband had let her down in comparable circumstances. 'He's never going to be there when she needs him.'

'I think I've remembered him at last,' said Melanie, with some excitement. 'It was the long coat that put me off. Has he got a very high forehead? And a squeaky laugh?'

285

'I haven't met him, so I don't know,' said Moxon. 'But I agree he sounds rather dubious husband material. He runs his own business supplying solar panels.'

Ben made a scornful sound and Moxon turned to him. 'Most likely the bloke who tried to swindle my mother. Doing well, is he?'

'As far as I know, he is. We get a lot more sun up here than people realise.'

Ben opened his mouth to argue the point, but Melanie tapped his arm and shook her head. 'Leave it,' she said. Ben, to Simmy's surprise, obeyed her.

Moxon pressed his hands together, as if drawing things to a sort of conclusion. 'Anyway, as I say, none of that has any bearing on the investigation.'

Melanie and Ben both kept their counsel, exchanging a glance that made Simmy think of intrigue in the playground. She and Moxon were inescapably the adults in the room, holding the bounds of good sense and due focus.

'And what about *Kathy*?' Simmy groaned. 'It's even more important to find her, now Joanna's poorly.'

Moxon gave her his full attention. 'I'm sorry. Is she still missing? I rather assumed, when I didn't hear from you early today, that that particular problem had resolved itself.'

Simmy felt a painful inner conflict. On the one hand, her instinct was to tell him the whole story about the email and the visit from Baz and Jo that morning. On the other, she wanted to save him extra work, as well as belatedly obeying Kathy's injunction to keep the police out of it. She compromised with a brief summary. 'She emailed me, making a lunchtime appointment,' she said. 'So I think we can assume she's okay. I've still got no idea where she's been or what was going on.'

'But it's all under control now?' said Moxon.

'I've just thought of something,' said Melanie slowly. 'We never talk about poor Mr Braithwaite, do we? He should be the *only* one we really care about and yet we've barely even said his name so far.' She gave Moxon a wide-eyed look of enquiry. 'That's not right, is it?'

The detective smiled at her. 'Very creditable, I'm sure, but you needn't worry. There's a great deal of police work going on behind the scenes. You don't see it, over on this side of the lake, but Coniston is buzzing, I can assure you.'

'I bet that Pamela Johnson's having a fine old time, then.'

'Who's Pamela Johnson?'

Simmy answered for Melanie. 'The woman I told you about in Coniston. The one who sent the flowers to Maggie Aston. She says the police questioned her.' She wanted to add *Do keep up*, but bit it back. There was bound to be a whole team of police detectives working on the case,

287

with nobody apprised of every detail.

'Of course,' he nodded. 'I didn't speak to her personally.'

'She came here early today, saying much the same sort of thing as Mrs Crabtree. Neither of them enjoyed their police questioning.' She smiled. 'I must say, you made it all quite easy the first time it happened to me.'

'It's *never* happened to me,' said Melanie, with a hint of envy. 'I always miss the most exciting parts.'

'You saw Selena Drury last night,' Simmy reminded her. 'That must have been quite exciting.'

'More than waiting for Joe to say something interesting, that's for sure.'

Moxon cleared his throat. 'Selena Drury? Don't tell me . . . girlfriend of the Somali bloke. Where was she last night, then?'

'Kendal. Having an Indian meal with Ninian Tripp. And no – you don't need to know who he is. He isn't involved in anything. His sister was – is – Selena's friend, that's all.'

'At least she wasn't with Daisy's fiancé,' said Ben. 'Where was he, I wonder? Out kidnapping your mate Kathy, I expect,' he answered his own question.

Moxon's groan was closer to a howl of rage. 'Kidnapping? Who said anything about kidnapping?'

Simmy couldn't remember exactly what she had told him about Kathy, but she thought there might have been some faint implication of the sort. His refusal to pay serious attention to her friend was both hurtful and a relief. Neither did he seem at all concerned about poor Joanna and her anaphylaxis or whatever it was. A thought occurred to her, causing her to bite her lip.

'What?' demanded Melanie.

'Latex. What's made of that, then?' She eyed the youngsters apprehensively, wishing she'd never had the idea.

'Condoms,' said Ben brightly, with another flash of Catullus before his eyes. 'She must have been having sex with someone.'

'Baz,' nodded Simmy.

'Off for a quickie, the moment they left here!' gasped Melanie.

'Er . . . ?' Moxon attempted.

'Nothing for you to worry about,' Simmy said quickly. 'They're not breaking any laws.'

'Just university regulations,' said Melanie sourly. Then she added with a grin, 'Fancy being allergic to that. Isn't that what you call nemesis?'

'I suppose it is.' Simmy smiled in spite of herself.

Ben glared impatiently at them all. 'So – what about Mr Braithwaite?' he reverted to the earlier issue. 'We're still not talking about the most important thing.'

Moxon made a strange gesture with his elbows, which was the closest Simmy had ever seen to somebody throwing up their hands. The meaning was plain: he had had enough. 'I knew all along I shouldn't have come,' he muttered. 'But when I heard the call for an ambulance go out, I didn't have much option. Not when I heard the address.'

Simmy almost felt like comforting him. He seemed young and confused and oddly embarrassed. 'It's all a big muddle,' she said. 'But you're sure to catch whoever did it, in the end.'

'It's just a matter of seeing the big picture,' said Melanie.

All three of them looked at her. Simmy had been told from the first – by DI Moxon – that seeing the big picture was her special talent. Ben reminded her of it repeatedly, in Melanie's hearing. Now the girl was producing it with a straight face as if it was the single thing the police detective had to bear in mind.

Ben laughed. 'She's right,' he said. 'All these flower deliveries and mean messages are a smokescreen. They're not the important stuff at all. We've already decided they have nothing whatever to do with the Hayter and Braithwaite business.'

Nobody answered him at first. There was an implied insolence in his tone, but his words were quite possibly a very accurate summary of the situation. Then Moxon spoke heavily. 'A smokescreen implies a deliberate concealment of the truth. If that's what you mean, then they are relevant, aren't they?'

Ben puffed out his cheeks. 'S'pose so,' he admitted.

'In any case, I trust you can depend on us to make all the appropriate investigations? Whether or not that includes those people named to us by Ms Brown is for us to decide – don't you agree?'

Ben nodded, his face reddening. 'Sorry,' he mumbled.

'No problem, sonny. Just try to keep in mind where the line comes, all right? And while we're about it, I could also suggest that a little more respect for the dead wouldn't come amiss. I understand how it is – it happens with some of my younger colleagues as well – but the fact is, there's nothing more serious than the taking of a life. Try to imagine how you'd feel if it was your own brother, or even an uncle you don't often see. You can't, I know. So let me tell you it's a very big thing.'

*Poor Ben*, thought Simmy. He'd had a week of being put in his place by various people. But she was on Moxon's side, more or less. Ben *had* been flippant, when he shouldn't have been. 'He's learning,' she said, putting an unwise arm around the boy's shoulders. 'Enough of the lecture, okay?'

Ben wriggled free and moved to the back of the shop. Melanie gave Simmy a small shake of her head, warning her to leave him alone. Simmy felt overwhelmed by the need to coddle fragile male egos; Moxon wasn't much better than the boy.

'I'd better go,' said the detective again. 'You'll be wanting to get some work done.' The total absence of any customers during the time he'd been there was impossible to ignore. Simmy felt a fraud, like a child merely playing at shopkeeping.

The three of them watched him go, their heads swirling with names and theories and the solemn facts of murder.

# CHAPTER SEVENTEEN

'He's right,' said Simmy. 'Might as well shut up shop for the day. We're just wasting time here.'

'You can't,' said Melanie. 'It's only half past eleven. Loads of people could come in yet.'

'They won't, though, will they? And I should be doing something about telling Kathy about Joanna. Whatever daft game she's playing, she'll want to know what's happened.'

'What if they've taken Joanna to Barrow?' said Ben. 'If Kathy's car's out of action, she'll never get there to visit.'

'I can take her.' The prospect of a two-hour round trip did nothing for Simmy's delicate bones, which began aching in anticipation. 'I suppose. After I've found her in Coniston.'

'We're all stunned,' said Melanie. 'Look at us – just standing here, with no idea what happens next.

But I bet they've taken Jo to Kendal, not Barrow. She'll have responded to that jab they gave her by now, and just need observation for a bit.'

Simmy and Ben offered no argument to this. 'Sounds as if you know the routine,' said Ben.

'When you've got as many relatives as I have you learn a lot about medical services. I've got four grandparents, five great-aunts and uncles and about twenty assorted cousins and siblings. They're all pretty accident-prone. Kendal hasn't got a casualty department, but they do most other things. It's nice in there.'

'How will we find out?' Simmy had a vision of Joanna languishing in a strange ward somewhere and nobody knowing where she was.

'She'll phone somebody. Her dad, probably.'

Simmy remembered Moxon's gesture, as if throwing everything aside, and was tempted to do the same. 'I'm furious with Kathy,' she realised. 'Going off in the middle of everything. What on earth has possessed her?'

'I think she really might have been kidnapped,' said Ben warily. His wounded feelings were recovering rather slowly. 'It would explain quite a lot.'

'Kidnapped by who?' Simmy demanded angrily. 'Nobody up here even knows her. And people don't get kidnapped in real life, do they? Only the children of millionaires, and even then it's about once every twenty years.'

'*Something's* going on with her, though, isn't it?' Ben retorted. 'After we've had murder and suicide and malicious messages, why is kidnap such a daft idea?'

'Good question,' nodded Melanie. 'And the answers to the whole thing could easily lie with whatever's happened to Kathy. And that means we have to go now and find her in Coniston. All of us,' she finished firmly.

'Wilf and Scott are there already,' Ben belatedly told them. 'They might have found something.'

'What do you mean, Wilf and Scott are there?' demanded Simmy.

'They're fell walking up there somewhere,' said Ben with a grimace. 'Because of Mr Hayter's death, sort of.'

'I can't imagine what you think they could have found,' said Simmy. 'How do you find evidence to explain a suicide, for heaven's sake? He's not going to leave a note tucked under a stone out on the fells, is he?'

Ben smiled at the image. 'Probably not. I think, really, they just wanted to get out there as a change of scene. Wilf likes to do that when he can.'

'In a freezing cold gale?' Simmy objected. 'It must be absolutely awful out there today.' She peered outside, angling her head to see the sky above the buildings. 'Look at the way those clouds are racing past!' She shivered. 'No way am I going any further than the centre of Coniston.'

'You might change your mind when you've heard what Kathy has to say,' Melanie suggested. 'Sounds as if she's got quite a story to tell.'

Simmy said nothing, but started carrying flowers from the shop into the room at the back, where they would sit in the chilly temperatures until Monday morning. A few red roses remained, which she planned to incorporate into bouquets early the next week. Idly, she assembled a rich colour scheme more appropriate to autumn than spring, adding some rather gaudy tulips that had been forced in a foreign field. It made her think of her own neglected garden in Troutbeck, where there would be frothy white blossom on the blackthorn and hawthorn that formed her hedge, in another month or two. Most of the colour tended to yellows and white, even in summer, and she found herself planning bolder hues for the coming seasons.

Why, she asked herself, couldn't she be left in peace to do her modest cultivating, instead of being forced to rush around the country lanes in a car with a broken wing mirror? If Melanie and Ben were both coming, she couldn't take the van. The whole Coniston business might well have nothing whatever to do with her, if Ben was right in thinking the floral deliveries were simply a smokescreen. Kathy was, of course, the answer. Somehow her friend had got into trouble, and Simmy's assistance was required. There had even been a hint, expressed by Ben, if she remembered rightly, that Kathy was in fact involved with Mr Braithwaite's murder. She could have seen something on Thursday that meant she had to be kept silent. Apparently nobody had set eyes on her friend for twenty-four hours. She sighed in resignation. When it came to the crunch, she knew she really did want to find out the truth. She just didn't want to get hurt or scared in the process.

Ben had followed Simmy to the front of the shop when she went to look at the sky. Now he shouted, 'Oh – there she is!' and pulled the door open before anyone could react.

'There who is?' asked Melanie.

'A girl,' said Simmy. 'Look.'

Ben had approached a fair-headed young woman bundled in a big black coat, as she walked along the pavement with her head down. She stopped and stared at him when he spoke. Simmy and Melanie could just hear him urging, 'Please come in for a minute. We'd really like to talk to you.'

'I bet I know who that is,' said Melanie.

Simmy's mind was working more slowly. All she could think was that it was one of Joanna's college friends, working up at Coniston. But then, how would Ben know her?

Unprotestingly, the newcomer followed Ben into the shop. 'This is Daisy Hayter,' he said. 'I saw you earlier on at the police station,' he explained. 'With Solomon Samalar.'

Daisy looked around the shop in bewilderment. 'Why do you want to talk to me?' she asked. 'Who are you all?'

Even Ben had difficulty in answering that coherently. Simmy did her best to concentrate, wondering what indirect connection they could justifiably claim with this person – who did indeed resemble Scarlett Johansson, with pretty pouting lips and curly fair hair. The boy made an impressive attempt to explain. 'We know about your father, you see,' he began. 'And the other man, Mr Braithwaite. They lived together – didn't they? Your father went missing. We know he died. We're very sorry,' he went on clumsily. 'It must have been horrible for you. We know you're getting married, as well.'

Daisy took a step backwards. 'That doesn't tell me anything. What do you *want*?'

'Well . . .' Ben turned to Simmy for rescue. 'Nothing, really. We just . . .'

Simmy stepped in. 'I took some flowers addressed to your father to the Coniston house last Monday. They had a message wishing him well in his new job. But I gave them to the other man, because he told me he was Mr Hayter. Then on Thursday, the police asked me to tell them whether the other man, when he'd been murdered, was the one I gave the flowers to. And he was.'

'Well done, Sim,' murmured Melanie. 'Clear as mud.'

But Daisy seemed to have found a glimmer of reason in the little speech. 'Tim,' she said. 'My father was his tenant. They didn't really live together in the way you mean.'

'That's not what the neighbours thought,' said Melanie.

Daisy ignored her. 'I remember seeing the flowers, when I went there with Uncle Nolan on Wednesday. But we didn't find a card with them. Did you say they were for a new job? That doesn't make any sense. He wasn't starting a new job.' Her voice faltered, and tears filled her eyes. 'Unless you count battling against oesophageal cancer a new job.' She stumbled over the long word, leaving out at least one syllable.

'Oh dear,' said Simmy. 'Come and sit down.' She rolled her eyes at the others, warning them to stay quiet and not make things worse. Daisy passively did as Simmy ordered, mopping her eyes with a tissue and sniffing.

'Sorry,' she said. 'It's all very raw. My mother's being so awful, as well as James being such a plonker. They're both just making it all worse.' She attempted a rueful laugh. 'And then Tim gets himself killed, on top of everything else. It was bad enough before that, but now . . .'

'It must be overwhelming,' said Simmy, trying to reconcile the 'Uncle Nolan' person with DI Moxon.

'It is,' Daisy agreed wholeheartedly. 'Just one horrible thing after another. Now I don't even know whether I'm really getting married on Saturday. I don't know if I even *want* to.'

'I did the other flowers as well,' Simmy admitted. 'Which is why I know so much of the story.'

'What? What flowers are you talking about now?'

*Oh God*, thought Simmy. Didn't she know about that? Hadn't Moxon just said that she did? Yes, he definitely had. 'The ones to Miss Drury . . . from your fiancé, Mr Goff. James, is it?'

'Did you? That was such a rotten thing for James to do. What was he *thinking*?'

'Have you asked him?'

'I can't find him.'

'Is he *missing*?' Ben demanded, unable to stay quiet another moment.

Daisy lifted her head proudly. 'Of course not. What do you mean?'

'Well . . .'

'My *father* was missing. Nobody knew where he was. He went out onto the fells on Monday night and died there from an overdose and exposure. He wasn't found until Wednesday. It's

300

not like that with James. He's just . . . worried. Nervous. Overwhelmed,' she concluded with a grateful look at Simmy. 'And he wanted to make a point, I think.'

'A point?' Simmy said, puzzled.

'Oh – it's hard to explain. Men have always chased after me, since I was about sixteen. I've been engaged a couple of times before, actually. One was to Jasper Braithwaite, Tim's son. He's really nice, but I realised I couldn't marry him when he decided to become a vet. I mean – I just wasn't ready for that sort of life. He's doing farm animals, you see.'

'Not really,' murmured Simmy. 'Are you scared of cows or something?'

Daisy smiled weakly. 'It's not that. But I want to live in a city, with plenty of night life and music and all that. James has his own business. He's doing very well for himself.' She lifted her chin defiantly. 'I'm going to handle all his paperwork for him. We'll be partners in every sense.'

'Who was the other one?' asked Ben suddenly.

'The other what?'

'Fiancé.'

'Oh, that was a really bad mistake. He was before Jasper, when I was only eighteen. My dad was absolutely furious about it, which made me more stubborn, of course. It all seemed so romantic at the time.' She looked wistful. 'He was much older than me, lived in a little cottage miles from anywhere, making pots, living on virtually nothing.'

Simmy's heart pounded painfully. Melanie spoke for her. 'He wasn't called Ninian, was he?'

'What? No, no. His name's Jeremy. He's gone now. He emigrated to South America or somewhere, years ago.'

It took a while for Simmy's pulse rate to subside, and even longer for her to talk herself into a calmer frame of mind. Implications were pressing in on all sides, but this was not the moment to address them.

Daisy also gave herself a little shake. 'Why are we talking about me, anyway?' she wondered. 'You were telling me about the flowers that somebody sent to my dad, on the day he died. And you don't know who – right? I mean, nobody ever does that, do they? Send flowers to a grown man, wishing him luck in a job he wasn't going to have. It's mean and nasty. It might even have driven him to do what he did.'

'I hope not,' said Simmy faintly.

'It's okay – it wouldn't be your fault. Didn't somebody say that all suicides are selfish by definition? I've been thinking about that and it's true. He couldn't have given a thought to my wedding when he did it. That makes me so *angry* with him.' She wept gently. 'But I'm also terribly sorry for him. They told him the cancer would kill him by Christmas and he wouldn't be able to eat properly for the rest of his life. He was already awfully thin. And he hated hospitals and pills and having to rely on somebody to look after him. So I can't exactly blame him for what he did. Especially with my mother making everything worse.'

'Were they divorced?' Simmy asked.

'Separated. She's got another man now, ten years younger than her. Bill, he's called. He's a builder.' She giggled miserably. 'Bill the builder. He's not very nice.'

'What about Tim?' Ben asked, with a cautious glance at Simmy. He seemed to think that questions were allowed now that Daisy had started to make disclosures almost without prompting.

'What about him?'

'He was *murdered*. Somebody stabbed him in the back with a long knife. That's the only thing the police are interested in. You're probably one of the few people who see how all this connects up – if it does. You're really *important* to the case.'

'Ben! For heaven's sake!' Simmy gripped his arm and shook him.

Again Daisy showed a fighting spirit. 'He's right, though. You two are clever, aren't you?' She looked from Ben to Melanie and back. 'I get your point. Poor old Dad's been upstaged by Tim Braithwaite – again. They've never been proper friends. Dad always blamed bad luck for the way he constantly got the short straw. He lost three jobs before he was forty and ended up driving vans for a living, which he hated. Tim was rich and successful. When Mum threw him out, Tim came to the rescue, letting him live in his house, but that wasn't working out. Then the cancer got him. When you think back over his life, it isn't even very surprising.'

'Poor bloke,' said Melanie. 'No wonder he topped himself, after all that.'

'It must have taken courage,' said Simmy.

'That's the funny thing. He never lacked courage. Even the van driving was quite brave, in a way. Getting up early, going off to places he didn't know, having to stay cheerful when people moaned about stuff being late. But those flowers,' she repeated. 'Wishing him luck in a new job. That must have really upset him, because he'd kept the driving job for two years and was determined to hang onto it until the last minute. Even though he could hardly lift some of the boxes he was supposed to deliver, he wasn't going to give up. No way was he getting a new job.'

They were back full circle, Simmy realised. 'We really need to know who sent the flowers,' she sighed.

'You think it's the same person who killed Tim?'

'No evidence that it is,' said Ben. 'But if it's not, then there are at least two people out there with evil intent.'

'"Evil intent!"' Melanie echoed scornfully. 'What's that? One of your Latin poets?'

'It's a technical term, actually. It means exactly what it says.'

'Shall I make coffee?' Melanie said tightly. 'We should have had it long before now.'

'What time is it?' asked Simmy, looking at her watch. 'Ten to twelve! How did that happen? There's no time for coffee now. We need to get going.'

'Where are you going?' asked Daisy.

'Coniston. Look, we should let you go. It was a bit awful, the way Ben dragged you in here. Thanks very much for being so open with us.'

'That's okay. I've got nothing to hide. And you all seem to be nice people. I should get back to Coniston as well – but I think you've made me miss the bus.'

'Come with us,' Melanie invited. 'We can drop you in the middle of the village.'

'All right, then. Thanks. My mother's sure to want to talk about wedding stuff.' She sighed heavily.

'Where's it to be?' asked Simmy.

'The church in Coniston. It's bound to rain.'

'Where Ruskin's buried? That's lovely!' Simmy was trying not to think about another wedding, four months earlier, where she had done the flowers and it had rained and a very young man had been killed.

'Yeah. Well. First catch your bridegroom.'

Daisy smiled again. 'He'll show up. He does this disappearing act sometimes.'

'Did he grow up around here?' Melanie asked. 'Because if so, it's a local habit. People just take off into the hills for no good reason.'

'That's what we thought my father had done,' agreed the girl, with another big sigh.

# CHAPTER EIGHTEEN

Kathy could hear voices above her and tried shouting to them, but her throat was too dry to make a decent noise. It was finally morning, she supposed dully. She had slept in brief uncomfortable snatches, very much like being on an overnight long-haul flight. She had passed beyond fear some time ago and was now angry and determined to get even with the beast who had done such horrible things to her. It was cold and dark and airless in this dungeon where he had pushed her the previous evening, after she had managed to escape for an hour. A futile escape that did her no good at all.

He had kept her in his van for most of the day, apparently parked somewhere remote, because nobody came when she banged and kicked on the sides. 'I won't hurt you,' he said repeatedly. 'I just can't afford to let you go until everything's finished up here. I can't trust you, you see.'

'I won't tell anybody anything,' she promised hopelessly. 'And there will be a huge search for me by now. They're bound to find me.'

There should have been a chance to escape when he drove her to Cockermouth. But he stood over her while she telephoned Simmy's home from a phone in a corridor that the pub landlord said they could use, and by then she was too stiff and bruised to contemplate running anywhere. She tried screaming, but the sound that emerged was nowhere near loud or urgent enough to attract attention. It wasn't easy to scream or shout, she discovered. Inhibitions against making a spectacle of yourself overrode even being kidnapped, it seemed.

'Leave a message,' he ordered. 'Tell her you're perfectly all right.'

She saw no way of making a coded reference to her situation, but simply hoped that Simmy would find the whole thing so strange that she would defy instructions and notify the police. She was desperate for the loo, which her captor knew full well and used as a means of controlling her. As soon as the phone call was over, he had allowed her to go to the ladies in the pub they'd gone to. He was clever, she had to admit that. No way would he use his own phone, only to have it traced in no time. He made sure nobody else was in the toilets who might lend Kathy a mobile. While she was in there he bought her a soft drink and a sandwich and waited while she ate and drank. He was unobtrusively presentable and not one of the handful of people there gave them a second look. If she had stood up and yelled, 'This man is holding me hostage' nobody would have believed her.

If she staggered out into the street, clutching the sleeves of passers-by, he would easily catch her and make it seem that she was merely annoyed with him. British people were notoriously slow to interfere in anything resembling a domestic tiff. They would either stand passively staring, or take the man's side, because he was the saner-looking of the two. She had untidy hair and grubby clothes. Nobody would take her seriously, whatever she said.

He locked her back in the van and went to use the gents in the pub. She was in a windowless self-contained section of the vehicle, with no access to the driver's seat. She couldn't hoot the horn or break a window. Banging on the side was an option, of course, but she'd tried that already. They were in a town now, but it was getting dark and few people were on the streets. Nobody was going to risk breaking a lock and investigating muffled sounds. That way lay far too much unpredictable trouble. Even if they suspected illegal people trafficking, they wouldn't feel equal to confronting it personally. The chances of a pair of police officers patrolling the mean streets of Cockermouth on foot were minuscule. She was aware of her own self-defeating thinking, of her loss of fight. She was disappointed in herself. But she had never even imagined a situation like this. She had never thought through how she would behave, with clever tricks and subterfuges to outwit her captor. The sheer shock of it was paralysing. Her main concern was the worry that must be consuming her daughter, husband and friend. She was desperate to contact them, and despite its misleading words, she was glad to have at least left a message to reassure Simmy that she was alive.

They drove for an hour or so, with Kathy still in the back where there were no seats. She lay face down flat on the floor, cushioning her head with her arms, and keeping herself rigid to prevent rolling over the floor every time they went round a bend. Already her hips and shoulders were bruised from the ridged metal base. There was a thin cloth covering which was a very slight comfort. She ended up wrapping it round herself, making a cocoon and trying to formulate plans for an escape.

When she heard the gears changing down and felt the van slowing, bumping over ground that could surely not be a road, she unwrapped herself and sat up close to the back door. As much for her own self-respect as anything else, she knew she had to make a bid for freedom. Afterwards, when she told the story, she did not want to sound feeble and passive in her own ears. Neither did she want to invent heroic deeds that never happened. So she crouched, bouncing on the balls of her feet, testing her knees for strength. Squatting had been part of her exercise regime for years, all her joints in full working order as a result. She would surprise him by leaping out and running away before he knew what had happened. After that, everything was in the lap of the gods.

It worked, after a fashion. She pushed the slowly opening door violently into his face, with a loud cry, and jumped down onto cold scratchy heather. Then she ran into darkness, with no idea of where she was going. 'Come back, you fool!' called the man. 'You'll fall and hurt yourself.'

His concern surprised her. Hadn't she just banged his face with a heavy metal door? But there was no way she was going to obey him. Instead, she paused and looked all around. Ahead of her and on a lower level were lights. A glow from a town, where there would be houses and telephones and people who might shelter her. She glanced behind and saw a looming shape against the sky, black against very dark grey. Its outlines were sharp, at the extreme edges of her vision, as she tried to understand what it was. The mountain, she realised. Very likely the same mountain she had been exploring when the man had popped out of the ground that morning.

He was still at the van, slamming its door and

calling out to her again. 'You can't go anywhere. Get back here, you stupid woman.'

Then a light flashed and she understood that he had a powerful torch. Quickly, she made use of the light to run forward, towards where the town of Coniston must be. She jumped over the tufts of heather and other vegetation, spotting a rock not far ahead. She reached it safely and glanced back. The torchlight was zigzagging all around, as he tried to locate her. It seemed impossible that he couldn't see her as clear as day with such a strong beam. Old films about prison camps came to mind, but in those the light came at predictable intervals and you could count on dark shadows for whole minutes at a time. This was very different – he was swinging it wildly, erratically, and presumably scanning the area intently as he did so.

She could see another rock not far ahead, and the hint of a third beyond that. Getting down onto her front, she slithered uncomfortably along the prickly ground, assuming the man would be instinctively looking for an upright figure. Movement, however, would attract his attention, so she crept slowly, despite every nerve telling her to hurry.

It worked for a long time. She progressed downhill for probably two hundred yards, with the man still shouting and flashing his light, until suddenly it went dark and she realised the battery had died. She knew they didn't last long on those powerful torches. Now she was free to stand up again and jog determinedly down to Coniston.

But he defeated her all too easily in the end by turning the van and beaming the headlights in the direction he guessed she had gone. He drove the vehicle slowly down the hill, over the bumpy heather and stones, and found her in about two minutes. Leaving the lights on, he ran and caught her and bundled her back into captivity with remarks more of reproach than anger.

'You never stood a chance, you know. The way you were heading doesn't lead to the town at all. You have to go way over to the right before there's any kind of a path.'

He had brought her back to the Old Man, and now he was telling her it was already after nine and nobody would be anywhere near her again that night. He drove the van over frozen bumpy ground, and then got her out and pushed her ahead of him off the track into dark prickly terrain. They reached the hole from which he had emerged so many hours earlier, and he ordered her into it. 'Don't worry – it gets wider once you're through,' he said. 'It's only for one night. I'll let you out in the morning.'

He had forced her down the tunnel, then tied her hands together and left her there, a long way below the surface, in something she assumed must be an old copper mine. It was pitch-dark and very cold. 'I'll die down here,' she whimpered. 'What if something happens to you? Nobody will ever find me.'

'Oh, they will,' he assured her. 'I'm not the only one who knows about this place. If I drop dead, there'll be others around tomorrow afternoon. Now, just one more thing. I need your email account details. Address and password, if you please.'

She resisted for a few minutes, before giving in. Why, after all, did it matter? What further harm could it do? He might even inadvertently leave some clues as to what was really going on.

He pulled some sort of obstruction over the hole, once he'd climbed out. There were metal rungs set into the tunnel, which rose at a sharp angle but was far from vertical. A combination of climbing and crawling was required to get in and out, relatively easy for all but the most infirm. At the bottom was a pitch-dark space the size of a small bedroom with old timber supports that she repeatedly bumped into.

'Don't touch the equipment,' he ordered her. 'It's at the back. You can lie down well away from it. There's a bit of water.'

'Come back!' Kathy screamed, at the very last minute, knowing he would ignore her.

She had the whole night to review the situation. Her kidnapper was also her daughter's seducer. There could be no good outcome to all this for poor Jo, who would either feel a painful self-disgust, or a towering sickening rage against the man – or both. Baz was a maniac, intent on his scientific researches at all costs. At some point he had evidently lost all sense of proportion, dreaming of glory to come as a result of his findings. That alone was bad enough, given the alarming involvement of her daughter. But a man in Coniston had been killed with a knife only the day before, and that made it far, far worse. It meant she could neither believe nor trust him because he was probably fleeing from the police, who would arrest him and charge him with murder the moment they caught him. This was what had been in her mind when she said 'What if something happens to you?' No way had she imagined that he would simply drop down dead.

The cold was actually less severe than she'd expected. Wasn't there something about the temperature underground remaining the same all the time? They'd said that when she'd gone down to some amazing caverns in the south of France. Baz had given her a blanket, and with her coat, she felt warm enough. She also had a bottle of water and two slabs of Kendal mint cake, which seemed a witty sort of touch – although the contortions required to get at them were unpleasant. Unable to use her hands, she had to lift the bottle in her mouth and tilt her head back to get a drink. She achieved two good swallows before dropping the bottle and losing the rest of the water. The candy bar had been helpfully unwrapped, so it was now slightly gritty and also in danger of getting lost.

Even if nobody came for her, she thought she could probably crawl up the shaft to the surface and use her back to push aside the large rock or whatever it was at the entrance, once it was daylight. An escape into the dark fells with every sort of hazard to trip and ensnare her would be worse than foolish. If that failed, there was still a good chance of people coming past the next day, so she would climb as high as she could up the tunnel and make a great deal of noise. Eventually she must surely attract attention. It would be a Saturday and there would be weekend walkers, even in February.

Darkness, she had discovered, could be a friend if you managed to develop the right attitude. Where most people might imagine rats and huge spiders and wriggling insects waiting to pounce on them, Kathy visualised a warm enveloping blanket, keeping all such beasts at bay. The very restriction of it was a kind of comfort. She felt around her awkwardly shuffling in a rough circle about a yard in radius and leaning back on her bound hands. The ground was packed hard and smooth and blessedly dry. There was nothing within reach except a stout wooden box, presumably containing Baz's 'equipment'. Other than that there was not a stone or stick or wriggling insect. All she could do was curl up, close her eyes and try not to think.

When she failed to fall asleep, she was disappointed with herself. After all, sleep was by far the best way to pass the time. But hands tied behind one's back made it impossible to find a comfortable position. Her shoulders ached and her wrists were chafed and sore. She tried to pretend that she was holding them there deliberately, like a Victorian gentleman out for a stroll. Her hands were crossed over, elbows bent, so the binding rested somewhere between her kidneys. After many passive hours, it occurred to her that she might just be able to work her bottom through the space between her elbows and bring her hands to a far more comfortable and useful position over her stomach. She wasn't fat or unfit. But she wasn't thin and athletic either. At eighteen she could have done it easily. At forty-five it was a very different matter.

She wriggled and stretched until all the muscles from neck to elbow screamed in protest. She would dislocate her shoulders if she carried on like that. Her buttocks were still firmly refusing to fit between her arms, whichever position she adopted. She was sure there must be a trick to it, known to acrobats and contortionists but obscure to everybody else.

She gave up, panting and hurting. The whole attempt had been counterproductive on every level. She now felt she was a stupid old failure. For the sake of a bit of extra comfort, she had wrenched a whole lot of ligaments and given herself a stiff neck. It wasn't as if her life depended on it, she told herself. She would be released in the morning anyway.

Hours rolled sluggishly by until finally she heard the very faint rhythms of human voices far above her. That was when she tried to shout, only to discover that her throat had dried up and all she could manage was a feeble croak.

Never mind, she told herself. She was going to be let out very soon now.

# CHAPTER NINETEEN

Ben and Melanie sat in the back, chattering incessantly as Simmy drove them all the way to Coniston, Daisy in the passenger seat beside her. It was still cold and windy, the water of the lake riffling in wild patterns as the turbulence hit it. Birds were giving themselves up to the tossing like teenagers at a funfair, rising and dropping for the sheer exhilaration of it.

Ben was still wrestling with the question of why someone should kill Tim Braithwaite. He ran through all the motives he could think of, which amounted to somewhere close to twenty. Only five or six of them were remotely sensible. Melanie and Simmy both reproached him for flippancy when he suggested the man might have said something rude about Donald Campbell and been ritually executed by the outraged burghers of Coniston. Daisy remained quiet, to begin with, having reassured Simmy that the chatter wasn't upsetting her. 'It's nice, in a way, that they care so much,' she said.

Ben seemed to forget she was there after a few minutes, asking her no questions and making no apology for his lack of sensitivity.

'Well, but it's possible,' the boy protested when chastised. 'Local heroes are not to be mocked.'

'There's not a shadow of a hint that he did mock him, is there?' said Simmy.

'The trouble is, we know almost nothing about him,' Melanie complained. 'Not even whether he was gay or straight.'

'He was straight,' said Daisy, coldly. 'Honestly, I do think you're starting to take it all a bit too far now.'

'Sorry,' said Melanie. 'Of course, you'd know about that. And other things. *You* knew him pretty well.'

'There's a lot I don't understand,' the girl admitted. 'The main thing is whether Tim knew about Dad being dead. I mean – was he killed before they found Dad's body? Nobody can answer that, and it's obviously important.'

'Is it?' said Simmy.

'It is to me. For everything to just *end* like that – it's horrible.'

'I know,' said Simmy sadly.

'He was a scientist, right?' Ben said. 'Mr

320

Braithwaite, I mean. Do you know anything about that?'

'Not much. When I was with Jasper, they both tried to explain it to me. Jasper would argue with his father all the time, saying his unproven theories were influencing the government, and DEFRA and making people's lives difficult.'

'DEFRA?' asked Melanie.

'The ministry that deals with agriculture and animals. Don't ask me what it stands for.'

'Department for the Environment, Food and Rural Affairs,' said Ben automatically. 'So Jasper is on the side of the orthodoxy where climate change is concerned?'

'I don't know what he thinks now. I haven't seen him for ages.'

'You'll see him at his father's funeral,' said Simmy. An unworthy thought about flowers entered her head. A big funeral of a prominent local man should bring in some welcome business.

'That's another thing,' said Daisy miserably. 'Both the funerals are bound to clash with my honeymoon. We were going to be away for three weeks. It looks as if we'll have to change all the plans now.' Simmy was intrigued by the girl at her side. With the looks of a bimbo, engaged three times, daughter of a failure of a father and a brainless-sounding mother, she was evidently both bright and ambitious. Her choice of husband seemed hard-headed rather than emotional.

Her grief for her father was real, but well under control. Whatever feelings she might have had for Tim Braithwaite were hard to detect. 'I suppose it might be a bit awkward, seeing Jasper again,' she guessed.

'Not really. He's moved on since we were together. He won't be too upset about his dad, either. They were always fighting, as I said.'

Simmy remembered Moxon's little speech on that subject. 'You can't be sure about that,' she said gently. 'It's often people in those sorts of relationships that feel it the worst. Fighting might just be their way of being together – a sort of substitute for real closeness.'

'Hey, Simmy – you've gone all psychological,' Melanie teased. 'Where did that come from?'

'I don't know,' shrugged Simmy. 'I was probably thinking of Kathy and her mother. They used to fight all the time, but when the mother died, Kathy was distraught. Took everybody by surprise.'

'Talking of Kathy, I hope she's there by now,' said Ben. 'I'm starving. We can all have lunch, can't we? You might have to lend me some cash, though. I forgot to bring any.'

They had passed through Ambleside and were heading west towards Skelwith Bridge on the A593. 'At least I don't have to go to Hawkshead again,' said Simmy. 'This is more direct.'

'Of course you don't.' Melanie sounded puzzled. 'Why would you?'

'Only that I did last time, taking flowers to Mrs Crabtree. That road's very spooky, somehow. I don't think I like it.'

'I do,' argued Ben. 'It's so *timeless*. You can imagine Wordsworth wandering about in the country lanes.'

'Not to mention the sainted Beatrix Potter,' sighed Melanie. 'I tell you what – if the Braithwaite man was rude about *her*, he might get himself killed.'

'My father says Fletcher Christian's brother went to school in Hawkshead,' Simmy recollected. 'He's always interested in that sort of lesser celebrity. He's got quite a list of them in his head. He tells the guests about them at breakfast, poor things.'

'Being somebody's brother doesn't make you a celebrity,' said Ben.

'We're going to be really late,' said Melanie. 'Can you go a bit quicker?'

Simmy had been slowing down to admire the views from a road she had not often used. Winter woodlands, grey fells, glimpses of lakes and river – Ben was right about the timelessness of it all. She knew very few of the names for the howes and woods and garths and thwaites, finding the old Norse derivations abidingly foreign to her ear. The deceptively English 'Hawkshead', for example, was actually something alien originating from a Norseman's name. Nothing to do with hawks or heads, anyway. The landmarks, down to the smallest clump of trees, were all likely to have been named a thousand years ago by invaders of one sort or another. It sometimes felt like borrowed land, used by the English only on sufferance. The Norse invaders had grown deep roots and taken firm possession of a region the softer natives had found too inhospitable for serious settlement.

'I keep wondering about Pamela Johnson,' said Melanie. 'There's something about her that feels wrong to me.'

'Oh? Like what?' Ben was evidently intrigued.

'It's as if she's been deliberately seeking Simmy out to tell her things that aren't really at all important. I can't work out what she's playing at.'

'You think she's laying a false trail,' said Ben with a solemn nod. 'That could well be.'

'No, no. She's just a village gossip,' Simmy disagreed. 'The world's full of them. She wants to feel she's at the heart of things.'

'Maybe she is absolutely at the heart of things. Maybe she's actually the killer,' said Ben.

'I know her,' said Daisy. 'She's a pain in the bum, but that's all. Dad quite liked her.'

'You know something?' said Melanie. 'We never actually checked with Mrs Aston to see if she did speak to Pamela about those flowers. For all we know, the whole thing was made up. That would leave the real sender still a mystery.'

Simmy moaned. 'Forget Mrs Aston. We can assume the police have spoken to her, anyway.'

'Never assume, Sim. That's a first principle.'
Ben's solemnity was deepening. He held up a finger
and wagged it so that Simmy could see it in the rear-
view mirror.

Simmy was lost for a reply. The Old Man of
Coniston would be visible soon, beyond Yewdale,
with the suggestions of endless wilderness in
which you could lose yourself. People shrank
to little dots out there, their lives rendered
trivial and fleeting in contrast to the implacable
landscape.

'Ten minutes and we'll be there,' said Melanie.
'This is going to be exciting.'

Simmy remembered that on previous adventures,
Melanie had managed to get left out for various
reasons, so she shouldn't blame her for feeling as
she did. Even so, it jarred. 'I hope it won't be,' she
said. 'I'm too old for excitement.'

'It's more likely to be just a boring lunch,' sighed
Ben. 'You'll talk about the weather or holidays or
cars or something.'

'I doubt it. After all, Kathy has been missing. She
must have *something* interesting to tell us.'

'Besides that, *you* talk about holidays as well,'
Melanie accused him. 'All those exotic travels your
family goes in for.'

Ben snorted. 'I do not. I haven't talked about that
for months. Although . . .' he allowed himself to
be diverted, 'my dad *has* just booked a self-catering

fortnight in Denmark. Wilf's not going, but the rest of us are.'

'All right for some,' muttered Melanie. 'What's that costing, then?'

'Thousands,' said Ben airily. 'Most of it earned by my mother. She's had two good commissions this year already.'

'I thought Denmark was all bacon factories and featureless landscape,' Simmy said.

'You thought wrong, then.'

'Nearly there,' Melanie announced. 'Are we dreadfully late?'

'A bit,' said Simmy, without even looking at her watch. In the circumstances, lateness didn't strike her as very significant. Coniston came into view, with its pubs and hotels looking dormant, the car park almost empty and the church dark and chilly. Unsure of whether the Yewdale offered its own parking area, she turned into the town park, which was close by. 'What're you doing?' Melanie demanded. 'You'll have to pay if you park here. Use theirs, where it's free.'

It made sense to Simmy and she reversed in an arc to face the exit. As she did so, her wing mirror, inadequately bound on Thursday evening with sticky tape, fell apart with a clatter. 'Damn! I meant to get my dad to fix that, but there hasn't been time.' She switched off the engine and got out, once again collecting fragments for reassembly. 'You three go on in, and I'll follow when I've found somewhere to park.'

They obediently got out and went off, while Simmy put the pieces on the passenger seat and then followed them in the car. She was only two minutes behind them, but that was enough for her to suddenly start worrying about keeping Kathy waiting. The wording of her email had been going round her head for much of the drive, increasing her bewilderment with every mile. *Under duress*, she had said. And *wear walking boots*. How was she supposed to do that, anyway, when her boots were in a cupboard up in Troutbeck? The whole message sounded silly at best, and thoroughly sinister at worst. And yet there was an insistent normality surrounding everything that had happened. Even the delivery of no fewer than four provocative bouquets through the week had an underlying ordinariness to it. Flowers couldn't kill. An assortment of people had used Simmy as a messenger. That was all. Even if Kathy's brief disappearance was inexplicable it was apparently not life-threatening.

But this was all rather beside the point, she admitted to herself, because a perfectly nice man had been murdered. That was not ordinary or normal or explicable at all.

Then she saw a familiar car parked behind the hotel, next to the space she had chosen to use. A blue Subaru with the double '1' that showed its year of manufacture, looking clean and undamaged, did much to reassure her that at least something was going to be all right.

The reception area was deserted, so she went through into a long empty lounge containing leather sofas and a big window, looking for her people. Voices were coming from an area around a corner to the left and she followed them. The three youngsters were standing together, all of them looking agitated.

'What's the matter?' she asked.

Before anyone could reply, a man spoke from behind Simmy. 'I'll take you to your friend. Come with me.'

'Baz?' Simmy looked at him. 'You know where Kathy is?'

'I do,' he agreed. 'Come on. I'll show you where she is.'

He eyed Melanie and Ben irritably. 'You two as well, I suppose. I never expected such a crowd.' Then he examined their feet. 'Not what I'd call walking boots,' he observed.

Daisy took a breath. 'And me. Can I come as well?'

'Yeah. You'll have to, I guess.'

He looked around, assessing the degree of attention they were attracting. A man on the reception desk looked as if he was about to ask some questions. Simmy knew she ought to do something, but she had gone completely blank. The presence of Joanna Colhoun's group leader suddenly transformed into a possible kidnapper made such an utter lack of sense that her brain had frozen. She looked hopefully to Ben, who might be keeping up rather better than she was herself.

At least he could speak. 'Why isn't Kathy here? Is she hurt or something?'

'She's fine. We just needed her out of the way for a bit, while we finished off the work. Now you can go and collect her, and no harm done. She's not going to make any trouble, with Jo so fond of me, is she?'

'Joanna's in hospital, did you know?' Melanie put in, obviously expecting a dramatic reaction.

She was disappointed. 'Yeah, but she's okay,' said Baz. 'Just her allergy thing again. She called me an hour ago.'

'An allergy to *latex*,' accused Melanie. 'Which we assume came from you. You let her go out into the street, almost dying of the reaction to your condoms.'

Baz blew out his cheeks disbelievingly. 'Nah! That wasn't it. She's allergic to chestnuts as well, apparently. There must have been some in the weird breakfast we got this morning. Some sort of home-made granola, it was. They think that must have been it.' He widened his eyes, challenging Melanie to retract her accusations.

She thought for a moment, and riposted, 'That

can't be it. She'd have reacted much sooner if it was.'

'Okay. Well she must have bought a snack bar or something. They haven't got to the bottom of it yet. The point is, it wasn't a condom – right?'

Melanie shrugged, aware that the matter was of little significance.

Baz jigged impatiently. 'Look – let's get going.' He looked again at their feet. 'Nobody got proper boots?'

'They're in the car,' said Simmy, thinking quickly. 'I can't drive in them, can I?'

Melanie frowned at her. 'When . . . ?' But Simmy quelled her with a look. A faint idea was stirring. If she could get some time alone in the car park, she could phone Moxon and tell him what was going on. While Baz was behaving with superficial reasonableness, there was a look in his eyes that she found alarming. Whatever the truth of it, by his own admission he had forcibly prevented Kathy from returning to Troutbeck the previous evening, and that made him potentially dangerous.

'We'll all go, then,' said Baz. 'Stay together. Go on.' He ushered them out like a shepherd with a nervous flock. Simmy glanced back at the man on reception, hoping he would have finally detected something unusual. But he seemed to regard them as just another walking group.

They all moved out into the car park, and Simmy realised her stratagem was never going to work.

330

Even so, she approached her car, with Melanie and Ben close behind her. Baz hung back with Daisy.

'Can you distract him while I make a phone call?' she whispered to Ben.

'I doubt it. He's sure to see you.'

'Not if I'm half inside the boot of the car, rummaging for my boots.' Even in the drama of the moment, she heard her father's ghostly chuckle at the two meanings of the word.

'Okay – I'll try. Mel – you'll have to help me. Go and say something to him.'

Melanie obediently turned round and took a few steps towards Baz. 'How far is it?' she called. 'I'm not walking about out there if it rains. Not for anyone.'

Ben followed her and stood at her side, creating a screen to shield Simmy. 'You'll miss the fun if you don't,' he said. 'You won't like that, will you?'

'It's a mile or so,' Baz replied. 'You're coming, whether you like it or not.' He looked at Ben. 'This is just a game to you, then, is it? Like something you'd play on your computer. Well, let me tell you, it's real this time. People have really died because of all this, and they're not going to be the last. It's a war now. Total bloody warfare.'

Simmy had her phone in her hand, her head and shoulders crouched inside the car boot, starting to key in Moxon's number, when she found she'd forgotten part of it. It would be in the memory somewhere, after making so many calls to him, of course. But then she realised she wouldn't be able to say more than a few words before Baz snatched it away from her. A text would be safer. But it was hopeless, as she'd known already. Baz was only a few yards away. He would be losing patience after about half a minute. Even so, she had to try. If only her brain wasn't working so slowly, with none of that surge of brilliant inventiveness that gripped people in books when this sort of thing happened to them.

'Warfare?' Ben repeated. 'Who's against who, then?'

'Not now. We've got to go. I'd have thought you'd be more bothered about your friend in the mine. She'll be cold and scared, wouldn't you say?' He became aware of Simmy's fumblings and stepped sideways to get a better look. 'Hey! What're you doing?'

'I can't find my boots. They're not here. I was *sure* I had them.'

'That's a phone,' he accused, marching forward and grabbing it. 'Who're you calling?' He squinted at the screen. 'What have you done?'

'Sent a text to the police,' she bluffed. 'They know where we are now.'

'Garn!' he said, rudely and rather funnily. 'You haven't had time.'

'It doesn't take long.'

'You've got the cops' number in your phone, have you? Don't tell me you texted 999, because nobody does that. It's not doable.' He put the phone in his pocket, and made his shepherding gesture again. 'Okay, you others – I want all your phones, now. Come *on*. We're not going anywhere till you've done what I say.' Reluctantly, as if parting with precious treasure, three phones were handed over. Baz took Simmy's out of his pocket again, and threw all four into the boot of the car. 'They'll be here waiting for you when you get back,' he said.

'Good try, Sim,' muttered Ben.

They straggled out of the hotel grounds and turned southwards, Simmy leading the way and Ben close behind her. 'You know where we're going, then?' he asked her quietly.

'No idea, but I'm worried about Kathy. He'll say if I go the wrong way.'

'Aren't you scared? He's acting very strangely.'

'A bit. But there's four of us against just him. I don't expect there'll be any trouble. But poor Kathy! She's been up in these fells all night by the sound of it. He can't be right in the head, can he?'

'Seems not.'

'Sshh,' warned Daisy. 'He'll hear you.'

But Baz was arguing with Melanie, who was loudly protesting that she couldn't possibly walk a mile uphill on rough ground. 'You don't have a choice,' he said firmly.

'If I just turned round and ran back to the hotel and told them what you're doing, how do you think you'd stop me?' she demanded. 'Why've we all got to go, anyway?'

'You've got nothing to accuse me of. I just thought you'd want to make sure your friend's okay. You can leave if you like.'

'You took our phones,' she reminded him. 'That's theft, for a start.'

Simmy turned round to speak to him. 'Our friend is the mother of your girlfriend. She's not going to think very favourably of you after this, is she?'

'Who cares?'

'How did you do it, anyway? Make her stay out here all night, I mean?'

'With this,' he said tightly, and pulled his waterproof jacket aside. On his hip was the sheath containing his knife. 'It's very sharp and I'm very quick with it, if I have to be.'

'You killed Mr Braithwaite with that,' said Simmy faintly. 'Didn't you?'

'Don't be stupid,' he said. 'Now keep walking.'

# CHAPTER TWENTY

Simmy was breathless with fear and exertion, stumbling over the rough ground in soft trainers. It was stony underfoot, despite the path being well used for most of the year. Baz had a knife around his waist, in a sheath, like a cowboy with a gun. Even though he hadn't shown them the blade, she could all too vividly imagine it. A knife had killed Mr Braithwaite, which made it obvious that Baz was the killer, even if he did deny it. And everybody knew that if a person had killed once, it was all too easy to do it again.

Her damaged bones were starting to complain at the climb as the path grew steeper. The mountain above looked huge and indifferent, no more benign than it appeared from a distance. Sheep peeped at them from behind the rocks and a sharp wind whipped at their faces. Baz and Ben had hoods.

None of the women did. The ones with long hair found it blowing across their eyes and their noses ran.

She tried to imagine Kathy, alone somewhere up here, bewildered and frightened. Her friend's suffering completely outmatched anything she herself might be enduring. As for Melanie, who regarded walking on the fells as one of the daftest of activities, her complaints were quickly becoming annoying. She had asked to come, after all. Ben remained silent, which gave Simmy cause for hope that he was working out some clever ruse for overcoming Baz and setting everything right.

The sense that all four of them were spineless and pathetic for so meekly obeying Baz began to fade. What if he was the only person who knew where Kathy was? If they collectively attacked him and got him carted off by the police, he might refuse to speak for days – in which time Kathy would die of cold or thirst. The only possible thing to do was to let him show them the place. After that, things might become very different. She clenched her fists at the prospect of punching or kicking the lunatic following behind them. If they could grab both his hands, he wouldn't be able to use the knife. If four people – five with Kathy – couldn't accomplish something as simple as that, then they ought to be ashamed.

They walked for half an hour in the cold, deserted landscape. The settlement of Coniston was scarcely visible below them, its church and few shops every bit as indifferent as the Old Man above them. Stone walls and rough paths were the only signs of human activity, and they gave no comfort. Farm buildings might be glimpsed on the slopes running down to the lakeside, but their occupants would have no interest in the small dots of humanity meandering up the hill towards the old copper workings. They would be tending their sheep or completing their claims for subsidies beside the warm fire, and not watching walkers.

Suddenly Baz called 'Stop!' and they all obeyed, looking around in confusion. All Simmy could see was a rough semicircle of rocks, some piled on top to suggest a sort of crude, low doorway. The mossy ground covering had been scuffed, with small black clods of soil showing.

'That's a copper mine,' said Ben, with implacable certainty.

'So it is,' Baz smiled. 'Or, to be more accurate, it's a side vent, made for emergency evacuation, as well as providing extra ventilation.'

'Not very deep, then?'

'Wait and see.'

'Are we meant to go down there?' Melanie's voice was a squeal of panic. 'Is that why you've made us come all this way?'

'Um . . .' said Ben. 'Can you see what I see?' He pointed to a hollow, fifty yards away.

Everyone looked. Simmy saw the top half of a blue Transit van. 'Is that yours?' she said to Baz.

He smiled again. 'This is where we part company. I've done the decent thing. You can take it from here. I'll be on my way, if it's all right with you.'

Nobody spoke for a moment, all blinking at Baz and each other. Then Ben spoke. 'No. It is not all right with us. You're a killer and a kidnapper. We're not going to just let you go.'

'That's right,' confirmed Melanie uncertainly.

'I'm no killer,' shouted Baz. 'Why do you keep saying that?'

'Because you've got the murder weapon round your middle,' said Simmy impatiently. 'You showed it to us.'

Baz spluttered in frustration, sensing a checkmate situation. He took a step towards his vehicle, and then stopped and stamped his foot. 'I'm no killer,' he said again, like a little boy. To emphasise the point, albeit irrationally, he drew out the knife and waved it at them. 'Just stop saying I am, okay?'

'What, then?' Ben challenged. 'What's this all about? What the hell are you playing at?'

'Ask her.' Baz tipped his chin towards Daisy. 'She knows.'

The girl's eyes widened and she put up a defensive hand. 'Don't you put this on me, you pig. I've been trying to stay out of it all along.'

'For heaven's sake!' Simmy exploded. 'My

friend's down there in the dark and you lot just stand here arguing. Kathy's what matters, now. How do we get into this mine, anyway?' She kicked at a stone, jarring herself painfully. 'Ouch!'

'She's right,' said Melanie crossly. 'We're supposed to be a rescue party.' She pulled a face. 'Otherwise there's going to be a second body out here on the fells.'

'Not to mention a third down there in Coniston,' muttered Ben.

'The entrance is behind the rocks,' said Baz. 'It's got a stone slab over it. Just lift it up and there should be enough light to show you the way. I forgot to suggest you bring a torch.' There was still a childish sulk in his voice, as if he was being badly misunderstood and didn't like it. 'I'm going now, so don't try to stop me,' he added defiantly. 'I'll be out of the country by teatime, and in a few days, the results of our experiment will be hitting the headlines.'

Simmy ignored him and walked round the stones to discover a square concrete slab, as Baz had described. 'Help me do this,' she ordered, addressing all three youngsters equally. 'It looks heavy.'

Daisy was the first to join her, and they had the trapdoor lifted a few inches before Melanie came to their assistance. Together they heaved it aside, ignoring the men who were still squaring up to each other like stags or fighting cocks. Simmy had a pang of alarm at the thought that Baz might actually stab Ben, but her greater worry was for her friend.

'Kathy!' she shouted. 'Are you down there?' The tunnel ran obliquely downwards, as far as she could see, which was only eight or ten feet in. Beyond that it was invisibly dark.

A muffled cry floated up, producing a mixture of fear and relief in Simmy. 'She's there! Come on, we've got to get her out.'

'Um . . .' said Melanie, eyeing the tunnel. 'There's not space for all of us, is there? I mean – just one person can do it, don't you think?'

'Melanie Todd, you're a coward,' flashed Simmy. 'Kathy! It's me, Simmy. I'm coming to get you.'

She crawled head first into the hole without another thought. Realising there were rungs fixed to the side of the tunnel, she withdrew her head and turned round, backing in, and feeling for the strips of metal with her feet. The tunnel was about four feet in diameter, the walls dry and reasonably smooth. The worst thing was the darkness, which became almost total as she blocked the light with her own body. Something scratched her cheek, but she kept going, trying not to think about the return climb, with Kathy somehow beside her.

It was a much shorter distance than she had expected. She felt something under her foot as she took another fumbling step down. The thing was making wordless sounds. She cautiously lowered herself, realising she had passed the final rung, reached out and found a shoulder, then a face, with hair. It was cold. 'Simmy!' Kathy croaked. 'I tried to scream, but my throat's too dry.'

'It's okay now. It's all going to be fine.' She realised the shoulder she'd felt had been at an odd angle, and traced her friend's arm down to the bound hands behind her back. 'Gosh, this must be painful,' she muttered. 'I'll see if I can untie it.' But the knotted cord had pulled tight, and in darkness it was impossible to unpick it. 'Sorry. I can't do it. We need a light and a knife. Hang on.'

'Ben!' she yelled. 'Her hands are tied behind her back. We'll never get her out like this. We need a knife.'

The boy's voice came back to her, much closer than she'd expected. 'We haven't got one,' he said. 'We'll have to push her out between us. Stand clear – I'm coming down.'

'Where's Baz?'

'We let him go,' said the boy tersely. 'For now.'

'Good. Except we could use that knife of his.'

Suddenly the boy was on top of them, literally. The resulting tangle took some moments to sort out. Simmy felt a patch of cold dampness somewhere on Kathy's lower regions and realised with a sad sort of horror that she'd been forced to wet herself. That alone implied that a lasting trauma might well result from her experience.

'Kathy, Kathy,' she whispered. 'We'll have you out in no time. Then we . . .' she stopped, wondering what exactly would happen next. They had no water with them, no means of carrying Kathy back to warmth and comfort. 'Then we'll get you some help,' she finished feebly.

'What's happening?' called Melanie from the top of the tunnel. 'I can't see anything.'

'We've got Kathy, but she's tied up. We'll try and push her up to you. Can you reach in and help her when we get near the top?' Simmy's voice sounded muffled in her own ears, the underground acoustic subdued by the enclosed space. Claustrophobia threatened to grip and paralyse her, the air feeling thick and cold in her lungs.

'Okay.' Melanie sounded doubtful. 'Hurry up, then. There's something happening over by that van.'

'Come on,' Ben urged.

'There's no way she can get up there with her hands behind her back,' said Simmy flatly. 'You'll have to go and find something to cut the string. Even then, she's going to be dreadfully sore and stiff.'

'Can't we *pull* her up somehow?'

'If you can get that box open, it might have something useful in it,' croaked Kathy. 'Baz said it had his equipment in.'

'If it has, he's going off without it. It can't be anything important.' Simmy felt desperately useless.

'I can't see a box, anyway. I can't see *anything*.'

'It's there just behind you. Made of wood with sharp corners.'

Simmy felt cautiously around, and located the chest. To her surprise, the lid lifted easily, once she had grasped the front two corners. Kathy, of course, could never have managed it with her useless hands. Inside was a jumble of clattery objects that felt like tools, some balled-up paper and a piece of rope. The tools raised a hope that she might find something to cut Kathy's binding, but they resolved themselves into two hammers and a trowel; nothing so useful as a saw or chisel. 'Rope!' she said, trying to assess its length. 'Or some kind of halter, maybe. It's got a knot in it that slides up and down.'

'Let's have a feel,' said Ben. She clumsily passed it to him. 'If we can loop it round Kathy, under her arms, one of us can go in front and use it to take her weight. Then the other can guide her from below. She can step up the rungs, can't she? So the rope would be more for balance.'

'Sounds very risky to me,' worried Simmy. 'How do we loop it under her arms, for a start?'

'She can step into it, and we work it up her body.'

'Who's going in front?'

'Me, I suppose,' said the boy. 'It'll have to go round my middle, because you're still getting over broken bones in that area.'

'Is it long enough for that?'

343

'Just. I think.'

'We ought to get Melanie down here. She's stronger than either of us.'

'She's too big,' he said.

It was true. Melanie's size would be a hindrance for several reasons. 'Try it, then,' she invited him. 'Kathy, he seems to know what he's doing. Is it okay with you?'

'Just get me out,' rasped the prisoner.

In a darkness that had slowly grown less absolute, they fumbled and wriggled, with false starts and slipping knots, until Kathy and Ben were bound together in a clinch that saw her head wedged between his knees. Somehow he straightened them out, and began a slow painful climb upwards.

Kathy was a dead weight at first as she failed to find any purchase with her feet, and Ben groaned from the strain and urged Simmy to do what she could from below. Simmy did her best to raise her friend far enough for her feet to connect with the lowest rung. Her legs were rubbery, the whole exercise impeded by her numb exhaustion. But gradually, rung by rung, they crawled upwards. It grew lighter and Mel's voice sounded closer as she kept asking for a progress report. At last Kathy's weight lessened, as Melanie grabbed her under both arms and exerted her own not insubstantial efforts. Like a painful forceps delivery, Kathy finally slid out onto open ground, leaving Ben and

Simmy to scramble out after her, panting hard.

They all lay there for a minute, blinking at the light. Simmy heard men's voices shouting not far off, and looked round. 'Where's Daisy?' she asked.

'Over there,' said Melanie, pointing at the hollow containing the blue van. 'There's a man.'

'What man?' The question was foolish, but Simmy's mind was not functioning quite as it should. Almost all of her attention was on her friend, who was weeping helplessly.

'Kathy, you're all right now. All we need is a knife to cut this bloody string round your wrists.'

'Here. Let me see,' said Melanie. 'Gosh, that must hurt! It's cutting right into your skin. I think I might have something, though. Hang on.' She rummaged in her jacket pocket and brought out a cluster of keys. 'I can probably unpick the knot with one of these.' She knelt behind Kathy and set to work. 'Fancy using such thin string. He's a real amateur, isn't he. Sorry!' Kathy had squealed as the key accidentally jabbed her sore wrist. 'It's coming now.' Using her fingernails, she gently loosened the knot, strand by strand, until it was free. 'There!'

Kathy's arms parted slowly and stiffly. 'Aargghh!' she moaned. 'That hurts.'

'She needs water. And a blanket,' said Simmy. 'Ben?' She blinked. 'Where is he?'

'Over there,' said Melanie again. The whole group seemed to be reforming in the hollow, where important action was clearly going on. 'We're going to have to phone for help or else use that van. It's not over yet, Sim.'

'Why is he still here? I thought he was going to drive away and leave us.'

'There's *another* man,' Melanie explained. 'I think he must have been waiting in the van all along. I suppose he's an accomplice of some sort, although there's been a lot of shouting. Ben's gone to find out what it's all about.'

'Well, it's lucky for us, then. We can get him to take us back down to Coniston. Kathy can't possibly walk all that way. Look after her for a minute, okay.' And she marched over to make her demands, trying as she went to make sense of Baz's behaviour.

The new man was dark-haired, quite young and dressed in an odd outfit including waterproof trousers and a tweed cap. The cold wind was buffeting him, gaining in force, so they all had to speak louder to make themselves heard. The elemental contribution did much to raise the sense of drama. Daisy's fair hair was blowing about and Simmy pulled her jacket more tightly around her.

'Listen!' Simmy said with an authority she hadn't known she possessed. The only basis for it was that she was at least ten years older than anyone else present – not counting Kathy. 'I need to get my friend to a doctor quickly. She's cold and dehydrated. Since you've obviously changed your mind about driving

346

away, you can damn well take her to a hospital.' She faced Baz full on, prepared to shout him down if he demurred.

'Fat chance,' he said. 'Look.' And he pointed at the blue van.

It took Simmy a moment to understand the problem. Then she saw that both the back tyres – which were all she could see – were completely flat, the rubber buckled. 'Oh!' she moaned. 'What happened?'

'This bastard slashed them. Front ones as well.' He pointed at the new arrival with a shaking finger. He looked very nearly as deflated as his tyres. Only then did she become aware that Daisy was holding the arm of the second man as if trying to stop him from doing something.

'Who are you?' she asked him.

'At a guess, I would say this is Jasper Braithwaite, son of the murdered Tim,' said Ben. 'The logo on his vehicle is the giveaway.'

Simmy looked round and saw a battered Discovery with 'Ambleside Veterinary Group' stencilled on the side.

'Why would he slash these tyres, then?' She stared at the newcomer. 'You're DI Moxon's godson,' she accused. 'What would he think of such behaviour?'

'He'd be proud of me, I should think. I've just prevented the escape of a murderer.' He looked fondly down at Daisy. 'Isn't that right?'

The girl let go of his arm and moved out of reach. She addressed Simmy and Ben. 'I did wave him down, when I saw the Discovery,' she explained. 'And asked him to come and help. He's been out on the fells doing something with sheep.'

'The tyres?' Simmy prompted.

'It seemed a good way to keep him here, without using force,' shrugged Jasper. 'He doesn't seem to be interested in making a run for it. I imagine because he's got something important in the van that he'd rather not leave behind.'

They all looked at Baz, who seemed to be quietly weeping. 'My samples,' he blurted. 'None of it'll be any good without the samples.'

Ben approached him. 'Samples of what? I thought it was all weather data. Wind speeds, temperatures, rainfall – what *samples*?'

Baz gave him a sneering look. 'It's nothing to do with *weather*, you idiot. It's copper. From the mines. I told all those students to check rainfall and the rest, while I was down there finding a whole new seam of *copper*. If I follow the rules, I can claim a percentage of the proceeds. That's all I need. But nobody in this country can be trusted to follow up on it. I might have to take everything to Argentina, where they're serious about this kind of thing.' There was a schoolboy bravado to him, a detachment from reality that made everybody blink.

Nobody spoke for a long minute, while they adjusted all their various assumptions. Then everyone expressed themselves at once. Kathy and Ben were loudest. 'But what about Joanna?' demanded Kathy, who had limped over, assisted by Melanie, in pursuit of Simmy.

And 'So where does that leave the murder in Coniston?' wondered Ben.

Daisy's voice broke in. 'And who sent those flowers to my dad?'

Confusion reigned, with little sense emerging from anyone, apart from Jasper. He looked down at his one-time fiancée and said easily, 'Oh, that was me.'

Another silence, before Ben said, 'Explain.'

'It was just a joke. I'd been chatting to him in the pub, trying to jolly him along, what with the cancer and everything. He was saying he wished Daisy had stayed with me, because he didn't much fancy being father-in-law to James Goff. He didn't think solar panels were a very reliable long-term prospect. Anyway, all I meant was to cheer him up, and make him smile.'

'You wished him good luck in his new job,' said Simmy slowly.

'Right. The job of being father-in-law to Goff. It was a *joke*. Why – didn't he get it or something?'

'We're not even sure he ever saw them,' said Daisy tearfully. 'He died the day they arrived.

He was out when they were delivered. Your dad took them instead. Would he have understood the message?'

Jasper grimaced. 'Doubtful. He might have thought Jack was trying to get new work, I suppose. He liked to think the cancer could be cured and everything carry on as it was for a lot longer.'

'Nobody even unwrapped them or put them in water,' said Simmy.

'You know something?' Ben was evidently thinking hard. 'I've been wondering just what happened to suggest Jack Hayter was missing.' He looked at Daisy. 'He never showed for your dinner party on Tuesday night. But *before* that. Wouldn't Braithwaite have missed him during the day and wondered where he'd got to?'

'He said he thought he was away on a driving job,' said Daisy. 'He was the first person I spoke to on Tuesday. I phoned to ask where Dad was. He said he had no idea.'

'They might have had a row or something,' suggested Jasper.

'Unless . . .' Ben looked round at the circle of faces. 'Unless Hayter did kill Braithwaite, and then saw no option but to kill himself as well. Hasn't that been the most likely explanation all along?'

'No, Ben,' Melanie corrected. 'The police are sure Mr Hayter died first.'

Ben adopted a stubborn expression. 'It's never

easy to establish the exact time of death, you know.'

Before anyone could reply, there was a shout from further up the fell. 'Hey – it's Wilf and Scott!' Ben realised, waving a welcoming arm.

The arrival of two more young men galvanised everyone into action. Ten minutes passed in recriminations and theories while Kathy's injuries remained untended. The fact that she could walk and talk had removed any great urgency from most minds, but Simmy felt bad for letting other matters override her concern for her friend.

Jasper was instructed to drive Kathy, Melanie and Daisy down to Coniston, where help was to be found, both for Kathy and the undrivable Transit van. Kathy had developed a profound case of the shakes, apparently after learning from Melanie that her daughter was in hospital. What to do with Baz remained unresolved.

Ben hurriedly tried to explain the situation to his brother and friend, but only succeeded in confusing them utterly. 'Is this bloke a murderer, then?' asked Wilf, eventually, looking at the thin-faced lecturer.

Simmy and Ben exchanged a glance, and then fixed on Baz. 'He might be,' said Simmy, with a frown. So much information had just poured forth that it was difficult to sift through for this crucial fact. 'But Ben thinks it could have been his lodger after all.' She held up a finger. 'Wasn't there a reason why it couldn't have been?'

'The timing probably doesn't work,' Ben acknowledged.

'I didn't kill him,' shouted Baz. 'What reason would I have to do that? I've never even *heard* of the man.'

'We don't have to stay here, do we?' asked Wilf. 'Can't we walk down to somewhere a bit warmer?'

'I'm not leaving my samples,' insisted Baz. 'You lot can go if you want.'

The three youths blinked at each other, and then turned to Simmy for guidance. 'Yes, come on,' she decided. 'We can't stand here all day, can we?'

# CHAPTER TWENTY-ONE

It took twenty minutes to reach Coniston, at a very brisk downhill trot. Baz mutinously watched them go, shaking a melodramatic fist at them every time one of them looked back. 'It'll be up to Kathy to decide what happens to him,' said Ben. 'She'll have to press charges against him, with us as witnesses.'

'You don't think he killed Tim Braithwaite, then?' asked Simmy. 'Even though he's got that knife?'

'What's the knife like?' asked Scott, who had said very little until then. He was middle-height and fair-haired. His front teeth were overlarge and his ears likewise.

'Long and sharp,' Simmy said.

'Serrated edge?'

'I don't think so. Was it, Ben?'

'N-o-o,' he said, not quite certainly. 'Why?'

'The murder weapon had serrations. I read the

pathologist's report, and he was definite about that.'

Wilf made a hissing noise. 'Nasty,' he muttered.

'He knows a lot about knives,' Ben explained. 'Working in a kitchen, see.'

At the Yewdale, where they automatically headed, there was considerable activity in the car park. Almost everyone seemed to have a mobile phone clasped to the side of their head, including Daisy Hayter and a very unexpected DI Moxon. There was no sign of Kathy or Melanie. 'What are you doing here?' she asked the detective, ignoring his telephone conversation.

He said 'Hang on a minute,' and took the phone from his ear. 'I'm investigating a murder,' he told her calmly. 'What do you think?' And he returned to his mobile.

She rolled her eyes and went to speak to Jasper Braithwaite. 'What happened to Kathy?' she asked him.

'An ambulance came for her. It left five minutes ago. She's very dehydrated and cold, they said, but no other damage as far as they can tell. Your assistant went with her. Fine girl,' he added thoughtfully. 'You let him go, then? The kidnapper?'

'He's still with his van, I think. He doesn't want to leave it.'

'Not much chance of a low-loader getting up there. Someone's going to have to take four new wheels in a jeep. Should be me, I guess. Do the cops know he's there?'

Simmy shrugged. 'Only if one of you told them.' She looked at Daisy, who was still talking urgently into her phone.

'Calling the boyfriend,' said Jasper. 'She's been on the phone for about twenty minutes now, telling him the whole sorry story. She wants him to come and get her, apparently.'

'Her mother lives round here somewhere,' said Simmy vaguely. 'She'll be all right. I dare say the hotel people are a bit miffed about all this going on in their car park.'

'They'll get over it.'

Daisy finally concluded her phone call. 'He's almost here,' she announced, mainly to Jasper. 'He didn't want to come at first. Said he's got too much to do.'

Simmy noted idly that the fiancé must have been speaking on his phone while driving – something she deplored. And yet there often seemed to be little alternative. Very dimly, she recalled a time when people had fixed phones in their cars, and could speak into them without using their hands. Something that had apparently failed to catch on amongst ordinary citizens. Her mother, of course, could remember a time when there was no such thing as a mobile phone at all.

There was a strong sense of anticlimax. The injured victim had been whisked away. The man responsible was weirdly alone on the slopes of the Old Man, guarding his precious samples. Despite all the bustle and phoning, nothing significant appeared to be happening. Ben evidently felt the same. He came over to Simmy. 'Wilf can take me home, if that's okay,' he said. 'I'm starving. We never got any lunch.'

'I suppose I should go as well,' she said. 'Unless we pop into the hotel for a quick snack?'

He shook his head. 'Better get going,' he said. 'Although I can't stop thinking about it all. There's still about fifty unanswered questions nagging at me.' He rubbed his forehead, as if to stimulate even more thoughts. 'Baz said none of this was to do with climate. But when he was down here with us, he ranted about a war. What was that all about, then? Are they fighting a war about copper? I don't think so.'

'It doesn't matter now, Ben. Stop agonising about it.'

Then a throaty engine was heard, slowing down as it squeezed its way into the car park.

'That's Jamey!' cried Daisy, running to the car as if nothing else mattered. A man quickly unfolded himself from the driver's seat and put his arms around her. He was at least a foot taller than the girl.

Ben spoke, almost to himself. 'That must be James Goff, Daisy Hayter's fiancé. The one who sent the flowers to Selena Drury. The one who sells solar panels for a living, and needs all the theories about man-made climate change to be right, or he's going to find himself in a right old mess.'

'For the Lord's sake, what does that have to do with anything?' Simmy snapped.

Ben looked at her, eyes wide, brain firing on every cylinder. 'A lot, actually. Pretty much *everything* in fact. Remember we googled Tim Braithwaite, and came up with some vague stuff about carbon dioxide emissions? Well, I looked into it a bit more when I got home. Mr Braithwaite was under a lot of pressure to reassess his findings. He was coming up with all the wrong answers. And our friend Baz up there was trying to help him with his little team of students providing hard data. Amazing what a difference that was making. But mad Baz thinks there's a great big government conspiracy, you see. He's convinced they're out to get him because he's on the wrong side, same as poor old Braithers.'

'I thought Baz was just pretending to do the climate stuff, when really he was mining for copper,' said Simmy.

'Both. He was into both. The climate experiments were real enough, but he could hardly fail to notice that they were doing them on top of old copper mines. Most likely he went exploring one day and got lucky. He's a physics tutor. He'll understand how to spot signs of copper ore.'

Daisy was dragging Goff over to speak to them. He seemed impatient to get back to his car, Simmy thought, giving him a long scrutiny. She was still stumbling through the foothills of

Ben's monumental accusations, and very slowly grasping their significance. 'You sent those flowers to Selena,' she accused the man in front of her. She was remembering the long brown coat and the high balding forehead. 'Why did you do that?'

Jasper Braithwaite was standing equally ruminatively, at her shoulder. 'That's not important now,' he said. 'The main thing is the cold-blooded murder of my father.'

As if alerted by a loud buzzer, Moxon's head swivelled round, and his mobile went into his pocket. 'Goff?' he said, striding across the five or six yards to the group. 'James Goff?'

The man bowed his head in acknowledgement.

'He's the murderer,' said Ben, in little more than a whisper. 'I've got it all worked out.'

'What?' screamed Daisy. 'What are you saying? You're insane.'

'No, he's not, Daze,' said Jasper kindly. 'It all makes perfect sense. This boy's a genius,' he added admiringly.

Daisy clung to her fiancé's arm. 'Tell them, Jamey. Tell them they've got it all wrong.'

Goff stood tall and firm, chin held high. 'I've nothing to say,' he announced. 'I have no idea what any of you are talking about.'

'Solar panels,' said Ben, holding up his left hand and ticking each item against a finger. 'Braithwaite a climate scientist. Hayter out of the picture, leaving

358

the way clear. When was it, eh? Early Tuesday, is my guess. I bet you knew Hayter was dead by then. You might even have said something to him that drove him to it, sometime on Monday evening?'

'That's enough,' said Moxon. 'More than enough, to be honest.'

'No, but . . .' Ben persisted. 'We need to get the whole picture.'

'Time for that later. Leave it, son. You've done your bit.'

Daisy was weeping, not surprisingly. Simmy quailed at the effect Ben's words must have had on her. But the girl was not silenced. She stared up at Goff's face with an appalled expression. 'It's all true, isn't it? My dad kept telling you there'd be trouble. He warned you to get out of the solar panels business before it all went bad.' She shook her fiancé's arm roughly. 'But you wouldn't listen. Just laughed it all off. Until you met Baz and Joanna and started to think it might be serious, after all.'

'Shut up,' he told her, yanking her hand away from his arm. 'Don't you understand what they're accusing me of?'

'James Goff, you are under arrest on suspicion of unlawfully killing Tim Braithwaite,' said Moxon loudly.

'No, Uncle Nolan. No!' begged Daisy.

'Is he really your uncle?' asked Ben.

'Just a friend of the family,' Moxon replied

for her. 'She's always called me Uncle.' He was beckoning urgently to a pair of uniformed police officers who had been sitting unobtrusively in a car in a corner of the park.

Before they could respond, Goff had taken something from his pocket, and now flicked it open with a shake of his wrist.

'A knife!' breathed Ben, superfluously. Simmy and he both backed away, holding onto each other like small children. 'That clinches it,' Ben added.

Jasper Braithwaite had not retreated with them. Instead he closed with Goff, snatching in vain at the hand holding the knife. 'Be careful!' Moxon shouted at him. 'Get away.'

Jasper ignored him and the three men were crowded together with Daisy dancing agitatedly around them. Goff was lunging mindlessly, clearly intent on doing as much damage as possible before he was overcome. 'Jamey!' Daisy bleated. 'Stop it. Oh, *please* stop it.'

Shaking off her paralysis, and with no conscious thought, Simmy plunged recklessly into the fray. Where Jasper had failed, she managed to grip the arm behind the knife, and wrenched it sideways. He jerked and writhed and a man cried out in pain. Then Moxon, from a strangely low level, came to her aid, pushing her quarry to the ground and lying across him, leaving Jasper to stamp hard on his arm. The air was full of noise and the smell of male clothes. Hard bodies clashed together. There was

360

something warm in an odd place in Simmy's middle.

Agonisingly slowly, the parts separated, the picture resolving into its constituent elements. Daisy was squatting on the ground beside the prone body of her fiancé, a uniformed officer beside her. Moxon was kneeling very close to Simmy, groaning and holding himself very tightly across the chest with both arms. Ben and another police officer were a few feet away, eyes and mouths wide with shock.

'Get me to a car,' Moxon ordered his men, who responded with belated alacrity.

'Can't you walk?' Simmy asked him, shaking her head to clear it.

'I don't think so,' he gasped. 'I've been stabbed.'

'Oh!' She knelt up to give him a proper look, her own movements jerky and uncoordinated. 'That must have been my fault.' She relived Goff's flailing arm as she tugged at it, the lethal weapon bucking and flashing towards Moxon's unguarded chest.

'You . . . you . . .' Moxon was trying to speak to Simmy, but he was obviously having trouble breathing.

'Shush,' she said. 'Don't worry. We'll get you fixed. He's not going to do it again.'

'You've dislocated his arm,' said Ben admiringly, before coming closer. 'Simmy . . . *Simmy?*'

'I think . . . it feels as if . . .' She looked at a growing patch of blood on her lower left-hand side. 'I'm bleeding!'

'Oh, God!' howled Daisy, not because of

Simmy's injury, it seemed, but simply because she could endure no more.

'Shut up!' grated Goff. 'Just shut your stupid mouth.' He looked at Ben intently. 'You were wrong in just about everything,' he sneered. 'All that baloney about the solar panels. Nothing's going to stop the business now. It's a gold mine.'

'Not a copper mine, then?' Ben quipped weakly. His confidence was ebbing rapidly, Simmy noted.

'Ben,' she said. 'Do you think we might leave this till later?'

Goff was sitting up, cradling an arm that certainly looked dislocated. The two policemen were preparing to carry Moxon to their car, leaving the attempted arrest uncompleted. They muttered as to the best means of achieving this, whilst avoiding any risk of further injury. The knife had been abandoned, kicked carelessly under Simmy's car. She could see it clearly, with blood on it. Jasper was blinking foolishly, kneeling beside his godfather.

Daisy was the first to see the opening. 'Jamey!' she hissed. 'You can get away now, if you're quick.' Apparently his unpleasant snarl at her was already forgiven. 'Come on,' she urged. 'I can drive.'

For a moment, he seemed willing to cooperate. He put his weight on his good arm, and started to gather his tall body together in order to stand up. But the long brown coat impeded him and his knees became entangled. He tried again, and then gave up. 'No,' he said. 'I'll have to take what's coming to me. I'm not going to spend years of my life in hiding.'

Ben was standing helplessly over Simmy, too embarrassed to examine her wound. She found herself oddly disappointed in him. They both looked around for help, and believed they'd found it in the shape of Jasper, despite his dazed appearance.

'Can you go into the hotel?' she asked him. 'Find somebody who's done first aid.'

'What?' He gave himself a shake. 'No. You're all right. It's him we need to worry about.' He indicated Moxon. 'I need a syringe. Could you get the metal case from the back of my car?' he asked Ben.

The boy was there and back in seconds, and Jasper revealed an array of medical equipment.

'I think it's a pneumothorax,' he said. 'We've got to release the pressure. He's not breathing.' He took a large syringe out of the case, and attached a needle from a sterile pack. Then he tore at Moxon's clothes. It took him five seconds to locate a safe spot and plunge the point into the man's chest. Simmy instantly revised her opinion of him, in two opposite directions. Firstly, he had become amazingly capable. Secondly, he had become an object of an irrational suspicion. He was, after all, an unknown quantity. If he could pierce flesh with such unflinching deftness, then that surely meant he could perhaps have stabbed Tim Braithwaite just as easily? *Don't be stupid*, she admonished herself. The man was a vet. He plunged needles and knives into flesh every day.

Jasper drew back the plunger, bringing a murky brownish fluid with it, filling the syringe. Withdrawing the needle, he expelled it onto the ground, and then repeated the process. 'Nasty!' he muttered.

'It's working,' said Simmy, who was now cradling Moxon's head.

'It's too small, though. There could be pints of muck in there by now. We need a drain tube to do any real good.'

Simmy's head began to swim and she looked round for a substitute nurse, worried that she might cause a fatal distraction by passing out in the middle of the delicate emergency procedure. What was wrong with the uniformed police officers? What were they doing? Why didn't they make themselves useful?

Before she could suggest anything, one of the men in question was by her side, staring at the spreading patch of blood. 'Here,' she said. 'You can take over. I'm feeling a bit woozy.'

Gently they changed places, while Jasper watched Moxon's chest. 'You need to get him to a hospital,' Jasper said tightly. 'He's still bleeding into his thoracic cavity.' The second policeman was speaking into a phone, hovering uncertainly over the bizarre tableau at his feet.

Simmy stumbled towards her own car, pulling open the driver's door and flopping in. It felt like a haven, despite being cold and shadowy. A large fir tree grew overhead, shutting out the fading light. *I wonder what time it is*, she thought, before sliding into a faint.

When she came round, Jasper and Ben were both standing over her. 'You're hurt,' said the vet somewhat superfluously. 'Let me have a look at it.' He unceremoniously pulled up her jumper and shirt and examined the wound. 'It's very slight,' he said. 'Lucky it's the left side. No vital organs there. But you ought to have it dressed, of course. Someone in the hotel ought to be able to fix it. I'll go and ask.'

She took a minute to reacquaint herself with the situation. Very little appeared to have changed since she blacked out. 'Actually,' she corrected his retreating back, 'I'm already feeling a lot better.' She raised her head 'Ben – you should go after him. He needs to stay here and make sure Goff doesn't escape. He might change his mind.'

Ben laughed. 'Not much wrong with you,' he observed. 'Bossing everyone around.'

'Shut up,' said Simmy.

Ben looked at Goff, who had got to his feet and was standing only a yard or two away, supported by Daisy. 'Why?' he asked. 'Why did you do it?'

'Hayter and Braithwaite saw me with Selena,'

came the exhausted reply. 'They gave me a tongue-lashing I won't soon forget. I *told* them it meant nothing. I was more than happy to marry Daisy. Selena and I were just . . . it was just an old-time's-sake thing. But they kept on, saying they'd tell Daisy I was rubbish, the wedding was going to be cancelled. She'd never see me again, yadda, yadda, yadda. Her old man wasn't as bad as yours,' he told Jasper. 'Old Braithwaite was incandescent, for some reason.'

'Because he wanted Jasper to marry Daisy, of course,' said Simmy. 'And when she chose you, it was a kick in the teeth for them both. Him and his son. No wonder he was so horrified when he realised you were cheating on her.'

'Horrified isn't the word. He made every sort of threat. Including – ' he looked at Ben 'assuring me that solar power was doomed to oblivion, taking me with it. He laughed about it.'

'So you stabbed him,' said Daisy, in a choked voice. 'A perfectly decent man, who prized truth above everything.'

Goff did not respond to this, but pursued his own need to tell the story as he saw it. 'Hayter couldn't take it, on top of all his other trouble. All this happened in their house, late on Monday night. Hayter went out, and Braithwaite just kept on and on at me, making one threat after another. I got away in the end, at about midnight. Went home, fetched my knife, waited a few hours, and then got back first thing Tuesday. Took him round the back of the house and stuck it in him. He wasn't even surprised. All he could think of was Hayter and why he'd never come back. Kept saying it must have been the flowers that came – that they were a mockery too far and he couldn't take any more.'

'Um . . .' said Simmy. 'I know all this is important, but *please*, would somebody help me?'

The car that should be containing Moxon was inexplicably still standing empty in the car park. A police officer was bending over the back seat, apparently preparing it to take the detective away, if only somebody could give him the necessary authorisation.

'Oh, damn it,' said Simmy, 'what are they waiting for?'

'An ambulance,' said Ben.

'They should set out to meet it halfway, save some time.'

'They'll be scared to move him,' said Ben.

Jasper returned from the hotel and shouted at the police officers. 'You need to get him to hospital *now*. Preferably in a bigger vehicle, so he can lie flat. Better take my Discovery.'

The officers made no immediate move to comply. Simmy watched as they finally managed to carry Moxon to the big vehicle and laid him in the back. Then she struggled out of her car and caught up with

Jasper. 'Is he any better?' she asked, peering over his shoulder. What she saw made her yelp with distress. The inspector's lips were blue, and his breath came in tiny shallow gasps. 'Oh, God! And it's all my fault,' she moaned. 'Look – I'm going with you. I'll sit next to him and make sure he's all right.' Quite how she planned to do that was a matter she didn't pause to consider. 'Just get on with it.'

'But there isn't room for you,' said Jasper.

'Yes there is,' she argued, and slid herself onto the seat, lifting Moxon's head and shoulders onto her lap. 'Drive!' she ordered. 'Straight to the nearest hospital.' It felt to her that there had been a dreadfully long delay in getting all this arranged. A lack of leadership, she diagnosed, and a set of events that deviated from any script in the training manual.

Jasper leaned in after her. 'His lung's collapsed,' he told her. 'Most of the bleeding's internal. All you can do is try to keep him breathing. He might be okay if the other lung can function at least slightly. I'd come with you, but I don't think there's enough space.'

'Might?' she echoed bleakly.

The policeman at the wheel of the car wasted no more time. His partner got onto the phone and somebody medical at the other end started to give advice and instructions, which he relayed to Simmy.

Simmy found herself ferociously determined

to save the injured detective. 'He's going to be all right,' she insisted, at the same time registering his closed eyes, clammy skin and barely perceptible breathing. Unless expert medical help was swiftly available, she could see all too plainly that he would not be all right at all. 'I can see some movement in his chest. He is getting some air. How long is it going to take?'

'The nearest A&E is Barrow. Best part of an hour away,' the driver told her.

'Is that where we're going? He can't last an hour, can he?' Panic flooded through her. Moxon was going to die in her lap, crammed into the back of a speeding Land Rover.

'There's an ambulance meeting us at Newby Bridge. That's ten minutes away. They'll keep him oxygenated until they can get him into a theatre.'

The ten minutes passed like ten seconds, as she watched the faint fluttering of Moxon's chest. His clothes had been only partly pulled clear, leaving her to watch a window, six inches square, through his shirt. There was only a sprinkling of blood to be seen. The knife had lunged in and out again, doing its damage inside, and leaving a swollen red wound in the middle of the man's torso.

At Newby Bridge, people in yellow jackets came and went, handling her with considerably more gentleness than they had earlier in the day when dealing with Joanna Colhoun. While almost all the activity revolved around Moxon, someone took the trouble to examine her own injury, wiping a sharp-smelling fluid across it, and covering it with bright-white gauze. She was very tired, she decided. And she felt rather sick. When someone pushed her down onto a narrow shelf-like bed, she was glad. It had been a very long day, she thought, and nobody could reasonably expect anything more of her.

She woke up to Melanie's voice. 'Sim? *Simmy!* You can wake up now. I'm taking you home.'

'What time is it?'

Melanie rightly ignored the question. 'I've got your car outside. I hope it's insured for me to drive.'

'What time is it?'

'Who cares? Why does that matter?'

'I don't know. It just does.' She felt like a stroke victim or an old woman with early Alzheimer's. When everything else swam confusingly and terrifyingly before one's eyes, the clock offered a small point of stability in a shifting world.

'It's five o'clock, okay? Just after.'

'Thanks. Where are we?'

'Kendal. I was here with Kathy when they brought you in. She's coming with us as well.'

'That isn't right. How did my car get here, then?'

'Scott brought it. We couldn't just leave it in Coniston, could we? Ben and Wilf have gone home.'

'Did they arrest Goff, then?'

'Who?'

Simmy felt weak. Not only did she have to bring Melanie up to date on the solving of the murder, but she would have to endure the girl's outrage at yet again missing the final act.

'Goff. Daisy's fiancé. He killed Tim Braithwaite.'

'"Go green with Goff",' Melanie remembered.

'What?'

'That flyer, for solar panels. Is it the same bloke?'

'Oh, yes,' said Simmy. 'It is indeed.' Then, 'How's Moxon? He didn't die, did he?'

'Not to my knowledge. They've still got him under the knife in here somewhere, I think.'

'Not Barrow?'

'Seems not. They can do most things here. They had plenty of time to get ready while you brought him from Coniston.'

'My parents are going to freak.'

'Yup. Ben called me. He says you threw yourself between a man with a knife and DI Moxon. What do you expect your parents to say about that?'

'Did I?' She tried to recapture the scene. 'Well, I suppose he'd have done the same for me. It just seemed right, somehow.'

'He *loves* you, Sim. And you don't love him. I don't really get why you'd save him like that.'

'I think you just put your finger on it. I felt so sorry for him. I do hope he doesn't die.' She fell quiet, thinking unhappy thoughts for a little while. Then, 'Where's Kathy?' she asked.

'Downstairs. We can go now.'

'What about Joanna?'

'I forgot to say. She's coming as well.'

They found mother and daughter in the hospital foyer, and went out into the cold dark evening together. Simmy was still trying to recapture the exact sequence of events that would account for so many hours having passed. 'I'm never going to explain it all to my mum and dad,' she groaned. 'I can't even remember half of it. What happened after we got to the ambulance?'

'You passed out,' Melanie told her. 'For most of the journey to Kendal.'

'Did anybody tell you that Jasper Braithwaite jabbed a dirty great needle into Moxon and pulled out a lot of gunk? He's a vet, so he knew what to do.'

'He seems nice.'

'Daisy was an idiot to pack him in and take up with horrible Goff.'

'Are we going to talk about murder all the way to Windermere?' asked Kathy.

'Probably,' Melanie shot back. 'Why – what do *you* want to talk about?'

'Jo?' Kathy queried. 'Is there anything you want to say to Simmy?'

'Sorry, Simmy,' said Joanna, like a five-year-old.

Simmy was bemused. 'Why are you sorry? What have you done?'

'Well . . . causing you so much bother this morning. And . . . I suppose . . .' She gulped. 'Actually, I don't think I *am* sorry, really. All I did was fall in love. I still don't understand what happened with Baz. Mum said he kept her all night in a mine underground. And Melanie says he was secretly digging for copper down there. I can't believe any of it's true. He *loves* me. He's been risking his job for me.'

'It is true,' said Simmy. 'All of it. I don't think he's entirely sane, if that's any consolation.'

'Of course it's not,' shouted the girl. 'Where is he? What's going to happen?'

'Last I saw of him, he was crying over four flat tyres on his van,' said Simmy heartlessly. 'If he stayed there for long, he'll have been arrested by now.'

'Crying? Oh, *poor* Baz. He loves that van.'

'Altogether too much love going on around here, if you ask me,' said Melanie. 'All it does is cause trouble.'

'You can say that again,' Simmy agreed. 'Even Mr Braithwaite's murder was about that, in a way.'

'You'll have to explain that.' Melanie spoke crossly, her frustration inescapable. 'Ben said it was all about solar panels and climate change.'

'Ben's wrong. Partly, anyway. Mr Braithwaite was threatening to tell Daisy he'd seen Goff with Selena Drury, in the hope of making her cancel the wedding.'

'I don't get the climate stuff at all,' Melanie complained. 'Who's right? Everything you read and see on the telly makes it seem obvious that we're all doing it with our cars and coal and stuff. But Ben's no fool. He seems sure it's not that simple.'

'I don't know,' sighed Simmy. 'But I can't believe Ben's likely to be right. Kathy – what do you think?'

'Don't ask me. Jo's a lot more clued up than me on that subject.'

'Jo?'

The girl spoke carefully. 'We have found some good data, but it won't actually prove anything globally. I guess you have to go with the majority. Scientists have been misquoted a lot. The real question has to be what we do about it. Don't you think?'

'I'm with my Dad,' said Simmy. 'He says it's too big a question for simplistic headlines. And he says it makes his head hurt when he thinks about it, so he prefers to let other people worry.'

'Which is the best we're going to get,' summarised Melanie. 'So what else was going on? Back to the love interest, by the looks of it. Sounds to me as if Goff really does love Daisy, even though he's not very nice to her. And he *was* seeing Selena. He sent her those flowers, after all, knowing it'd cause trouble with Solomon.'

'People do that sort of thing,' said Joanna softly. 'Even when they know it'll get them into trouble. Men, especially. I saw Baz kissing one of the other students, a month or so ago, but he swore it never meant anything. He said men sometimes couldn't control themselves.'

'Rubbish!' said Kathy and Melanie in one voice. 'Total rubbish,' added Kathy.

'They just do what they think they can get away with,' Melanie elaborated. 'It's not the same thing.'

'Next year, I think I'll go away for the first half of February,' said Simmy. 'And miss Valentine's altogether. It obviously makes everybody crazy.'

'No you won't,' laughed Melanie. 'You'll be madly in love with somebody yourself by then, and as gooey as everybody else.'

Simmy found nothing to say to that, thinking about the suffering DI Moxon, and how careless she had been with his feelings over recent days.

'I bet you I'm right,' Melanie went on. 'I even bet I know who it'll be.'

'That police detective, I suppose,' said Kathy. 'He's obviously keen on you.'

'Please don't say that. It makes me feel terrible.'

'I wasn't thinking of him, anyhow,' said Melanie.

# CHAPTER TWENTY-TWO

Angie and Russell reacted very badly to the appearance of a damaged daughter on the doorstep. 'Is that blood on your leg?' Russell demanded, as she stumbled into the kitchen and lowered herself into the chair by the Rayburn.

'Just a little cut,' she said. 'It probably isn't even mine. It's been a perfectly horrible day, Dad. Everything got a bit out of control, I'm afraid.' She gave a brief and rather garbled account of events to her appalled parents.

Angie was at first incredulous, then furious. 'I can't *believe* you'd be such a fool,' she shouted. 'It's as if you *deliberately* put yourself in danger. Why must you do that? What perverse spirit possesses you?'

'It wasn't deliberate,' Simmy argued calmly. 'One thing led to another, and at no point did I feel I had a choice. There were men with knives, for God's sake. They threatened us. And I had to rescue Kathy. There was definitely no choice about that.'

'None of this makes the slightest sense,' complained Russell. 'Why was Kathy in Coniston in the first place? Who *are* all these people?'

'It doesn't matter, really. Except one of them killed a perfectly nice man, who was a friend of DI Moxon. Now he's in hospital, fighting for his life. Moxon, I mean. The nice man is dead.'

'Fighting for his life?' repeated Angie sceptically. 'That's tomorrow's headline, is it?'

'Probably. He was stabbed in the chest and nearly died. I was collateral damage, you might say.'

'You should have stayed right out of it.'

'I know. I agree. I have no idea what I thought I was doing. It just seemed unfair that he should be hurt when he was only doing his job. Actually, that isn't really true. I didn't think anything at all at the time. It was all just instinct. I dislocated the murderer's arm,' she added proudly. 'Moxon was trying to arrest him, and he pulled out this awful knife.'

'If the murdered man was his friend, shouldn't he have been taken off the case in the first place?' asked Russell.

'Possibly. But apparently nobody was too worried about it. I'm still not sure why he was in Coniston at all. Somebody must have phoned him.'

An idea occurred to her. 'Most likely the man on reception. He was obviously suspicious when Baz took us all up the mountain with him.'

'I wish I knew some of these people,' Angie complained. 'What was the motive, anyway?'

'Ben says it was all about solar panels, and climate change not really mattering, and renewables being doomed to oblivion. But it wasn't just that. Basically, it was all about love.' She sighed. 'Most crimes are about that, aren't they? When it comes right down to it. Jealous love. Frightened love. People terrified of losing somebody they depend on for their happiness. If that's threatened somehow, they see red. It's amazing, really, how powerful it is.'

'Can't see that stuffed-shirt of a detective ever falling in love,' remarked Angie.

Simmy sat up and glared at her mother. 'He's not a stuffed shirt. Not at all. He's totally human, with a full set of emotions. Melanie thinks, believe it or not, that he's in love with *me*.'

Angie stuck to her guns. 'Sounds as if every man involved in this case was trying to impress a woman. Bloody fools.'

Russell put a hand on his wife's arm. 'Steady on, old girl. It's not all bad, you know. From what I can understand, it hasn't worked out so terribly, by and large.' He smiled at Simmy. 'I know there's a lot more you haven't told us, but for now, you need a bit of peace and quiet.'

'Okay,' she agreed. 'But before that I need *food*. I haven't had a thing since breakfast.'

On Sunday afternoon, she went with Ben and Melanie to visit Moxon in Kendal. Melanie drove Simmy's car again, Russell having made a sterling job of mending the wing mirror with gaffer tape. Ben insisted on coming, overriding the protests from his mother. 'She doesn't really care,' he said. 'She just wants people to think she does.'

Moxon was in a single room, with the usual array of wires and monitors, and a mask over his face. His eyes were open and they brightened considerably at the sight of Simmy.

'I'm terribly sorry,' she blurted, before she had even sat down. 'It was all my fault.'

He pulled the mask away, and gazed earnestly at her. 'How do you work that out?'

'I got in the way.'

'You saved my life. I was totally unprepared for such an attack. He'd have got me in the heart without you.'

'Oh. Surely not? You must have done self-defence training.'

He smiled. 'I was paralysed,' he admitted. 'It all went right out of my head. I've always been more scared of knives than any other weapon.'

'They'll easily get him for it, won't they? There's the knife. Traces of his hair or skin or whatever in the Coniston house. Evidence from Selena and even Daisy. Even I can see there's an excellent case. Whatever he says, you'll nail him with all that against him.'

His eyes twinkled. 'I'm sure you're right,' he mumbled from inside the mask.

When she got back to Windermere, Kathy turned up to say goodbye before driving back to Worcester. '*Can* you drive?' wondered Simmy. 'With your arms so stiff?'

'Jo's coming, too. She'll take the wheel. And look – I wanted to show you this.' She revealed a large pottery vase. 'It's one made by your friend Ninian. I went to his cottage this morning and bought it.'

'You *what*? How did you know where it was?'

'I asked Melanie. It's lovely up there, Sim. You really ought to go and see it.'

'I keep meaning to. I just haven't got round to it.'

'Well, he says to tell you he'll come in and see you today. Probably any minute now. Listen, Sim – I really am terribly sorry for all the trouble. I used you, in a way. I was more worried than I let on to you about what Jo was doing. Claudia had warned me there was something I should worry about, after she'd gone to see Jo at college a few weeks ago. She wouldn't say much. Didn't want to be disloyal, and she could see how besotted Joanna was. I was out there hoping to bump into Baz, when he popped out of that mineshaft. It never crossed my mind that he'd turn out to be such a nutcase. I really did think he'd stab me if I gave him any cause. I was a complete wimp. I had absolutely no idea how terrifying it can be when somebody breaks all the usual rules of behaviour. It just turned me to a jelly.'

Simmy thought about her own reckless assault on Goff, and wondered. 'Don't worry about it,' she advised. 'Jo seems to be taking it quite well.'

'Maybe,' said Kathy dubiously. 'Although I doubt if she'll speak to me all the way home.'

Ninian turned up ten minutes after Kathy had gone. He was clean and brushed and profoundly concerned. 'I made you something,' he said, producing a piece of pottery.

It was an intricately fashioned porcelain rose, painted yellow. Each petal was perfect in shape and colour, the whole a piece of artistic splendour. Perched in the centre was a small bee.

'It's my version of a Valentine,' he said, shyly.

Simmy's smile, as she met his eyes, was every bit as shy. 'Thank you,' she said.

IF YOU ENJOYED THE LAKE DISTRICT MYSTERIES,
YOU'LL LOVE OUR OTHER BOOKS
BY REBECCA TOPE . . .

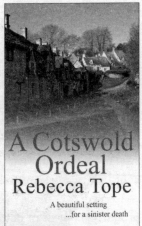

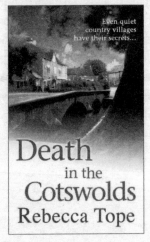

To discover more great books and to
place an order visit our website at
**allisonandbusby.com**

Don't forget to sign up to our free newsletter at
**allisonandbusby.com/newsletter**
for latest releases, events and exclusive offers

⬛ **Allison & Busby Books**
🔲 **@AllisonandBusby**

You can also call us on
**020 7580 1080**
for orders, queries
and reading recommendations